PRAISE FOR

BELOW THE BELT

"Characters who are simply magnetic and refreshingly multi-dimensional . . . With plenty of gritty, sensual and scenic details, and a number of intriguing, empathetic supporting characters, this is one series that readers should check out as quickly as possible." —*RT Book Reviews*

"A series for fans of uniforms, discipline and athletic prowess . . . The core romance is strengthened by a playful sense of humor and real chemistry between the characters, as well as steamy bedroom scenes. A colorfully memorable supporting cast." —*Publishers Weekly*

"Wonderfully entertaining . . . Fun, sexy, and the characters are so likeable you won't want to put the book down." —Wit and Sin

"An engaging story with plenty of humor and heat." —Harlequin Junkie

"A delightful read with a fascinating and engaging cast of characters." —The Reading Cafe

"A fun read with interesting characters and great dialogue." —Cocktails and Books

continued . . .

FIGHT TO THE FINISH

JEANETTE MURRAY

BERKLEY SENSATION, NEW YORK

BERKLEY

An imprint of Penguin Random House LLC
375 Hudson Street, New York, New York 10014

FIGHT TO THE FINISH

A Berkley Sensation Book / published by arrangement with the author

ISBN: 978-0-425-27928-1

PUBLISHING HISTORY
Berkley Sensation mass-market edition / March 2016

PRINTED IN THE UNITED STATES OF AMERICA

10 9 8 7 6 5 4 3 2 1

Cover photo of Young Muscular Sports Guy © Martin Valigursky / Shutterstock.
Cover design by Rita Frangie.
Interior text design by Kelly Lipovich.

Penguin
Random
House

*For Nurse Geri, who watches over her school like
a hawk and has magical sponges. You're awesome!
Thanks for the help!*

*And to Jen from iHeartOrganizing for answering my
blogging questions. You were an angel for taking the time
to answer all my silly or serious inquiries. Thank you!*

*And lastly, Josayn, for being open and helpful as
another awesome resource. You're a doll!*

(Any and all mistakes made were mine and mine alone.)

CHAPTER

1

How did someone just knock on the door of the sexiest man ever? One who sent your pulse racing, your blood pounding, your knees weakening, and one who you could never actually be with?

Kara breathed in, then out. In one more time through the nose, and out, two, three, four . . .

"Mom!"

She jerked from her yoga breathing and looked down at her son. Not as much "down" as "over." In the last three months he'd grown nearly three inches. Her little boy was no longer so little.

"What?"

Zach indicated the door with both hands, which were still gripping the three bags of allergy-approved potato chips she'd brought so he didn't feel bad being left out of potato salad. There was always potato salad at a cookout. "Are you going to open the door? My hands are losing their grip here."

"Be glad you aren't one of those animals whose mothers

eat their young. I'd be tempted." With a sigh, she knocked on the door. There. That sounded like a normal knock. "Where'd a ten-year-old get such a smart mouth, anyway?"

"I come by it naturally," he said with a grin that had her flashing an identical one back at him. The kid was incorrigible. It was one of the things she loved about him.

The door opened a moment later with her best friend, Marianne, standing in bare feet, jean capris and an oversized Marine Corps boxing T-shirt. "Hey! Why'd you knock? We said to come in."

"I like to be polite when I haven't been to someone's house before."

"I have," Zach reminded her, gliding past Marianne with a curt "hey," before dashing off to the backyard.

"He's so refined," Kara said with a groan. "Mr. Manners, for the win."

"He's ten. If he wasn't a little obnoxious, I'd worry." Her friend pulled her inside and gave her a side hug while closing the door. "But you know you're welcome to walk in. Graham said as much."

"Graham said as much," Kara muttered under her breath. "Am I overdressed?"

Marianne surveyed Kara's sundress and wedge heels that had seemed like a good idea in her closet, and now appeared very out of place. "You're cute. It's a cute dress. Let's put that away. Zach's dessert?" she asked as she took the glass dish and walked it to the fridge.

"Says so on the label. He's got some chips he can eat, though there's plenty of that to share. Just have to—"

"Keep the utensils properly labeled for zero cross contamination. Graham's already on it. He went out and bought big plastic blue serving spoons, because that's Zach's favorite color, and has warned everyone that using them improperly is punishable by death."

Kara had to bite back the misty tears that threatened at the sentiment. "That's . . . a little extreme, but sweet."

"He's a sweet guy." Marianne popped the dessert in the fridge and hooked an arm around hers, linking elbows. "When are you going to let him take you out? The man seriously has it bad for you. You know it. I know it. Everyone knows it."

"It's not a good idea, and you know exactly why." Feeling like an idiot because she couldn't fix what wasn't her problem to begin with, she shook her head. "I agreed to come over here because everyone else would be here and it's a get-together and I could bring Zach, not a one-on-one thing. If you think my being here is giving him the wrong impression, I'll grab Zach and we can go."

Marianne's teasing eyes softened at that. "Don't go. I'm kidding. Not about him wanting you, that's true. But you shouldn't feel bad about it. He won't make it uncomfortable."

That was a fact. Though he had hinted and made her very aware of his presence and desire, Graham Sweeney had not once pushed the issue of asking her out. It was as if he sensed the invisible male-repelling force field she had erected around her life and Zach's, and respected it by standing just outside of it. Every so often, his toes might bump against the edge, but he remained outside the shield.

"Guess who's here!" Marianne walked out through the back door and announced them with a flourish. "Which isn't much of a guess, since Zach came out here five minutes ago."

Reagan, all five-foot-ten goddess inches of her, stood from the patio chair and came to give her a hug. "Yes! Now we're not outnumbered."

"Hardly," Graham said by the grill, hooking an arm around Zach's head. The boy put up a token protest and squirmed, but Kara saw him grinning. "Us men still have four, to your female three."

"Sorry, I wasn't counting those who couldn't drive yet."

Reagan blew Zach a kiss, which caused him to blush and run for a soccer ball in the corner of the yard to practice dribbling.

"Nice." Kara settled down in a free chair and smoothed the skirt of her dress down primly. "What are we talking about?"

"First match," Brad said. "Not for practice."

Gregory Higgs, upon whose lap Reagan was perched, groaned. "Man, we're here for fun. Don't bring work into it."

"But it's something we all have in common," Marianne pointed out. "We're all connected to boxing, or the Marine Corps team, in some way." She flushed as she looked at Reagan. "I mean, uh . . . okay sorry."

Reagan waved that off. "I got my job back. But it's not for me. Watching you guys box sort of made me queasy to my stomach. I'll be looking for a new job after this for sure."

"Then what else do we have to talk about?" Graham set a plate of burger patties on the table. "Hey, kid! Food!"

Kara bristled, then realized Zach liked the nickname and took no offense. He sprinted over to grab a burger, slap it on a gluten-free bun and take off again.

"Guess he was hungry," Graham said with a smile.

"Are those—"

"They're from a peanut-free factory," Graham assured her.

He settled in a chair beside Kara, crowding into her space without even moving close. The man was just . . . potent. That was the only word for it. Potent. It was as if he took over everywhere he was.

"He was. Hungry, I mean. I didn't let him chow down on lunch like usual. Uh, the food—" she began, but stopped short when he held up a hand.

"I made some potato salad without mayo or hard-boiled eggs. Extra relish and mustard so it's almost soupy, how he likes it. I double-checked your blog to make sure the brands were the right kinds, without any of the cross contamination stuff. And no tomatoes for the burgers."

She stopped, stunned. "Thank you."

"I like the kid." He shrugged and sat back with a beer. "I'd rather he didn't keel over in my backyard."

So many danced around her son's serious allergies, or made them something sacred they had to talk about in hushed tones, or treated them like the most annoying inconvenience in the world. Graham simply made it normal, and didn't seem to shy away from using them as a good-natured joke.

So, tally time. The man looked like a Greek god, was smarter than anyone else she'd met, had the body of a serious athlete, and was conscientious and sweet about her son's limiting allergy needs.

The man had to be stopped.

SHE was fire and light. Energy, amusement. Everything a man needed to survive. Kara was everything he wanted.

Zach, Graham thought as he watched the boy spend thirty futile seconds attempting to kick the soccer ball from its wedged position in the corner of his fence before resorting to his hands, was a brilliant bonus.

Kara leaned forward, animatedly talking to Marianne about something. He caught a glimpse of the tops of her breasts, with a few freckles dusting the creamy skin. The straps left her toned, muscular shoulders and arms bare. Yoga and Pilates had definitely done her body good. And the frilly hem fluttered around her calves, tanned and toned from summer yoga sessions outdoors.

Her dress was the perfect showcase for what she was, class and femininity encased in a tough exterior that took no shit and managed to keep up with a tireless young boy by herself.

He'd been attracted from the moment they'd met. Her single mom status had given him a moment's pause—dating a woman with a child wasn't something he'd considered before—but he'd very quickly moved past that nonexistent hurdle. The fact that she was still single amazed him. Either the men in this town were morons, or she was very good at hiding herself away.

"Any new yoga stories?" Marianne asked, settling down on the bench with her legs draped over Brad's thighs, a plate of the trifle-like dessert Kara had brought balanced on her knees. She brushed one hand over the back of his neck, as if she couldn't help herself. The Marine looked like he could slide into a puddle at her feet. Very different from how he'd been two months earlier . . . the stick-up-the-ass guy nobody wanted to hang out with because he was too intense for his own good.

"No new yoga stories." With a secret smile, Kara sipped her water and crossed her legs at the ankles. A delicate silver ankle bracelet winked in the fading evening sun. "I've been dealing with these guys too much. Well," she added, tapping a finger to the corner of her mouth, "there was that one . . ."

"Gimme!" Marianne leaned forward, upsetting the balance until Brad wrapped an arm around her waist and righted them again. "Spill. You know I live for these."

Her finger tapped once more, and he had the urge to press his lips against that corner. As if she knew tapping there would draw his attention. "I really shouldn't. Client privileged information."

"That's for lawyers and shrinks. Tell her, Sweeney," Greg prompted.

"That's for lawyers and shrinks," he repeated, deadpan, and they all laughed.

"Well, have I told you all about . . ." She looked up, scanned the backyard to see where Zach was, then ended on a whisper, "Shrink Wrap Man?"

Most shook their heads. Greg grinned and rubbed his hands together. "This is gonna be good."

"Okay. So you know how when you get hot dogs, they're all smushed together in a pack of eight? And the plastic is pulled tight over each of the hot dogs?"

Graham started to grin slowly.

Kara sat back and waved a hand as if she were telling a classy joke in a cocktail lounge. "His penis looks sort of like that in his skin tight leggings when he does Downward Dog."

Marianne burst out laughing, and Reagan gasped, eyes wide. "No!"

"Yes," Kara said solemnly, taking a sip of her water. "I wish not, but very true. I've actually considered having Marianne make one of her famous pamphlets about the importance of wearing clothes that breathe during yoga, so he stops wearing those pants."

"I'll do it," Marianne said with a gasp. "I'll do it, just for you."

"What's so funny, Mom?" Zach called out from the corner.

"Nothing!" she answered quickly, waving him off to keep him from coming closer. "You're doing great!"

Zach ignored that and ran closer to the group, scooping up a hot dog and taking a bite. Marianne burst out laughing, managed to squeeze out, "I'm gonna pee my pants!" and ran inside. The door slammed shut behind her.

"You should get a dog, you know," Zach told Graham around a mouthful.

"Zach, manners."

He shot his mother a chagrined look, swallowed, then said it again. "You should get a dog."

"Why's that? I've got you coming over here often enough to run around the backyard and eat my food. What do I need a dog for?"

Zach snorted and kicked the soccer ball into the back corner, sitting down beside him. Kara looked anxious, as if she didn't want her son to be a bother. To ease her mind, he slung an arm over Zach's chair.

"You need a dog 'cause you've got a backyard and you live alone. No mom or whatever to say no. Why wouldn't you have one?"

"I'm gone a lot," Graham reminded him. "Especially with practice. Probably better if I wait on that."

"I'd come take care of him for you." Looking to his mother, Zach continued. "Couldn't I? I'm responsible."

Graham glanced at Kara, who had a stricken look on her face. "Bud, it's just not the time for a pet right now."

The toes of Zach's tennis shoes scuffed the concrete pad of the patio. "Yeah. Okay."

"Hey, Zach, could you run back out to the car and see if I left my sweater?" Kara rubbed her upper arms and shivered. "I'm getting a little cold."

"Sure." With a shrug, Zach held out his hands for the keys she dug from her purse and took off.

"I'm sorry," she said to him softly after her son let the door bang on his way in. "He's been asking for a dog since, I don't know . . . he could say the word 'dog.' I said we couldn't because we don't have a yard, and you do, so . . ." She lifted her hands in silent confusion. "I guess he assumes anyone with a yard should have one."

"It's fine. Really. He's a boy, of course he wants a dog. I'm not offended." And if he thought for one minute Kara would let the boy claim ownership when he couldn't care for it, he'd go out to the pound tomorrow and pick up the ugliest son of a bitch mutt he could find. He loved dogs, too. But without someone around to care for the animal when he was gone, it wasn't fair to the animal.

"You didn't have a sweater in the car, Mom. But I found this sweatshirt on the couch so, here." Zach thrust the oversized red-and-gold hoodie into Kara's lap. She stared at it, a little horrified. "You said you were cold. Put it on."

"Zach, you can't just take people's things without asking." She glanced between the three men. "I'm sorry, whoever he stole this from."

Graham bit the inside of his lip to keep from smiling. He knew for sure she'd sent Zach to the car just to get him out of earshot. Now he'd have some fun with it. "It's mine, and you can wear it."

"Oh, I couldn't." Her eyes narrowed, and her lips drew into a firm line. If she could have poked him with her fork, she would have. "Here."

"I insist. As my guest, it's my job to make sure you're comfortable. Let me." Torturing her—and himself just a little—he stood and took the sweatshirt, holding it over her head. "Arms up."

His friends watched on with amusement, and Reagan's eyes twinkled as Kara sighed with resignation and lifted her arms. He wiggled until the sleeves were in place, then stuck her head through it and let the material drift down. His fingertips skimmed the silky underside of her arms before dropping away.

Even that one touch would torment him for hours. God, she had the most beautiful skin.

And a missing head. Zach's giggles caused him to look back. The hood had flopped forward, and Kara's hands—covered by the too-long sleeves—were unable to push it back so her face could pop out. He helped maneuver the fabric until her head emerged. She gasped, as if coming up for air from the crashing surf. Her hair, once a smooth line of auburn silk, was fuzzy and a little mussed. For reasons that bewildered him, the flustered look on her face and the hair draped all over only made her more beautiful.

She met his eyes from upside down, and for a moment, the whole world faded away. His nose was an inch from hers. Her hair caught on her eyelashes, which were nearly as light as the strands. Those aqua blue irises were piercing. Was it his imagination, or did he hear her breath hitch a little, like his did . . .

"Mom, are they all coming to my EpiPen party?"

Moment shattered, Graham jerked up and away.

"What'd I miss?" Marianne jumped back down from behind him out the back door.

"We were about to be invited to a party," Reagan said. To Zach, she asked, "What's an EpiPen party?"

"My pens are expired, so I have to get new ones. *And-plusalso*, I'm getting bigger." To illustrate, he flexed and showed off a puny adolescent biceps muscle. "So I get new pens and I get to play with the old ones."

"First off," Kara said calmly," 'andplusalso' is not a word, as I've told you a dozen times."

"Mrs. Wrigby says it," he said defensively.

"Mrs. Wrigby has twenty-five ten-year-olds she has to garner the attention of. I'm sure if she thought it would work, she'd teach you geography while doing an Irish step dance. She says it to be funny. And secondly, they don't all need to come." She sighed and looked at Marianne. "I was going to ask if you wanted to come over and check out his new pens, since the new pens are different, and you might watch him from time to time."

"Because I'm a baby and can't stay home alone," Zach added, looking disgusted by the thought.

"Because you're ten, and I'm not comfortable with it yet," she shot back. "When he gets a new set of pens, I use the old ones for a quick brush up on training."

"Can I come?" Reagan sat forward. "I'm interested. I've read your blog a little, and I'm intrigued. I can bring a movie and popcorn, and we can make a night of it."

Graham waited for Kara to invite them all. After all, the guys had hung out with Zach on occasion, and Graham had taken the chance to hang out—not babysit, as he would never use the offending B word—with the kid to get to know him one-on-one. But Kara said nothing.

"Sounds good. Tomorrow night?"

Both other women nodded.

She sighed and rubbed a hand over her knees. "I think we'll head out then. Thank you," she added to Graham as she stood, "for the sweatshirt and the invitation."

He shook his head as she started to pull her arm out of one sleeve. "Keep it until you get to the car. You know how chilly it is now."

She glanced up at the sky, with the sun that still hadn't quite set yet, and the balmy seventy-three degree weather. "Right. Zach, head in and grab the dessert dish. We've got to go."

He looked like he wanted to argue, but one fulminating glare from his mother had him nodding and going in. But he ducked his head back out again and said, "Thank you for inviting us," before closing the door behind him.

"Mr. Manners," Kara murmured before standing herself. "Girls, I'll see you tomorrow. Gentlemen, Tuesday at the gym."

"I'll walk you out," Graham said before she could escape. "It's not a problem."

She wanted to argue, but he sent her the same fulminating stare she'd given her son, and she simply stood and walked into the house. Zach was already heading through the front door to the car, so he had her in the house alone.

"Thanks again for coming."

She played with the strings of his hoodie. Though she was tall, the shirt swallowed her slender form. "You're really nice to keep asking us . . . I mean, including Zach and all. I know his allergies make stuff like this difficult." Her eyes, which had been wandering everywhere but at him, made contact with his. "I really appreciate that you made the effort."

He'd have done it even if he'd disliked the kid's mom. But the way she looked at him now, and the emotion in her voice for having made a simple potato salad . . . he'd keep a vat of the stuff in his fridge forever if she'd just keep looking at him that way. "It's seriously no problem."

"I've been doing this almost ten years. I know it's not 'no problem.'" She started toward the door, then, almost as a second thought, came back and kissed his cheek. "Thanks, Graham."

She took off before he could ask her to stay, or ask her to dinner, or ask her to marry him . . .

You know, the usual.

Probably best she made her escape now. He could tap-dance around a closing argument in court, and couldn't manage to ask a woman to dinner. Or not that specific woman. He needed more time to prepare, and be ready to handle any argument she tossed at him for getting out of it.

He'd see her again soon. And he'd be ready.

CHAPTER

2

Marianne set the serving tray with three glasses of wine, some cheese and crackers on the coffee table. "Where's Zach tonight?"

"Friend's house." Kara settled on the floor on the other side, while Marianne and Reagan took seats on the couch. "He got a last minute invitation and decided going there was much cooler than hanging out with Mom's friends."

"He's such a sweetheart," Reagan said. "He reminds me of my brothers, but cuter and less of a pain in the ass."

Kara smiled at that, then twisted her hair into a clip and grabbed a glass. She didn't often have wine at home—the decent stuff was too expensive, and the cheap stuff was worse than no wine at all—so she relished when someone brought a good bottle to her place as a hostess gift. Even more so if she was kid free for the night.

"Please tell me why," Reagan said as she nibbled on a cracker, "you have a free night from mommyhood and you are wasting it on us instead of going out with a hot man and getting some much-needed touching?"

"You're both free from mommyhood and you're wasting your night here."

"Because we love Zach and you and we want to be able to save the rugrat's life." Marianne pointed at her. "Plus, we're *always* free from mommyhood. And when we go home, we've got someone in our bed. You've got a book."

"Or a vibrator," Reagan said absently. When both women stared at her, she blinked. "Whoops. Said that one out loud, huh?"

"Nice one, Heels."

"They are adorable, aren't they?" Reagan extended one leg to show off her red patent leather Mary Jane–style three-inch heels. "Red is classic. Speaking of classic, you know who has those classic good looks? Graham Sweeney." She stared hard at Kara as she said it. "The Adonis with a good right uppercut."

"Do you even know what an uppercut is?" Marianne whispered.

"No," Reagan whispered back.

"I'm not dating Graham Sweeney. Or any other Marine." Kara gulped down the wine. Hell, she was kid free and had nowhere to drive tonight. She could go crazy and kill the bottle. "I'm not opposed to dating. I date."

"Rarely," Marianne muttered.

"I'm picky. That's not a bad thing. Not when I've got another soul to worry about." She crammed a cracker in her mouth in frustration. This argument was going to cost her serious calories. "I can't bring around losers. It's unacceptable."

"But why no Marines?" Reagan asked while Marianne shook her head vehemently. "Oh, uh . . . sorry. Ignore the question."

Kara sighed and waved her longtime friend off. "It's okay. Henry's an asshole. Zach's father," she explained to Reagan.

"Sperm donor," Marianne muttered into her wineglass.

"Sperm donor . . . unless Zach can hear me." Kara was firm on that. She couldn't rightly call him a father on a regular basis when he wanted nothing to do with his own son, but she still did her best to keep the negativity away from Zach. "He lives here, we all went to high school together."

"I'm almost a year younger than Kara, and Henry is a few years older. Just for your frame of reference." Marianne handed Reagan another cracker and took one for herself. "This one walked in graduation with a secret under her cap and gown."

"Five months along and nobody knew but me and Henry." That part made her smile. She'd been so relieved when she'd shared the news with him, and he'd supported her gut reaction to keep the baby. It had taken the pressure off. "Obviously I wasn't going to start college when I'd be giving birth midsemester, so I took what I told myself was a year off and started working the front desk at one of the gyms here. Henry supported that decision. He supported every decision I made." That made her grimace. "It took me awhile, and some maturity, to see he wasn't really supporting me so much as not emotionally investing. It was 'Whatever you think is best, I believe in you.' Or 'You know what you need, so go do it.' All talk."

"I can see where that might bolster your self-esteem though. Feed into the relationship." Reagan nodded. "So you had Zach. What'd your parents think?"

"What parents?" Marianne snorted, and Kara shrugged. "They were done with me when they realized I wasn't giving the baby up and wasn't going to college right away. It was my decision to toss my life away," she added, "according to them. So I had to live with it."

"Fuck 'em," Marianne said, holding up her glass in a toast. "My parents didn't like your parents, by the way. Did you ever know that? They never said anything until after Zach was born, because I think they were hoping once the baby arrived they'd snap out of it."

"No snapping," Kara said sadly.

"No snapping," Marianne agreed. "But you figured it out. Why? Because you're awesome. That's why."

"And because I had a great support system, which included Marianne's parents. I found another gym that let me bring in Zach and leave him with the child care people, unless they were swamped. Then he went in a sling with me at the front desk. I had amazing shoulders and back muscles that fall."

"I bet. How hard," Reagan murmured, "to be nineteen and doing it all on your own."

"Yeah. Zach wasn't much help in those days." She laughed. "I would watch all these yoga mommies—that's what my manager called them." She grinned when Reagan's eyebrows winged up. "You know, the ones who don't work, and come in carrying an iced green tea from Starbucks, wearing the matching, gorgeous yoga outfits that coordinate with their personalized yoga mats and their kids always match and look adorable, and they do the yoga class because it won't get them sweaty and then they all go out for lunch together. The yoga mommies."

"Huh." Reagan nodded slowly. "I could be a yoga mommy. Just, you know, without the yoga."

"It's required. Sorry. I would watch these women go in there, and I would think 'Wouldn't it be nice if coming to the gym was my break instead of the main stressor in my life?' So one day, after my shift, I stayed and did a class. I had no clue what I was doing. I looked like an idiot."

"I'm sure that's not true."

Marianne lifted a shoulder. "It's probably true."

Reagan slapped at Marianne's knee.

"It's true. I did. I was never really an athlete like some people." She shot Marianne a glance. "But afterward, I felt so . . . alive." That made her feel bad. "That sounds awful. Like having Zach wasn't living. But this was something just for me. Mine alone. So I kept going back. I was the loser in the back of the studio in the cutoff jeans and gym employee polo—because I couldn't afford real workout clothes—with the ungainly posture."

"And now you teach it."

"Teaching brought me more per hour than working the desk handing out towels. And I got bonuses if I had so many people per class. I added in Pilates because it complemented the workout. And I love it. It's not work anymore."

"See that dreamy look in her eyes?" Marianne grinned and bumped shoulders with Reagan. "That's how I want her to look at a guy someday."

"She will," Reagan said, looking defensive. "She's just not ready yet."

"One day," Kara said. "One day." When someone knocked on the door, she glanced at her friends. "Are the guys picking you up?"

"I told Brad I'd text him when we were done, since we would be drinking." Marianne checked her phone with a frown. "But I don't think that's him."

Kara stood and walked to the front door. A quick check at the peephole had her flattening her back against the door. "It's Graham," she whispered. "What do I do?"

Both girls looked expectantly at her. After a moment, Graham knocked again.

"Open it," Reagan mouthed.

Marianne pointed at Reagan and nodded in agreement.

"I can't," Kara mouthed back.

Marianne rolled her eyes and walked to the door, pushing Kara out of the way and opening it with a flourish. "Graham, hey."

Kara listened as Graham paused. "Where's Kara?"

She covered her face.

"Let's find out. Come on in." Marianne hauled him in and straight over to the couch. "What brings you to our little girl fest?"

"Girl fest? I thought this was where Kara was showing you guys how to use Zach's EpiPens? I wanted to come by and learn."

Her heart melted. She closed the front door and walked out from behind it. "Hey."

He turned, and her mouth watered. In a dark polo that looked amazing with his perma-tanned skin, dark hair and darker eyes, jeans and boots, he was delicious. "Where'd you come from?"

"Never mind that. You wanted to see the EpiPens?"

He shoved his hands in his pockets, looking a little embarrassed. "I didn't realize this was a girl thing. I can go."

She caught his arm as he started to walk toward the door. "No, stay." When he hesitated, she squeezed gently. It was like squeezing a PVC pipe . . . a thick one. "You're right, that was the main point of tonight's get-together. So let's do it."

When he raised a brow, she flushed. Oh God . . . "Not . . . I mean, not do . . . it . . ." she finished weakly. "I'm gonna go get the pens." She ran toward the kitchen before she said something stupid.

More stupid. As if there was something more stupid than that.

GRAHAM wiped his damp palms on his jeans and looked at the two women sitting on the couch, staring as if they were watching a movie in a theater. "What?"

"Nothing," Reagan said softly. "I'm just feeling a little warm. Is it warm?" she asked Marianne.

"Very," the trainer confirmed. "Have a seat, Graham."

He wanted to grumble at the innuendo and secret language they were sharing, but refrained. He perched on the edge of the armchair, looking around. "Where's the kid?"

"Friend's house. And here's the mom." Marianne stood and took the basket of oranges from Kara's hands and set it on the table. "I thought the cheese and crackers were snack enough."

Kara sat down in front of the table, across from the couch, and settled a plastic tote box full of slender boxes beside them. "They're not a snack. Everyone grab an orange."

Graham did, brushing his knuckles against Kara's as they reached for the same one. She jerked back, and the orange fell to the coffee table. Marianne cleared her throat. Reagan stared intently at a wall to the side.

"Sorry," Kara said, handing him the orange without touching. "Okay, so here's one version of a pen. These were his last version. This is the trainer, so you can test it first and see what it's like. No needle, no risk." She demonstrated pulling the cap off, then went through miming thrusting it into her thigh and holding it for ten seconds after a clicking sound. "Count, out loud, because too much is going on at once and you have to make sure you keep it there the right amount. Then immediately call 911, even if he looks like he's doing better. Anytime, anywhere you have to use the EpiPen, you should call 911, even if he seems like he's improving already."

"That seems violent," Reagan said as she took the trainer from Kara. "Why does it have to be so hard against your thigh? Why not more gently against the arm?"

"The thigh is the best place, because it spreads the medicine the fastest and is the easiest spot for self-injection. But you have to hold it there because there's a recoil. The thigh isn't flabby."

"Well, some are," Reagan said, patting her own curvy legs.

"Stop," Marianne said, taking the trainer pen and trying it out before handing it to Graham. He did the same, inspecting it closely after giving it a try.

The thought of having to use the pen on Zach's small body made his hand shake a little as he handed it back to Kara. She gave him an odd look, but then passed out another pen exactly like the first. Except it was a bit more colorful.

"Real pen time. Don't mess with it, it's got a needle. Hold the orange against the table or the couch, and you can feel what it's like injecting it."

Graham did so, marveling at medicine and how far it had come.

"And we have now officially used about four hundred dollars' worth of medication on fruit," Kara joked. Graham felt his eyes bug out at the number, but she waved it away. "They're useless to us now, so there's nothing better to do with them."

"Why did you have four?"

"Two for school, two for home. He had two that he carried with him at all times, too, in his backpack or in my purse, but we practiced with those this morning together."

He hated that Zach had to know all of this information. Hated that this was a vital part of his childhood . . . knowing how to save his own life.

"This is his new one. It talks." She grinned and passed around the trainer. When Marianne pulled off the cap, it began to speak the instructions.

"Niiiiice," she murmured, then passed it to Reagan, who passed it to him.

"More expensive, unfortunately, but worth every penny. In an emergency, you don't have to worry about relying on a shaky hand reading tiny instructions."

He looked up at Kara, wanting so much to offer help. She was a single mom, and though she hadn't told him the story, he could guess Zach's father wasn't exactly contributing financially to their lives. Or really contributing in any way, period.

Another knock sounded on the door, and Kara jumped. Marianne stood, saying, "I've got it." She let in Greg and Brad, who came in and immediately took residence on the couch with their ladies.

"Oh, oranges." Greg reached for one, and Reagan slapped the back of his hand.

"Trust me, you don't want that one."

Kara and Marianne laughed when Greg wrinkled his nose in confusion and rubbed his hand.

"Now that we've got our rides here to take our wine-soaked butts home, we're going to take off." Reagan stood, holding a hand out to Greg. When he raised both brows, she shook the hand, insisting.

"We just got here. Don't we at least get some cheese and crackers?" Brad asked. Marianne reached over, grabbed a cracker and shoved it in his mouth.

"And that's all, folks. See y'all at practice tomorrow morning, bright and early!" Marianne kissed the top of Kara's head as they passed. "Don't get up, we'll let ourselves out."

"But you—" The door snapped shut before she could even get out her sentence. "Wow. They're in a hurry," she said with a nervous laugh.

"They've got someone to keep them company tonight. I can't blame them." When Kara glanced at him, he shrugged. Then he stood and started gathering oranges into the basket they'd come from.

"You don't have to pick those up. I can do it." She reached for it, but he kept it out of reach. "Really, Graham, you should get going. I'm sure you've got plans."

"I have nothing. It's a school night," he added with a smile over his shoulder on his way to the kitchen. He pitched the oranges and set the basket by the sink. "Do you mind if I get a glass of water?"

"Sure thing," she called from the living room. He heard the jumble of EpiPens and knew she was putting them all away safely. "Glasses are in the cabinet beside the sink."

He opened the one to the right, and came face to face with a mini pharmacy. It took him a moment to catch his breath after seeing the medications. He hoped some were just for emergencies, and not all for daily use. He couldn't imagine Zach having to take that much regularly. He was a tough, smart kid, but even tough kids had limits.

Closing the cabinet quietly, he opened the right one and got water from the filter pitcher in the refrigerator. He carried it back to the living room and settled into the armchair. She'd want him to go, and he was fully prepared to miss all her subtle hints. He was about to be rude, on purpose, for the first time in his adult life.

"I'm sure you've got things to do."

Hint number one to get out. "I'm free."

"Really, I don't want to keep you."

Hint number two. "It was no problem. I'm glad I know about it now." He grinned when her hand clenched around the edge of the coffee table.

"I appreciate you coming by." Her voice was firm, but her hands shook a little as she started to sweep crumbs onto the platter. She wouldn't make eye contact. "Zach adores all you guys, and you taking an interest in his medical needs says a lot. Not every adult in his life cares enough to bother."

"Then they're assholes." Graham took a calm sip of water as her head snapped up. "He's got allergies, that's all. It's changing a few ingredients to a recipe here or there. Buying a different brand of food, or keeping an eye on the utensils. It's not the end of the world, far as I can tell from reading your blog."

She sat back on her heels. "You really did read it."

Hell yeah, I read it. I want you. I've wanted you for weeks. And I'll use everything at my disposal to get to know you.

All he said was, "Yep. It's a good blog, lots of easy-to-understand info. You could really make that a full-time gig."

She blushed, then continued scraping off the totally clean coffee table. "Thank you. That means a lot to me."

"Why do I make you nervous?"

She jolted, as if he'd touched her with a hot poker instead of just asking her a question. "I'm not nervous," she lied, not making eye contact. "That's ridiculous."

"You're cleaning the coffee table instead of looking at me. You've been trying to push me out the door since I got here. And you don't want to be alone with me. Why? What is it about me that freaks you out?"

"I'm not freaked out by you." She stood and gave him her back as she walked to the trash can with cupped palms and dusted the crumbs into the trash can. "I'm just not sure being alone like this is wise. Nothing can happen, and I don't want to accidentally encourage you, so . . ." She looked back at him, hands in the air in defeat. Her eyes were sad, like she regretted it more than she could voice.

"Kara." He spoke softly, and she instinctively walked to him on bare feet. "Kara, nothing *has* happened. I'm trying not to push you."

"I know that. And I appreciate it." She halted a foot away. "More than you know."

"But at this speed, we might make it to our first date when we're eligible for the early bird special. I like you. I hate games, so I'm telling you now, I like you."

There. Cards laid out. He wasn't kidding. Games were the worst. He watched game players all day in his office, and he did everything he could to avoid the bullshit in his personal life.

She swallowed, and he took a half step toward her. Closing the gap slowly enough she could move back if she needed to. But she didn't move back, only tilted her head up slightly to look at him. "Graham . . ."

His lips quirked. "Kara."

"Graham." Her voice had softened, almost to a slur, and her eyelids closed a fraction. "I—my phone."

He hadn't even heard it ring, he was so lost. "Get it later."

"I can't. Zach. Zach's with a friend." She patted the pockets of her jean shorts, did quick spins in place looking frantically for the still ringing phone. "Phone! Where's my phone!"

"Here." He found it on the floor beside the leg of the table and handed it to her just as it stopped ringing. He waited while she checked the call, then immediately called them back.

"Stacy? Hey, sorry, couldn't find my phone. Is Zach okay?" She placed a hand to her heart, and Graham dug in his pocket to get his keys ready to roll. If something happened with Zach, he'd be driving her there. No way could she drive if she was panicked about her son.

After a few moments, Kara sagged a bit, shoulders drooping. Her eyes closed and she let out a sigh. "Yeah, definitely. Oreos are one of his main food groups. No, it's fine, I'm glad you called. You know the deal . . . any questions, always call. I hope the boys are having fun. Sure, I'll say good night to him."

Sensing the call was coming to a close, and there was no immediate crisis, Graham decided to give her some privacy. He headed for the door, but as he opened it, he felt her hand on his back.

As he turned around, she leaned forward and gave him a quick hug, phone still up to her ear, then stepped back, out of reach. He smiled slightly, then waved and stepped out just as she said, "Hey, Zach, you doing okay?"

It wasn't quite how he'd envisioned the evening ending . . . but the spontaneous hug, started by her, would tide him over. For now.

CHAPTER

3

Tuesday morning brought yoga and Marines. Tuesdays were good days. Kara walked in early to the training room, ready for muffins and Marianne time, and stopped short as she caught Nikki, one of Marianne's trainers, with her butt in the air and her head stuck under the ice machine. Her skintight khaki shorts looked like they were painted on as she wriggled and scooted around.

Kara cleared her throat, heard a muffled, feminine curse, then Nikki emerged from under the machine. Her dark blond hair was pulled back into a messy bun, but not of the fashionably messy variety. There were smudges under her eyes, and her polo had dust on it. The girl was a mess.

"Hi." She stuck her hands behind her back and rocked back on her heels, looking younger than her early twenties, as Kara knew her to be. She looked like Zach when he'd been caught in the act and wasn't ready to fess up yet. "Marianne's not here yet. Did you need something?"

"Hmm." She couldn't say what, but something wasn't quite

right. Instead of backing out and waiting for Marianne in the more open gym, Kara let her bag hit the desk chair and settled the muffin basket on the desk. "I'll just wait in here."

"Oh, but . . . I'm cleaning." As if struck by sudden inspiration, Nikki's baby blue eyes lit with excitement. "I'm cleaning, and the smell . . . you don't want to sit in here with it. It'll ruin the taste of your muffins later."

Kara sniffed delicately. Smelled just like it always did in the mornings before the sweaty Marines invaded the room. Like faded cleanser and plastic. Not the most delightful scent in the world, but not the worst. "I'll be okay. Just do whatever you need to."

Nikki's eyes looked a little panicked, and she searched around before grabbing a rag and dry-wiping down the wall beside the ice machine. Kara huffed quietly and sat on one of the exam tables. She let her clogs clatter to the linoleum floor and stretched out, reaching her toes and holding. There was almost nothing a good stretch and some deep breathing couldn't solve, as far as she was concerned.

Okay, so stretching and breathing hadn't managed to solve her unfortunate, but unwaning yearning for one specific Marine boxer. But that's why vibrators and batteries had been invented.

Nikki continued to clean the same exact spot on the wall, without moving. Kara wondered what her motivation for being in the gym so early was. She could have been searching for a lost earring from the day before. Maybe they were her grandmother's and very precious.

Kara did her best not to scoff, even in her own head. More like she lost some cheap earring the night before after trying to climb on the lap of some unsuspecting Marine. The men, she gave them credit, all did their best to avoid giving her the wrong idea. But the young trainer-to-be seemed bound and determined to snag a Marine. Any of them. Pickiness was not in her personal dictionary.

"Hey," Marianne said, running in on a dash. If she were a cartoon character, there would be dust clouds billowing in her wake. "Sorry I'm late. Brad slept over, which he doesn't always do, especially not when I've got to get here early, and before I could get out of bed he—"

"Hey, Marianne!" Kara said loudly. "Look who's here early! Nikki!"

Marianne froze midstep, then looked around wildly. Her ice blond hair swirled around her shoulders, not yet pulled up in its typical ponytail. "Wha . . . oh. Nikki . . . what are you doing here so early?"

"Cleaning," came the curt reply. The woman turned and tossed the rag in a bin. "Why is that so weird?"

"It's weird because—never mind." Marianne cut herself off and let her tote bag drop on her desk chair beside Kara's. "We've got an hour or so before you need to be back. Why don't you go grab a donut and coffee at the Dunkin' Donuts on Mainside."

"I don't want a donut," she said, sounding to Kara like a snotty brat.

"Let's try this again." With a deep breath, and the patience of a saint, Marianne calmly said, "I want some privacy in my training room for the moment. You need to head out for a while. You can come back at your regularly scheduled time."

"You've let Levi come in early before," she said, looking a little hurt. Kara tried to feel some form of sympathy, but the young woman made it difficult.

"I've asked Levi to come in for a specific project where I needed an extra pair of hands. Right now, I'm about to have a meeting in my office, in which I need privacy. You're excused," she snapped when Nikki opened her mouth again, likely to argue. "I'll see you in an hour."

Nikki flounced, yes, flounced, out the door, grabbing her knockoff designer purse from the hook behind the door before she left. The door slammed shut behind her.

"God, she's insufferable. How the hell have you not sent her back yet?"

"She's twenty-one. We were all insufferable then. Well, maybe not you," she conceded when Kara raised a brow. "But you had a three-year-old. Hard to be insufferable when you're responsible for another human life. She's immature. She'll either grow out of it, or life will slap her back hard. She'll figure it out."

"Maybe slapping her now is the answer." Kara grinned as Marianne handed her a muffin from the basket. "I mean, metaphorically."

"Of course you do," Marianne said, then took a bite of her own muffin. "You're not in a very Zen place today. What's going on with you?"

"I nearly kissed Graham." Picking at the paper from the muffin, she didn't look up. She believed in honesty, especially with those closest to you. But she also believed you didn't have to make it harder on yourself than necessary. Right now, staring at her muffin made it easier. "The night you came over for the EpiPen demo. You left, he stayed, and . . ."

Marianne said nothing, and Kara felt an odd need to fill in the silence.

"It's not my fault. He's just standing there so, so . . . male. And caring, and he seems to really like Zach, and he's, you know, well, he looks like how he looks and . . ." The muffin crumbled on top of the exam bench, and Kara knew Marianne was listening intently, if she didn't scold for the crumbs on her pristine work space. "I don't know."

"First off . . ." When Marianne didn't continue, Kara finally looked up cautiously. Her friend's face was serious. "First off, crumbs."

Kara grinned. She couldn't help it.

"Secondly, hell yeah, you should have kissed him. What stopped you?"

"A call from Matt's mother. Matt was the friend Zach

was staying with." When Marianne nodded in understanding, she added, "He was fine. Just a question on snack food. But it definitely derailed the whole thing. And thank God," she added, wondering why her friend wasn't equally shocked by the entire ordeal. The silence meeting that statement was deafening. "Because it would have been a disaster."

"You forgot how to kiss?" Marianne smiled. "It's pretty easy. I'm sure he'd be more than happy to spend an hour or three practicing with you."

Kara held up a piece of muffin over the edge of the table, just waiting for a good reason to drop it on her friend's pristine floor.

"Okay, okay! Put the muffin down. Asshole."

"Jerkface," Kara shot back, very maturely, from the ease of long friendship.

"Come on, Kara. He's into you. He's an awesome guy. He's insane to look at, with all those bronze muscles and that dark hair. And you know how, even if he's shaved like, ten minutes ago, he still looks like he's got stubble? And those eyes . . ." Marianne sighed.

"Uh, remember Brad? The Marine you chose? And love? And are probably going to marry and make babies with?"

Marianne shook her head a little, as if coming out of a dream. "I'm taken, not blind. The guy's seriously hot. And he's awesome to boot. How many men are there in the world that have both the looks and the personality to match, with the added bonus of intelligence? Five?"

"And you and Reagan got two of them. Very unsporting."

"I know." Smug with it, Marianne took another bite of her muffin. "You really should sell these things, you know. They're actually good, as compared to some of those other allergen-free mixes we've tried."

"Owning my own kitchen and distribution and the start-up costs . . ." Kara sighed. She'd looked into it. Nearly ten years of baking and cooking for her allergic-to-everything son had taught her enough tricks of the trade that she could make most things palatable. Sadly, she knew they would never compete with the real deal, but as far as substitutions went, it was acceptable.

"You should at least create a cookbook. That's an almost zero startup cost. If you can't get it published, you could make one. Self-publish it. You've got such a huge blog following, they'd totally be behind you."

Somehow, that one hadn't pinged her radar. "Hmm." She broke off another piece and ate it thoughtfully. "Maybe. It's just that teaching and the blog and keeping up with Zach's schedule really keeps me so busy, it's hard to justify the additional time. I have to sleep at some point."

"Sleep is overrated." Brad walked in, waving to Kara and bending down to press a kiss to the top of Marianne's head. He made his way to the ice machine, well familiar with the routine by now, tossing his knee brace on the table next to Kara's.

"So you proved this morning with my wake-up call," Marianne said, a gleam in her eye.

"Ew. No. Stop." Kara covered her ears with her wrists—her fingers were too crumby—and hummed. "You two can't do that crap with an audience. It should be illegal."

"She's jealous," Marianne yelled at Brad, clearly for Kara's benefit. "She could be getting some but she's being *stubborn* about it."

Kara flipped her off, then hopped down off the table. "I'm setting up early and stretching. In the gym. In private. With no wisecracks from you. Brad," she added as she grabbed her tote from behind Marianne's back, "you've got your hands full with this one. Good luck." She grinned as her friend flopped a little with the force.

"I'll need it," he agreed as he settled the ice bag over his knee. Marianne growled and stood, probably to punch him in the arm. Kara left before she could get caught in the middle.

* * *

GRAHAM entered the gym with sweating palms. It was yoga day, which translated in his mind to Kara Day. Capital letters, because it was that important. He scanned quickly for Zach, but reminded himself that wasn't to be expected. It was enough that she was here.

Reagan clacked in behind him. He knew it was her before he turned around. The heels she wore habitually were unlike any other sound in the sweltering, dark gym. "Good morning, Graham. You're a bit early."

"Extra yoga practice." He flashed her a grin when she smiled. "You're here early," he shot back at her.

"Extra . . . never mind." Her smile turned a bit sly, and he shook his head and walked toward the pile of mats Kara had brought out from the storage room. He grabbed one and found her face down, arms at her side, doing a good imitation of a plank of wood on her own personalized mat.

"Hey."

Her back moved, a sign of her breathing, but she said nothing. Assuming she was deep in some trance, he left her to it and rolled out his own mat in the front. He normally preferred the back, because the more distance he created from Kara, the easier it was to watch her without her noticing. The easier it was to keep his hands to himself.

But, despite no longer being in charge of a mini platoon of Marines trying out for the team, he knew he should be in front. Yoga wasn't his thing . . . in fact, he sucked at it. But he still wanted to be a leader to the younger guys. Being one of the oldest meant he assumed the responsibility of being a good example. A task that wasn't all that difficult, under normal circumstances. He'd lost his wild edge years ago.

That long lost wild edge seemed to flare back to life anytime he caught Kara in a compromising position . . . yoga-related or otherwise. As she breathed deeply enough for him to hear, and rose her torso up from the mat, palms flat, arching her back, he bit back a moan. The position thrust her breasts forward, and the look on her face, eyes closed and serene, was akin to the look of a woman after a good, satisfying lovemaking session.

He'd be fighting a semi for the rest of practice at this rate.

The sigh of relief as she rotated her hips back and sank into Child's Pose—and wasn't it a kick he knew what it was called—made him smile. Then she rolled up, graceful as an otter in the water, and gave him a small smile of her own. "Hey. Sorry I didn't answer you earlier. I wasn't quite ready to move on yet."

"No rush." Except he felt the rush inside him, pushing him to move faster. It was like having a hive of bees rolling inside his skin, pushing every direction, and mostly toward her.

"How are you?" she asked, brushing her hands off and sitting cross-legged to fix her ponytail, which didn't look like it needed fixing to him.

So they were really going to play the Nothing Happened game. Fine. He could play for now. "Good. Great. Getting ready to morph into another scrimmage match this weekend. What are your plans for the week?"

"Nothing, really." She twisted, pulled and secured until her hair was in a silky bun at the top of her head. Having watched her work before, he knew it wouldn't be long into their yoga session before strands were falling down around her temples, framing her heart-shaped face. It was the hottest thing he'd ever seen. "Relaxing with Zach, for the most part. New school year means I'm at the ready for problems."

"He's a great kid. I'm sure there aren't too many problems." He heard a short bark, almost like a yell, but ignored it. "Maybe this weekend you could bring Zach to catch the match. We're just competing against the local Lejeune team. No travel."

She bit her pink bottom lip, looking worried. "I don't

know. It's a violent sport, and—" She turned as he did when a heavy door at the opposite end of the gym screeched open and shut, finding the source of the shouting as it grew louder.

Coach Ace, a burly black man who had muscle and heft and moved like a ghost, walked in, pointing directly at Graham. "You."

He stood slowly. "Yes, Coach?"

"What have you seen since you got here?"

Graham blinked, then looked down at Kara, who remained sitting on her mat. "Uh, nothing. Just talking with Kara, sir."

"You," he pointed at Kara, still speed-walking their way. "What have you seen?"

Graham bristled at the tone. She wasn't one of the Marines, or a teammate, to be barked at. But Kara unfolded her legs gracefully and started to stand. He held a hand down for her, and she accepted it on autopilot, barely giving him any of her weight to bear. "I've seen nothing, sir. I was in the training room, and then I came out here to stretch. Gra—I mean, Sweeney has been the only Marine to come through so far."

Coach Ace grunted, as if in disbelief. Graham wanted to ask, but he also didn't want to get in the middle of anything. But still . . . "Sir, is there a problem?"

"You could say that." Rubbing a hand over his dark face, the coach rocked back on his heels and looked heavenward. "Someone's vandalized the wall of fame."

Graham looked at Kara, found her looking at him, then they both took off at a jog. Coach Ace didn't join them. He skidded to a halt at the other end of the gym, at the doors that led to the mostly unused hallway containing photos of past boxing teams and champions. "Hold on. Let me check it out first."

"He said they *had* vandalized it. Not that they currently *were* vandalizing it. Pretty sure he wouldn't be asking you what you'd seen if he caught someone red-handed," Kara pointed out, clearly not listening to him. "Don't play the

'protect the womenfolk' crap with me. I'm a big girl. Now go."
She shoved at his shoulder, and he opened the heavy door.

Right away, he saw it. The photos of each boxing team
from the past several decades lined the walls, framed in
simple black or gold frames, with white mats and a small
plaque to indicate the year. On the glass covering the photos,
someone had used a marker or paint or something to draw
obscene images, write nasty messages and create lewd or
downright stupid pictures. A few were more simple, just giving each guy a dumb mustache or top hat. Others were more
graphic, with body parts and sexual suggestions scribbled.

"This is . . ." Kara's voice trailed off, and she cleared her
throat. "Juvenile. I know it's horrible, and so very disrespectful. But it's almost juvenile compared to the other acts. Right?"

He couldn't help but agree. Their vandal was losing
steam, or maybe losing ways to fuck with the team. Trashing
the bus, the training room, puncturing tires, creating a huge
publicity mess with paint . . . that had taken time, energy
and support away from the team. This was just disrespectful,
but not all that clever. It was the sort of thing you expected
from middle school kids who hated their principal and snuck
in after hours to doodle on his photo in front of the office.

"Maybe the handwriting will help the MPs figure out
who it is. Since they have to be connected to this building
or the team somehow . . ." She didn't say what they were
both thinking.

The vandal was most likely a member of the team. Or
had been. Or had wanted to be. It might be someone they
currently trusted. Someone they called a friend.

CHAPTER

4

Kara sank down on the couch beside Zach just in time for the phone in the kitchen to ring. With a sigh, she hefted herself back up. "Pause the movie, would ya?"

"Moooooom." His young voice whined at the command. "Hurry back. We can only watch it tonight before it's gotta be back to the red box thingie drop off tomorrow morning."

"A five minute phone call will not ruin our plans. The Avengers can wait a minute. Captain America waited, like, six decades."

He groaned at her joke, burying his face in a throw pillow.

She chuckled and answered the phone. "Hello?"

"Kara, hi." The voice of her attorney, Tasha Williams, cut through any good feelings she'd had about the evening. Her stomach sank, dread swirling to mix greasily with the handful of buttery popcorn she'd already consumed.

Her attorney never called unless there were problems. Big ones. Otherwise, she had her assistant send a simple email. "Do you have a minute to chat?"

"Sure. Hold on just a minute." With a sigh, she leaned out of the kitchen door. "Zach, go ahead and start the movie. I'll be on the phone for a bit."

He brightened and grabbed for the remote. His world, as he knew it, was right and perfect.

Kara's was about to get another ding. "Okay, what's up?"

"Henry is making another run at lowering child support."

She sank into the kitchen chair. "Of course he is."

"Something this time about how your job . . . I'm sorry, jobs"—her voice dripped with disdain on the word—"were too low paying. And that your choice to remain a freelancer rather than hold a regular nine-to-five job was irresponsible, and he shouldn't have to compensate financially to pick up the slack. Since you want to keep him full time, you should have more skin in the game."

Kara heard the unspoken "or else." "Let me guess, he made not-so-veiled comments about gaining custody again."

"Bingo. Never came out and said it, but as usual, it's his favorite go-to threat."

Super. Henry was, at the best of times, a negligent human. He didn't care much about anyone or anything beside himself, and mostly Kara thought that wasn't based on any malice toward others. Just a general lack of consideration and awareness. But when something inconvenienced him, he turned from negligent to nuisance to asshole in a hot minute.

He didn't want custody. Never had. His entire life would come crumbling down if he suddenly became responsible for another human being. The man couldn't be trusted with a goldfish. But custody had become that one thing he held up as a selling point toward being awarded less and less financial responsibility.

The idea of him taking Zach for a weekend chilled her to the bone. Zach as a ten-year-old was pretty self-sufficient. But with his allergies, and an uncaring, self-absorbed adult in charge for two days . . . it could be a disaster.

"Kara?"

She blinked. "Yes, I'm sorry."

"You'll need to come in tomorrow, if possible." There was a hesitation, and Kara saw dollar signs in it. "And you'll need to speak with the front office about the retainer."

"Mm-hmm. Sure." She hung up after agreeing on a time to meet, mentally calculating exactly where that money was going to come from.

This was Henry's plan. Not only did he know she'd fight to keep Zach from going to visit his dad routinely, but that she couldn't afford to play the lawyer game. It was a decision of whether to accept less money monthly, or spend greatly in chunks via attorney retainers.

She sat at the table for five minutes, giving her body a chance to calm down via deep breathing and visualization. When she felt calmer, she went back into the living room and sat beside her son. He grumbled, as there were plenty of other places to sit that wouldn't put them shoulder to shoulder, but didn't argue when she wrapped her arm around him and pulled him tight against her.

"Love you," she murmured into his hair.

He grunted in a very male sort of way.

She smiled, and watched the Avengers kick ass.

"OKAY, don't yell at me," Marianne said as she held up her hands. "But I have to tell you something."

Kara set her smoothie down and glanced at Reagan, who looked equally concerned. "What? What is it?"

"This smoothie sucks," Marianne said simply. "Whose idea was it to come here for drinks? When I think post-work cocktails, I don't think of one that includes a shot of seaweed."

"It's not that bad," Reagan said, sipping her own concoction. She managed to hold the face for a full five seconds before scrunching up her nose and waving her hand in front of her mouth. "Oh, there's an aftertaste. Oh, bad. Bad."

Kara sighed and sipped her own. "Acquired taste. And I didn't want to go to Back Gate, because if I went there, I might end up drowning my sorrows in five beers and having one of your manly men tossing me over their shoulder to haul me back up to my apartment like a drunken lush."

"Very classy," Marianne said.

"Ladylike," was Reagan's thought.

"Uh-huh. Speaking of classy, any updates on the vandalism?"

Reagan blew out a breath that shifted the fine hairs escaping her twist. "None. Since it looks like this time, the person popped the lock on the back door there in that never-used hallway, so it's impossible to tell when it was done. Nobody knows when the last time someone wandered back there was. Could have been ten minutes before Coach Ace found it, could have been days. The gym is almost solely used for practice right now, and that hallway's mostly ignored."

"It sucks. So disrespectful," Marianne said with an angry clench to her jaw.

"You know," Kara said softly, "Nikki was there early that day. And she acted surprised she got caught in the room early." When Marianne leaned forward more, Kara went on, "She was under the ice machine when I walked in, as if she were looking for something. But when I said hi, she acted like she'd been caught red-handed."

"No black marker in her hand?" Marianne asked hopefully. "It would be the perfect excuse to dismiss her."

"No black marker," Kara said. Much as it pained her to admit the next, she went on. "She's a crazy one, but I struggle to think she would do something like that. It's not her style. Ripping apart the apartment of an ex-boyfriend, maybe."

"In her mind, they might all be potential ex-boyfriends." When Kara and Marianne looked at Reagan in surprise, she blushed and looked down. "Sorry, that was stupid."

"No, go on."

"Well . . ." One finger drawing through the condensation from her glass, she continued. "She wants them. I don't think she cares who. She's a tag-chaser. But nobody is taking the bait."

"Levi has." With a sigh, Marianne pushed her smoothie glass farther from her. "Poor guy. He's smitten, and she either has no clue, or doesn't give a crap."

"Combination, fifty-fifty," was Kara's summation. "Continue."

"So what if she sees all of them as pseudo-exes? They've all turned her down, they've all scorned her. None of them want to be caught alone with her. They've rejected her, and she's annoyed with it. She's more than annoyed," Reagan corrected, scooting in her chair a bit as someone passed behind her in the crowded cafe. "She's hurt. And a hurt woman, especially an immature one, can do a lot of damage."

It was something to think about. "Speaking of being hurt . . ." Kara squeezed her eyes shut, then went for it. "I have to go back to mediation again with Henry. Zach's dad," she reminded Reagan, who looked confused. Storm clouds gathered in Marianne's eyes.

Her friend had never cared for the guy, even when they'd been teens. She'd wanted to tear the guy apart back when Kara had gotten pregnant, but that was just as much Kara's fault as Henry's. And they'd all been young and stupid.

As an adult, her friend had zero tolerance for the bullshit her ex heaped upon her regularly.

"What's that fuckhead's problem this time?"

"There are kids around," Kara admonished. "He wants to lower support—again. Or else he'll have to start taking Zach for more than what he usually does."

"Which is how often? I feel like he's always with you," Reagan said. "Which is great, because he's a good kid, but that has to be exhausting."

"It is, but the alternative is horrifying." Kara reached into her purse and dug out a receipt and jotted down a note to write a blog about being a single parent dealing with allergies. The lack of break was wearing. It was a good one for her readers. She stuffed the reminder back in her bag. "Anyway, I've got to figure this out, because Zach would definitely suffer if he were with his dad often. The guy isn't a winner in anyone's book. I'm sure he'd come back swearing like a sailor or telling me how horrible I am."

"When was the last time your ex saw Zach?"

"Zach was about three. His dad picked him up for lunch, then brought him back an hour later disgusted that he couldn't eat anything and demanded to know why I'd done 'nothing' about his allergies yet. Like there's some sort of pill I could give him to take all the allergies and intolerances away, and I was just too lazy to bother."

"Fuckhead," Reagan breathed. "I'm sorry, but she's right. He's a fuckhead."

That made Kara snort out a laugh, then laugh harder because the sound was so awful. Loud enough that a table by the window shot her the evil eye for disturbing their afternoon guava-infused beverages. "So now that I will be paying for my attorney—again—to beat my ex into a pretzel—again—this will be my last time out for a while." She toasted them with her protein smoothie and took another sip. "Such is life."

"Okay, don't yell at me," Marianne said.

"I am having déjà vu," Reagan murmured. "We know, you hate the smoothie."

"Not that." Wadding up her napkin, she tossed it at Reagan, who batted it away.

"If I weren't wearing my cute shoes, I'd kick you."

"All your shoes are cute." Kara looked under the table to catch a glimpse of today's footwear. Black and white polka dotted heels with a little bow on the back. "Yup. Cute."

"Back to me," Marianne said, clearing her throat. "You should ask Graham."

"For shoes? I doubt we're the same size."

"Why am I friends with her?" Marianne asked Reagan. Reagan shrugged. "Ask Graham for help with the custody issue. He's cheaper than a real lawyer."

"He *is* a real lawyer."

"Not what I meant." Marianne waved that away. "He might not be able to do a lot, but he can give you a ton of free advice, so you aren't wasting hours with your own attorney. You can get in, tell them what you want, and get out. Less billable hours that way."

Kara chewed on the straw a bit. A disgusting habit, but she couldn't quite stop herself. It was better than chewing her bottom lip raw. "I couldn't do that."

"Because he's so ugly and smelly and spending a lot of time with him might make you vomit."

"Marianne," Reagan scolded.

"No, obviously that's not it. The exact opposite, asshole. But I don't want to impose on him. He's got so much going on right now with boxing and matches coming up, and then the All Military games. It would be wrong of me to dump this on him, too."

"It's rather simple. You invite the guy over for dinner, you spend ten minutes laying out the issue, you spend ten minutes listening to him talk, and then you eat. Done."

Reagan patted Marianne's forearm. "It's not that simple, and you know it. There are feelings involved."

Smugly, Kara smiled at her friend. "Yeah, it's not that . . . wait. Feelings for who?"

Reagan looked disgusted. "Don't act like that. We aren't stupid."

"I'm not friends with stupid people, so of course you aren't. But I never said I was feeling anything."

"We've got eyes," she pointed out.

"I don't want to lead him on. Nothing will happen there, so . . ." She raised her hands and lowered them again. "I just can't."

Reagan looked like she wanted to argue, but ducked her head and went back to the bad aftertaste smoothie. Marianne simply shook her head and kept quiet.

When these two chatterboxes went quiet, Kara knew she had a problem.

REAGAN sat in front of the Marines, her top foot swinging over the other as she waited for Coach Ace to stop talking. Graham let himself zone out a bit, watching the high heel swing back and forth like a metronome. It was soothing, really, and he could almost feel himself float away to a place where his solar plexus didn't sting like a sonofabitch and his jaw didn't hurt.

God, boxing was fun.

"Dude." Greg elbowed him in the ribs as he hissed, "Are you staring at my girlfriend's legs?"

He blinked, shook his head to land back on this planet, and turned his head. "No?"

"Is that a question or an answer?" Greg, the easygoing, affable team member who could make anyone laugh, looked pissed. "Please tell me you're not actually checking out my woman."

"Chill, man. I zoned out. Her foot was in the way. Calm down."

Greg rolled his shoulders back, looking uneasy with the whole thing, then mumbled, "Sorry," from the corner of his mouth.

Graham started to say it was no big deal, when his head snapped forward. From the corner of his eye, he saw Greg's had done the same. They'd both received a head slap.

"Quit your gossipin' and listen," Coach Cartwright said from behind them in a low tone. "Don't make me separate you two like a bunch of damn kindergarteners."

Greg looked over and grinned at him in a way that said, *Business as usual*.

"And now, I'm turning it over to Ms. Robilard, who will be speaking about this weekend, as well as a few other pressing matters."

They waited quietly while Reagan stood, smoothing down her skirt with businesslike brushes of her hand. She took the spot Coach Ace left and cleared her throat. "We all know the match this weekend is an important one. It's the last one before the All Military games. It's also against men you've probably seen around, working out. Many of you came from Lejeune, so these are former teammates. It's important to note that while this is meant to be a training exercise, it is also designed to be fun camaraderie."

Graham thought several of the younger guys, with blood-lust in their eyes, could stand to be reminded a few more times before the match began. He'd be watching for them to go too hard, too heavy.

"We also need to talk about how we will be handling the vandalism." She took a quick breath, let it out slowly in a parody of their yoga breathing. She always presented a strong, polished front, but he had a feeling she was more like a master at hiding her real feelings. "We need to keep a sharp eye out. You guys are trained to notice details. You need that. I am not saying, nor do I want you to ever accuse one of the Lejeune team members of anything. I simply want you to be on guard. There will be more people in and out of the gym, and I'm asking you to be alert. Nothing more. If you see something, do not take it upon yourself to address the situation. Call the MPs."

Graham barely held himself back from snorting. He knew she was doing her job, asking them to bow to the closest authorities, but there was no way any of his teammates would see someone screwing with their gym and just walk away to get better cell phone reception. From the look on Greg's face beside him, he knew his friend was thinking likewise.

"Okay, so, uh . . ." She clapped her hands together. "Have a good practice!"

"Less than two weeks," Brad muttered as he walked over to join their group to stretch out before the afternoon practice. "We've got less than two weeks before we head to the games. And this junk just keeps on coming."

"So we do what the lady says." Lacing his fingers together, Graham stretched his arms high and felt the pull. "We keep our eyes open, our ear to the ground, watch everyone and pay attention. It's like when you're trying to deal with a large group of eyewitnesses. The odds are, more than one of us has seen something suspicious, but we didn't realize it at the time. Connected together, it might mean something."

"Lawyer boy just can't keep his fancy lawyering to himself," Greg joked.

"Maybe that's what slowed him down so much this morning during practice." Brad inspected the side of Graham's jaw. "You're not one to get caught so easily. You're always five steps ahead. How'd you get clipped?"

Because his mind had been with Kara, not on the sparring match. He shrugged. "Off day. Whatever."

"Short practice today, boys." Coach Willis walked by, his head barely reaching the tops of their shoulders. "Short practice. Coach wants you home early and resting. And by resting, he doesn't mean mattress gymnastics," he added, staring at Greg, who held up his hands in an innocent gesture.

"Short practice, thank God," Graham murmured. He could go home and soak in his tub, lay down and read a damn book. Block out the world, including one very fine yoga instructor. For once, luck was on his side.

CHAPTER

5

G raham rolled up to his home in Hubert, five minutes from the back gate, and wanted to sigh with relief. Short practice his ass. Short practice apparently meant, "We're going to murder you, and you're going to like it. And after we're done, we will let you leave early to find a ditch to crawl into and die."

He hurt everywhere. Even the roots of his hair were tingling.

As he hit the clicker for his garage door, a movement by his front door caught his eye. He glanced, and saw a short person huddled on his front step, arms wrapped around their knees. A hoodie covered their head, despite the warmth of the afternoon, their sneakers were untied and a bookbag rested at their feet.

Zach.

He was out of the car in an instant, the car door still swinging open as he dashed over and crouched down in front of the boy. "Zach. What's wrong? Are you hurt? Is it your mom?"

The boy looked up at him, so miserable it made Graham's heart rattle in his chest. "I'm sorry."

As he sniffled, Graham settled down beside him on the concrete, wrapping an arm around the kid. He decided to not mention the tears or sniffling. "Sorry for what?"

The boy's voice was a little muffled as he rested his forehead on his knees, but Graham could still make it out. "I came out here, and then you weren't home and I got scared but I'm okay and please don't send me back."

In his head, Graham listed all the reasons Zach might have run away. Fight with his mom, bad grades, bad behavior at the babysitter's, bullying . . . But it was overshadowed with pride and love that the young boy had come to him when he'd needed someone. Not Brad or Greg. He'd come here.

He gave Zach's shoulder a quick squeeze and cleared his throat. "I'm here now. How'd you get out here, by the way?"

"Taxi. I used my allowance."

Resourceful kid. Though it unnerved him that a cab had taken a ten-year-old boy anywhere alone. "Your mom has no clue you're here, does she?"

"I was supposed to ride the bus to the babysitter today. She's got yoga stuff to do. But instead I walked down to the gas station on the corner and called a cab."

So both the babysitter and Kara were likely freaking out. "You know we have to call them, right?"

Zach's small back heaved with a sigh. "Yeah. I just can't."

"I'll do it." And he'd work it out so the boy could stay, at least for a bit. Whatever was going on in his life, it was clear he needed someone besides his mom to lean on. Which was not at all a slap to Kara, because she was one of the most amazing mothers he'd ever seen in action. But sometimes, a boy just needed a man to talk things out with. Or even just an adult who wasn't a parent. "Let's go inside and get you a snack. I'm sure you're hungry."

"Starving," he said with a dramatic flair, clutching his stomach and rolling to his side. His sneakers kicked out and he twitched like a bug in the throes of death. "I think my stomach's gonna turn inside out in a minute."

"Now that, we can't have. Come on." He led Zach back into the garage and through the door into the kitchen. It was a mint green color, which he'd thought cheerful, unique and a nice contrast for the dark cabinets at the time and now felt stupid about. It was like living in a bowl of mint chocolate chip ice cream. He just didn't have the energy to paint it right now. Not when the mere idea of lifting his arms over his shoulders made him want to cry daily.

He opened the tiny pantry and waved a hand. "Pick a snack, any snack." For a moment, he expected to see a good rendition of a plague of locusts, descending on the free-for-all food. He kept his diet pretty solid, but stocked some junk food for when he had guys over . . . especially Greg, whose taste buds gave a toddler a run for his money.

Grabbing a bottle of water and a few aspirin for himself, he turned to see Zach carefully picking up each box of food and reading the ingredients thoughtfully before setting it back down. It tore at his heart, knowing this was his life. That he couldn't do what any other boy his age would do and grab an armful of snacks and chow down. That each bite he put in his mouth could have dire effects on his health.

"Oreos," he managed to choke out. "Oreos are good, right? I think I remember seeing that on your mom's blog."

Zach turned, blinking sad eyes at him. "Yeah, you don't have any in here though. Can I just have some lunch meat?"

Oh, you poor, sweet, smart boy. "I've got a special stash." He'd forgotten in the moment he'd decided to keep the cookies handy in case Kara ever happened to magically drop by with Zach in tow . . . you know, in his fantasy world. He'd put them in a hidden spot so Greg or anyone else wouldn't scarf them. He reached on top of the fridge, pulled down a small wicker basket and set it on the kitchen table. "There's regular and double stuff."

"Who even eats regular when you've got double stuff?" Grinning, Zach grabbed the package and dropped his book bag on the floor. He kicked his shoes off and they landed beside the bag. The hoodie came off next, landing somewhere in the near vicinity. "Do I have to eat them at the kitchen table?"

"Nah." Graham grabbed a bag of carrots and hooked an arm around Zach's neck. "Let's go watch something bloody and violent on TV."

He might have imagined it, but Graham thought he heard the boy sniffle a little before he let out a low, "Yeah."

KARA settled back in the break room of the gym, wondering how many more extra classes she would have to take before Henry backed down. She couldn't afford the retainer without working overtime, and she still had two more in-home private lessons to give before she was done for the day. She loved yoga as much as the next person, but even she had her limits.

Her phone buzzed in the outer pocket of her duffel bag, and she eyed it warily. If it was Tasha calling with more bad news, she didn't want it. Maybe that was childish, but she'd rather just have it pushed aside to deal with later. When her back didn't ache and her feet didn't hurt from walking on the hard wooden floor all day.

It stopped, then immediately started buzzing again. With a groan, she pulled it out and saw the babysitter's name on the screen. She answered, "Hey, Syl, how's Zach?"

"Uh, you did say he was supposed to come today, right?"

"All week," Kara agreed. "Why, is he telling you he shouldn't be there?"

There was a short pause, then the babysitter answered softly, "He isn't here."

The breath left Kara's lungs in one big rush that left her feeling hollowed out, empty, deflated. Her heart sank, she could actually feel it sink, down to land on top of her stomach, leaving her weak and nauseous at the same time.

Henry. Henry had come and . . . no. Not yet. He wouldn't do this yet.

Kidnappers. Had someone come and taken her beautiful boy? Human trafficking. Drug mule. God . . .

Her phone beeped with an incoming call, and she pulled it away to see Graham's name and face smiling at her. *Not now, not now.*

"Sylvia . . . you're positive he wasn't on the bus."

"I was at the bus stop when it drove by. It never even stopped."

"Did you call the school? Maybe he fell asleep on the bus, or got on the normal bus to go home instead. Maybe—"

"I called the school. No kids were on the wrong bus. I drove by your apartment really fast, to make sure he hadn't gone home, but he wasn't there. Or if he was, he wasn't answering the door when I knocked. Kara, I'm so sorry. I don't know where he is."

Graham buzzed again, and she nearly screamed with frustration. "Syl, I'll call you back. I'm . . . I'll call you." She hung up, but as she hung up, it answered the other call instead. She started to hang up when she heard Graham's voice.

"Kara? Hello?"

Ask for help. Don't do this alone. You need help. Biting back a moan, hand shaking, she held it to her ear. "Graham?"

God, she sounded weak. She sounded ineffective, weak, and young. None of which she really was, so she had to steel her spine and find her son.

"I've got Zach."

Those three words had relief soaring through her so fast

it was painful. Her heart started back again at a sluggish rate, and her lungs burned with the effort to drag in full breaths. "Oh my God. You have him." Her voice sounded like she'd pushed the words through a tunnel of jagged glass. She paused. "Did you pick him up from school? You shouldn't have been able to do that."

He waited a beat before answering. "We just got in. I came home from practice and he was sitting on my front step. Taxi," he added, answering her next question before she could ask. "Taxi and allowance money. Look, he's safe here, we're watching some TV, and I've got the rest of the night off. He said you have a lot of clients today, which was why he was going to the babysitter's. I'll keep him with me, and you can swing by when you're done."

She slid a trembling hand over her face. The adrenaline hadn't worn off yet. "I can't ask you to do that."

"You didn't. I'm offering. It's nice to watch sports when there's someone else to yell at the TV with."

"You don't have any of his food—"

"He's munching on Oreos right now, and we'll figure out dinner. I'll get some recipes from your blog." When she didn't say anything, he said, "Kara. We're fine. He's fine."

"I'm sorry I accused you." A lone tear leaked out, a weakness she could indulge in now that her son was safe. "That was rude of me."

"I can hear in your voice you're frantic. It's fine. Just come by when you're done."

She nibbled on her lip. "I really should get him now and drag him—"

"Kara." His voice was lower, as if he wanted to keep it a secret. The faint sound of the TV was gone now. He must have stepped into another room. "He's got something eating at him. So I'm going to keep him here and let him unload for a bit. Sometimes, talking to an adult who isn't a parent just works better when a kid needs to vent. Come get him later. Punish him later. Do the whole Responsible Mom thing later. But give him a little time first. Give yourself a little time, too."

She should scold him for giving her parenting advice when he had no experience. But he'd once been a young boy. She couldn't discount that. "I'll call you when I'm on the way."

"Perfect. We look forward to seeing you." He chuckled, then added, "Well, I do, anyway." Then he hung up.

She set the phone down on the bench beside the duffel and covered her face with both hands. Now that she actually had the time to cry, the tears wouldn't come. It was as if they knew she could afford the moment to self-indulge, and were stubbornly withholding.

Even her tear ducts were against her.

With a shaky breath, she quickly texted Sylvia to let her know, stuffed the phone in her bag, stood on wobbly legs and made her way to the parking lot.

HEADLIGHTS cut through his open front window, waking Graham from the drowsy, relaxed pose on the couch. He sat up, muting the TV as he did, and checked out the window. Definitely Kara's car, though she wasn't turning it off and getting out. Was she hoping to grab him and run?

No way in hell.

But even as he watched, prepared to go out there and pull the keys out of the ignition himself, she slowly let her head drop to the steering wheel. He could see the exhaustion and worry from the front door. She wasn't trying to grab-and-go. She just wasn't ready to deal with the stress yet.

He gave her another few moments and went to check on Zach. He'd hit a slump at about eight thirty. Early for a kid his age, but Graham had a feeling the adrenaline of running off plus the excitement of being able to hang with him for a while had taken its toll. He'd carried the boy—and what a trusting, humbling weight that had been to hold against his shoulder and chest—to his guest room and tucked him in. It was a school night, so no way would he stay. But until Kara could come back for him, it was a more comfortable place to rest.

Zach was still out, and snoring just a little. Graham smiled, then closed the bedroom door again and headed to the front door. He made it just in time to open it before Kara rang the bell and woke the boy up.

"Hey." He held it open and let her come in. She wore yoga pants that were cropped at the calves and molded perfectly to her long legs, a flowy tank top that skimmed the top of her spectacular ass, and her hair in a long braid that emphasized how slim and tempting her neck was.

She looked around the living room, then into the kitchen. "Zach?"

"Sleeping in the guest room. He zonked out early, and I figured you might need a few minutes before you got him to go home." When she just stood there, staring toward the hallway that contained the bedrooms, he added, "I'm sorry. I hope you weren't worried too much."

The look she shot him was so maternal, he wondered if she'd ground him.

"'Worried' is not the word I would use." She let her purse drop to the love seat and sank down beside it. Her head flopped forward into her hands. He took the sofa, sitting close enough to reach out and touch her. He wanted to. But he wouldn't. Not yet.

"'Worried' makes it sound like I sort of thought about it, but knew it would be okay. Like how I worry when he's taking a big social studies test because he hates to read about history. Or worry he'll leave his EpiPen at home . . . but never has." She looked at him then, eyes full of tears he knew she was battling hard to not shed. "Terror is probably more accurate. I couldn't breathe. Graham, I . . ." She fluttered a hand over her chest, and it heaved with the effort to draw in air. "I couldn't . . . oh, God." Her voice was thin, and he could see she was a hair's breadth from a full blown panic attack.

"Hey, hey. Come here." Without waiting for her to protest, he tossed her purse on the coffee table, sat beside her on the love seat and pulled her against him. When she clenched a fist in his T-shirt, he knew she was so far gone she didn't even realize who held her. He waited until her breathing subsided, continually rubbing at her back with the palm of his hand and making a lot of low, soothing sounds.

He flashed back to the thought of carrying Zach, and what a humble, trusting weight that had been in his arms. How right it had felt, how amazing. And thought to Zach's mother, the woman he held now. He wanted that same weight from her. Wanted her to freely hand him her troubles to help her carry them. Wanted to hold her and be humbled by her faith.

After a while, Kara's grip on his shirt loosened and she sat back, wiping under her eyes. "I can't believe I just did that."

"Don't apologize." *God, don't apologize.* "You had a scare. If you hadn't needed a minute to collect yourself, I would have been shocked. It means you're human, and you love him."

"Some days, I wonder why," she muttered, wiping once more below her eyelashes before shaking it off. "I can't believe I just fell apart like that."

"Kara, stop." When she looked at him, eyes wide in surprise at his tone, he gentled it a little. "You're allowed to fall apart. There's not one parent out there who can say they're strong all the time."

"And they've got a partner to pick up the slack." The monotone way she said it, and how her eyes dulled, made him want to find Zach's sperm donor of a father and beat him up. "I've got to stay strong or else I'll lose it, completely."

He didn't answer that, since it seemed as though there was no way for him to argue the point without it turning into a fight.

"I should collect him and get out of your hair. I can't believe he bothered you like this."

"In a minute." He rocked a bit, and was surprised as she leaned into the movement, letting him take her on the gentle wave.

"Bend a little," he said in a hushed tone, not wanting to break whatever moment had allowed Kara to give him this much trust. "You've got five people right here, at least, who want to be a safety net."

She murmured something he couldn't quite catch, then tipped her head back up. When her eyes half-closed, he took a chance and brushed his lips lightly across her cheek, ending just a breath from the corner of her mouth. Enough that it could be construed as a bolstering, friendly gesture.

Or not.

She turned more toward him, and their lips met more firmly. First tentative, then more bold, she nibbled on his lower lip, then swept her tongue across to soothe the sting before opening her mouth to let his own tongue in to taste.

Graham gripped the couch cushions hard enough he felt a few seams on the arm pop. But there was no way he could possibly touch her now. He'd ruin it, for both of them, and he was not giving up this moment for anything in the world. If she wanted more, she'd have to take it. And God, he'd give her whatever she wanted.

After another moment, she moaned and rose up on her knees to press more firmly against him, then straddled him. Her breasts flattened against his chest, her core settled firmly against his erection. Her thin yoga bottoms were of zero consequence; he felt it all. Everything. The pure heat of her, the way she opened for him. She had to feel the same.

And he knew what heaven felt like. Heaven was Kara, in

his lap, surrendering to him and the feelings they'd both been fighting for far too long.

He took the chance and let his hands rest on her hips, then cruise up to cup her breasts over the shirt. When she moaned and tore her lips from his, he froze, praying she wouldn't give him a slap or pull away. But she did neither, just moved to his ear, nipping playfully as his thumbs circled around her nipples. Though she wore both a tank and what felt like a thin sports bra, the tips puckered beneath the fabric enough they were easy to find. He pinched, rolled and played until she was thrusting her groin against his in an imitation of an act he so desperately wanted to move on to with her.

Then she was gone. Evaporated like smoke. He was left with his arms up, hands still cupped as if holding the comfortable, plush weight of her breasts instead of air. When he could unravel the knot of his brain, he blinked and found her across the living room, arms wrapped around herself as if she'd taken a sudden chill, back facing him.

Damn. No, damn it, *no*. This was the exact opposite of what should have happened. Pushing the point was going to be the death of his chance.

"Kara," he said hoarsely, then paused. He had no clue what else to say. "I'll get Zach."

"Wait." She turned to look at him, and she was so pale beneath her freckles. Her nipples were still tightly budded beneath her tank, and it was all he could do not to let his gaze linger there too long. "I . . ." When words failed her, he wanted to kick his own ass.

"I'll get Zach," he said again, then headed for the guest bedroom. When he got there, he found the boy still passed out, sprawled out across the bed, managing to take up three times his own body size in square footage. His hair draped over his forehead, and his shoes were still untied. This kid . . .

Gently, Graham scooped him up, carrying him in his

arms to the living room. When Kara saw them, her eyes widened and she started to hold out her arms, as if he were supposed to pass the boy off. When Graham just raised a brow, she shook her head, grabbed her purse and hurried out the front door, leaving it open for him. She waited while Graham settled Zach in the back, buckling in the mumbling, half-conscious child firmly.

Kara stood beside the driver's door, sheltered behind it, using it like an Amazon uses a shield. He approached with a few cautious steps, praying she didn't just run for the hills.

"Thank you, for getting him in the car. He would have been impossible for me to manage." Her fingers tightened around the edge of the door. "You were such a big help today. I'm sorry I . . ." She let out a ragged breath. "I'm sorry."

"Don't. Don't be sorry. Just let me help some more. Let any of us help some more."

She shook her head, but the sadness in her eyes said she wished she could.

"I know you have to get him home. I won't keep you." The relief that shone in her gaze was almost tangible. "But promise me something."

She let out a little laugh that sounded like a combination of confusion and frayed nerves. "At this point, I owe you a month's worth of favors."

He let that one go. He didn't want to be a debt to her. He wanted to be *there* for her. "Promise you'll come to the match this weekend. Bring Zach."

She was going to argue. He saw it.

"It's not as violent as you think," he said quickly to cut her off. "Not like a full-on match. And Zach might like seeing what we've been up to." He smiled a little. "We like showing off for the kid. It'll be fun all around."

She looked away a moment, and he saw her mouth tighten. "I'll think about it."

It was all he could ask for. "See you later."

With something akin to a deer-in-the-headlights expression, she sank into her car, closed the door and started off.

As Graham entered his quiet house, without even a kid sleeping in the guest room for company, he knew his life without those two would be a very empty one.

CHAPTER

6

"Should we be here? This late, I mean?" Kara passed the caution tape to Marianne and waited for her friend to loop it around the banister, then pass it back for her to do on her own side. "What with all the vandalism and other stuff going on, I'm not sure we should be here so late by ourselves."

"Three tough women against one vandal?" Marianne scoffed, then glanced down to where Reagan was shuffling around the gym floor in the slippers she kept in the training room. "We're good. Right, Reagan?"

Reagan held up a hand making the OK sign, and continued on her way with a measuring tape and painter's tape, marking off the set-up for the crew in the morning.

The match was the next evening, and according to Reagan, their dingy little gym would somehow be magically turned into an arena for spectators, mimicking the grandeur of a legitimate tournament. In the morning, hours before anyone would be admitted to the gym, a maintenance crew would come in and set up a ring, the bleachers and more. Since Reagan would have been setting up alone, Marianne had volunteered to stay and help, and called in Kara to complete the trio. Zach, to his disgruntlement, was at home with the babysitter.

"Plus, with us having the whole gym lit up like a Roman candle, I can't imagine anyone would want to come in here and stir up trouble tonight. It's obvious they'd be caught." Her friend ripped the end of the caution tape off and used a piece of duct tape to secure it to the top of the banister. "And now we do the other side."

"It's nice, having you guys help. Have I said thank you?" Reagan called from below.

"You're welcome!" Kara and Marianne said in tandem.

"Kara, I owe you a night of babysitting."

"No you—"

"She sure does," Marianne cut Kara off, glaring. "You paid for tonight's sitter, when you could have put that money toward an attorney. So yes, she can babysit for you another time."

"Only fair," Reagan agreed.

"I'm coming tomorrow, and bringing Zach," Kara said cautiously.

"Fun," Marianne said absently, winding the tape around the starting post. "He'll like it. He loves the guys."

"Yeah, he does." One particular Marine more than the others, it was turning out. Despite being in deep shit for his runaway stunt, Zach couldn't stop talking about the evening he'd spent with Graham. How the man had let him order dinner so he got the right food, how he'd not even complained once about the weird food Zach had ordered, that they'd watched a movie Kara likely wouldn't have allowed in her house, but also wouldn't object to, and that Graham had given him hell about running off like that, but in a cool way. A man's way.

It was like he was slipping out of her fingers, one month at a time. His need for a strong, healthy, positive male role model was becoming more apparent by the day. But she couldn't ask Graham to be his role model, not when the man had feelings for her. It sent the wrong signal. Plus, Zach would get attached and then Graham would be gone. Not because he was the kind of man to drift out of someone's life, but because he simply had no choice. He went where the Marine Corps sent him. And they had no option to follow, even if she wanted to.

But oh, after that kiss . . . she wanted to. Or at least, she wanted the option to. His hands had found all the right places, and he'd shown such restraint in the face of an unholy temptation. He would have been amazing in bed. All that golden tan skin, hardened by the workouts they went through daily, with that unflappable control and powerful need . . .

"Earth to Kara." Marianne poked her in the side. "Where'd you go? Daydreaming about something?"

Kara blinked. "Huh?"

Marianne sat back on her heels, cocking her head a little. "Your face is flushed, your eyes are glazed over and you look like you just left a very sexy man's bed." Her friend's mouth opened on a little *O*. "You were having a sex daydream."

"Was not." Her face heated, and she pressed a cool hand to one side.

"You were! You daydream slut! Tell me."

"Wow, when you put it like that, of course I'll tell you all my deep, dark secrets," Kara said dryly, then yelped when a hand settled on her back. She looked over her shoulder to find Reagan standing there, looking confused. "You scared me.'

"She's still in a sex haze," Marianne explained to an obviously confused Reagan.

"You had sex?" Reagan asked, sitting down on the bottom stair with a thud that didn't go along with her beautiful business suit. Her legs splayed out over the hardwood, and her feet tapped restlessly in their furry blue slippers. "With who?"

"With nobody. Calm down, I didn't have sex with anyone."

"She was having mental sex," Marianne clarified. "Daydream sex. And I know just the Marine who was starring front and center." When Kara glared, she shrugged. "You can't seriously think we both haven't realized you and Graham are dancing around the issue."

"He kissed me," she admitted softly. "The other day, when Zach ran off to his house. I came to pick Zach up, he was asleep, so we talked. And then we weren't talking, and then we were kissing, and . . ." She covered her eyes with her fingers, resting her hot cheek against the cool metal of the hand rail. "This is horrible. I'm such an idiot."

"Still missing the 'idiot' part. Unless you did it wrong." Reagan gave her a sympathetic pat on the knee. "Did you do it wrong?"

"I didn't do it wrong," Kara snapped as Marianne snickered. "Stop it. You didn't get half as much shit as I'm getting now while you were ignoring your feelings for Greg. Why am I the one getting all the comments?"

"Because Graham is basically your slave, and you know it." Serious now, Marianne settled down with her back to the wall, her feet extended until they nudged Kara's. The three made a very interesting picture in the stairwell. "I know, without a doubt, you aren't trying to lead him on. That's not how you work. He probably knows it, too. But if you are serious about never even giving him a chance, you need to give it to him straight. Don't play coy, or try to let him down gently. He's a lawyer. He can handle being rejected with normal lingo."

"And get into the whole, messy reason why I can't? Because I could." She whispered, "I wish I could. God, I wish . . ."

Reagan leaned her head against Kara's side in commiseration. "It's only eight years. Maybe . . ."

"No." Firm now, Kara cleared her throat. "It's not going to happen. I can't ask him to give up eight years of his life waiting for someone who can't leave the state for more than a vacation. That's unfair. It's cruel. I won't do it."

"You know what's best." The youngest of them sounded as if she only half-believed it, though. "I agree though. Don't let him down gently. Be firm. If it hurts, it hurts. But it'll hurt worse to be led on, even accidentally."

"You're right. Both of you." Kara sighed. "Bitches."

"That's what we're here for," Marianne said, running a hand over Kara's arm.

IN the locker room, Graham had seen a plethora of odd rituals. From singing to dance routines, and even a guy who had built a shrine in his locker—complete with candles—to the goddess Beyoncé. Some guys were into the weirdest shit. So it was no shock to him when he witnessed Tressler, a cocky kid with more than his own share of confidence, go through some half-assed chanting thing, then glare when other guys watched.

"That guy is so full of himself it's a wonder he doesn't sweat mini Tresslers," Brad muttered as he sank onto the bench beside Graham. "I get hyping yourself up, but man . . ."

"All a part of the act, brother." Graham bumped shoulders with him. "You're extra grumpy. I thought the smell of fresh competition would cheer you up."

"I'd be more cheerful if I hadn't had to sleep alone," Brad grumbled, scrubbing a hand over his hair. "You get used to someone being there, and suddenly they're not, and it's like you forgot that they haven't been there forever. Pisses me off."

"That feeling does? Or Marianne?" Greg asked with a grin, then dodged when Brad kicked a foot out. "Watch the knee, Grandpa. Can't have you blowing it out before the games."

Brad flipped him off.

"Nah. Unlike you, I didn't sleep alone. Probably because my girlfriend is fine breaking the rules." Greg sat opposite them and grinned. "It was the least she could do after I spent three hours sitting in a car, playing security guard, waiting for them to finish up the gym."

"Thanks for that, by the way." Brad reached behind him and grabbed a bottle of water, drinking deeply. "I felt better knowing you were nearby. Otherwise I would have given the big Hell No to Marianne coming back so late with those two and working on the place alone."

Those two . . . Reagan and Kara. "How were they when you saw them last night?" he asked casually, pulling on one of his soft-soled shoes. "Tired, after all that extra work?"

"Look at his ass, trying to be all nonchalant and shit." Greg shook his head. "Just admit you want to throw her over your shoulder, drag her ass back to your house and lock her in your bedroom for a week. We won't judge."

"I might judge a little," Brad amended.

"Shut up." He fought with the laces of his second shoe. "I don't want to drag her ass back there. I want . . ." Tug, tug. "I want her . . ." Why wouldn't the stupid laces unknot? "I want her to come . . . come . . . willingly!" The lace snapped between his fingers. "Is that so fucking much to ask?" He tossed the shoe on the floor, staring at it disgustedly.

"Well," Brad said after thirty seconds of silence. "You really showed that shoe who was boss."

Graham stood and walked off to the supply closet to grab another lace, ignoring the way his friends—supposed friends—chuckled behind his back. They could eat shit and die for all he cared.

KARA settled down on the uncomfortable bleacher and made room for Zach. The event was more crowded than she had originally anticipated. In her world, boxing had never been anything she'd thought twice about. It wasn't a mainstream sport, for the most part. So it surprised her that enough people cared to make it to the event. Reagan had clearly known, though, as she'd asked both sets of bleachers to be extended from the walls. She had done what she could to brighten the place up, but it was still a simple gym with minimal updates and bad lighting.

Frankly, it sort of added to the ambiance of an underground fight . . . although the event was closely refereed and completely aboveboard. Made it feel a bit more secretive, more intense. More thrilling.

"Mom, when does Graham go up?" Zach asked, bouncing beside her. "When?"

"There's no time schedule, so I'm not sure." She picked up the programs—done via Marianne's pamphlet software, she knew—and pointed. "Looks like he's second to last. So we might not be able to see him. That's a long time to wait."

"Mom. *Moooooooom.*" Her son turned, eyes wide, mouth dropped open in shock. "We can't leave before seeing Graham. He's the best one!"

"How would you even know that?" she asked, smiling a little even as she tried to keep a stern voice. "And remember, you're still on probation. You have very little wiggle room with which to bargain, young man."

He grumbled, but subsided.

Secretly, Kara had hoped Graham would go first. The butterflies in her stomach wouldn't settle. They hadn't settled since the evening of the kiss. Everything she'd attempted to keep pushed down, boxed up and closed off had sprung back to life after a minute in his arms. She couldn't have contained the butterflies even if she'd gone around chasing after them with a net. They were free to float around her system, causing her involuntary giddiness at a moment's notice.

And now she would see him, in his true element. Despite the fact that she'd never been a huge fan of contact sports, there was something primal and a little exciting about the idea of watching Graham battle against another male.

That probably made her a very sick woman.

Through the first few fights, Kara managed to hold back her revulsion in favor of keeping a close eye on Zach more than the action. Though one man ended up with a cut above his eye, and another a bloody nose, the entire thing was surprisingly less gory than she'd thought it would be. That helped. Zach, however, found the entire thing thrilling, to the point of standing up and pumping his arms when Greg entered the ring and dominated by turning his opponent in circles, dodging and weaving artfully and then throwing a few quick punches that had even Kara's eyes bugging out. The man was cartoon-superhero fast.

"Mom. Mom! Oh my god, Mom, he's amazing!" Zach sat back down, or rather flopped back down, his body practically vibrating with excitement and energy. "First he was like bam!" He jutted out a small fist. "Then wham! Bam!" Two more fists, the second nearly missing the head of the woman seated in front of him.

"Whoa, no way, dude." She captured his next ready-to-fly fist and pressed it down firmly. "Show me later. Make mental notes. Otherwise you're going to hurt someone."

He grinned sheepishly, face flushed with the thrill of it and the heat from all the bodies surrounding them. "Sorry."

Her little boy . . . who wanted so desperately to become a man. Meanwhile, she was doing everything she could to discover a way to slow down time. Before she could think about it, one hand came up to stroke down her son's head and cheek before resting on his shoulder. He squirmed, but didn't shrug the touch away.

That wouldn't last much longer, either.

"And don't say, 'Oh my god,'" she admonished belatedly,

settling down. Brad's round was next. She had seen a quick video Marianne had taken of him practice sparring with a fellow teammate before, but it was nothing compared to now. Even with his knee in a brace, the man was methodical and precise. And by the third round, as his opponent seemed to droop like an overwatered daisy, Brad was fresh and ready to go another three rounds. To Kara's untrained eye, it seemed as though he won less by talent and more by simply outlasting his fellow boxer, waiting for the other man to tire enough to make mistakes and capitalize on them. Since it worked, she couldn't see cause for complaint.

She couldn't hold back the smile as he stepped under the ropes and Marianne was beside him in an instant. First to give him a kiss on the cheek, then to walk with him to a corner to inspect his knee. Her friend was as protective of her athletes as any mama hen . . . but that one particular Marine certainly got special attention.

"He's next."

"Hmm?" Kara glanced down at her son, then at the program. "No, he's two from now."

"Didn't you hear?" He pointed up at the ceiling, which she took to mean he was referring to the announcement system. The gym's PA system was so old and outdated, it was difficult to make out anything said. She'd tuned it out from the start. "Things got shuffled around. A few people are hurt or whatever and they couldn't change the programs fast enough. He's next. Please say we can stay! Please."

Kara debated. Watching up to now had been difficult, but not impossible. She enjoyed teaching yoga to the young Marines, and had found real satisfaction in working with a bunch of testosterone-driven athletes who had initially scorned the practice and now gladly joined her sessions. But watching Graham get punched . . . her heart clenched a little at the thought. "I'm not sure I can stay, Zach. It's getting late, too."

"It would mean a lot to him." That had her blinking and looking back down at her son. "Graham told me he wanted me to see the match. He's good, too. I mean, I heard . . ." he muttered when her eyes narrowed. He broke eye contact and then sat up straight, staring across the gym.

She followed his eye line and found Graham entering the gym from the locker rooms, looking . . . different. There was no other word for it. Purely male, dominant, aggressive, a little mean.

If this had been the Graham from the other night, she never would have crawled in his lap for a kiss. He would have forced her on her back and taken it without asking, and damn the consequence.

The realization that he had this in him, this domineering, alpha aggressiveness built into his person, and tempered it enough to make her comfortable, to let her lead . . .

She shivered, and Zach gave her a peculiar look. "You can't be cold, Mom. It's like, a hundred degrees in here."

"Just a tickle. We can stay." That had her son's eyes lighting up. He had a bad case of hero worship all right.

Graham stepped into the ring, looking a little silly in silky shorts and shoes that looked soft enough to bend laced up to his ankles. His hands were encased in the thick boxing gloves, and in his mouth was a black mouth guard that should have looked ridiculous but only turned his face from a handsome work of art into a menacing gargoyle, uniquely beautiful in its ferocity. She shivered again, then leaned forward, elbows on her knees, to watch.

He met the referee in the middle, alongside his opponent, listened for a moment, nodded, then touched gloves carefully with the man he would be attempting to punch in the face in another minute. They both grimaced at each other, but she assumed it was more of a friendly grin, hampered by mouth guards.

Competitive sports had never made a lot of sense to Kara.

They separated, and Kara took the moment to soak in the sight of Graham's body before it would be pummeled. His skin was bronzed evenly, unlike many of the Marines before him with their cute, comical farmer's tans. His back faced her, and she could appreciate how the silk bottoms cupped and molded his very fine ass with each step, riding up as he did a few toe jumps to show impressively muscled thighs. As his arms stretched in front of him for a few practice punches, the muscles of his back moved and morphed in a way that had her salivating.

Probably not just her, either. A woman would have to be both blind and in a coma to not sense the presence of the very hot, very alpha, very desirable male in the ring. His maleness was just . . . overwhelming, really.

The sound of the bell made her shriek a little, and her hand flew over her mouth. Several people turned to give her odd stares, and a few evil eyes. Zach scooted a few inches away, as if he was embarrassed to be seen sitting next to the crazy shrieking lady.

Unlike several others, Graham didn't come from the corner swinging. He edged in, watching his opponent, circling with him, hands up. The first few punches all came from the other man, and Graham dodged them easily, without swinging back. His eyes were fierce, his dark brows furrowed in concentration. How the other Marine didn't collapse with fear beneath that intense gaze was beyond Kara.

The other man swung again, and this time Graham retaliated, throwing several punches in some amazing choreographed sequence that seemed to flow without thought through his arms. The other man's head snapped back, then to the right, then back again as he stumbled a few feet and hit the ropes. Graham then backed off, when she thought he'd pounce.

When the Marine came out swinging from the rope, Graham took one to the chin, and smiled. He actually smiled, though it was a sort of scary, threatening smile that had Kara wanting to look away.

His opponent landed another punch, and Kara covered her eyes with both hands. No more. No more of this. She couldn't watch him get kicked around. And the worst part was, he was allowing it happen. Even without understanding the sport as a whole, she could tell he was simply playing around, letting the other man get in a few shots of his own. He could stop it, and chose not to.

"Mom, what are you doing? You're missing all the good stuff!"

She resisted Zach's tugging on her arm, even after the bell ending round one rang out. "Just watch, and if anything looks too violent, close your eyes. Honor system."

Zach snorted, which she took to mean, *Yeah, okay sure, whatever you say.* Except the sarcastic version.

"He's letting the other guy get him," Zach said quietly, as if puzzling it out himself. "You can tell, he's dropping his guard a little sometimes."

"How do you even know what . . . never mind." The more she talked, the more she was tempted to look up again. And the bell rang for round two, leaving Zach preoccupied and her wanting to crawl in a hole until it was over.

How did Marianne and Reagan do this every day? How did they listen to the boxing gloves hitting flesh, the grunts and groans and the blood, and not go home with scars on their hearts? She'd cry daily if she had to witness such a violent sport on repeat.

When the third round's bell rang, there was a blessed moment of relief from both the crowd's noise and the sound of the male aggression while the winner was tallied.

Peeking from between her fingers, she found Graham kneeling in his corner, swishing water in his mouth before—*ick*—spitting it into a bucket held up by Coach Cartwright.

After conferring for a moment with the judges—three men

who sat at a folding table off to the side—the referee called both men back to the center, paused for a moment, then lifted Graham's still-gloved hand in the air victoriously.

Well, of course he won, Kara thought as she surged to her feet and clapped like a wild woman. Of course. There was never a doubt in her mind

Except when she'd covered her face for two out of three rounds.

Zach hopped onto the bleacher beside her and screamed out loud, waving his arm and jumping so much her shoulder felt like it was going to fall off when he grabbed onto her for balance.

"Zach, there's no way he can see you. Stop, or you'll fall!"

The jumping ceased, but the yelling and waving didn't. Kara rolled her eyes, but then when she looked back at the ring, she found herself looking directly into Graham's eyes. Against the odds, he'd found her in the crowd, and was staring intently at her, as if she were his next opponent. And he wouldn't go so easy on her.

Except the battle wouldn't be a violent one. Graham's war would be a sexual one. A fight of the body and heart.

At this point, Kara figured her odds of winning the battle were about as high as Graham's boxing opponent's.

That was to say, nil.

CHAPTER

7

Graham sank down on the bench in the locker room, letting Brad and Greg yank off his gloves and unwrap the tape from his knuckles and wrists. "Anything besides water around here?"

"What, like a flask? Save it for after the match," Greg suggested.

"I mean like a sports drink, you idiot," he growled.

"Water," Brad encouraged, grabbing a bottle from the table against the wall and plunking it down on the bench beside him. "Fill 'er up. It's best right now. You can grab something later, after you've rehydrated."

"Sweating bullets thanks to the shitty A/C in this place." He settled against the locker and wiped a hand over his brow. "It's affecting my sense of smell, too. Everything smells like something burning."

Greg looked at Brad, and he could sense they were silently wondering if he'd gotten hit in the head more than normal. When Brad leaned down to inspect his pupils, he shoved at his friend's shoulder. "Get out of my face. If anyone's giving me a checkup, it's gonna be your hot girlfriend."

Brad kicked him in the calf. "The asshole's fine."

"No, I think smelling burning stuff is a sign of a concussion." Looking uncommonly serious, Greg looked toward the door that led to the outer gym. "I'm not trying to be an ass, but if you're smelling something burning, I'm worried."

"You guys don't smell it? I thought it was the A/C working overboard to keep up with the number of bodies in there." Two of which had been Kara and Zach. Spotting them in the crowd had made the moment of victory a thousand times sweeter. Though Kara had appeared a bit pale, Zach looked like he'd never been happier. That she'd given him the chance to come watch, even when he should have been grounded, made Graham's day.

"Actually, I sort of smell it now, too." Sitting up straighter, Brad scrunched his brown and turned a full circle on the bench. "It smells . . . okay, yeah, he's not concussed. Something smells like it's burning. Coming from the vent?"

Greg shrugged his shoulders. "Can't smell anything."

"Maybe we should call maintenance. Something might have blown a fuse, or some motor burned out in the HVAC." Graham stood, shaking his legs out a little. "I'm gonna get dressed, watch the last match and then head straight home. I need some—No." He froze as the odor grew stronger. "It's in here. Start looking in lockers."

They didn't question him, only began flinging lockers open. Graham started in the back corner, where the smell of something burning was the strongest, though still not overpowering.

"Found it—Jesus H. Who does this shit?" Brad stood back as he opened a locker and thin, white smoke billowed out. There, at the bottom of the locker, sat a candle, flame flickering. The hem of a t-shirt hanging on a hook, dangling over the open flame, smoked, but there was no active fire yet. A pair of workout shorts dangled from the other hook, high enough that it wasn't in danger. Yet. From the look of it, the clothes were too damp with sweat to make a fire likely, for now. Brad grabbed the damp T-shirt from the hook and tossed it to the tiled floor, stomping on it a little just to be sure there was no live flame. Greg reached around him and blew out the candle.

They all stared into the locker, watching the swinging shorts and the black smoke tendril coming off the charred, extinguished wick.

"Whose locker is this? What asshole lights a fucking candle *in* their locker and then just shuts it? God." Greg ran a hand through his hair, which really needed a trim if he wanted to be within uniform regs. "How stupid could someone be?"

"They're babies," Graham reminded him. "They can't think straight with all the testosterone flowing through their veins, combined with the competition. It's someone's locker, so let's find out whose, give them the ass chewing of a lifetime, and make anything that could start a fire off limits from here on out. No more prematch ritual candle or incense."

"Guys," Brad said quietly, looking at the name written on the waistband of the shorts. "This wasn't an accident. These were Tressler's. He's not the candle-lighting type."

"Tressler?" Greg's jaw ticked. "That little pencil dick . . ."

"No." Brad shook his head and slapped a hand down on Greg's shoulder to contain him. Greg and Tressler had had an . . . altercation a few weeks ago after the younger man had made some inadvisable comments about Reagan. It wouldn't take much to have Greg's anger running loose where the young Marine was involved. "This wasn't him. Think. Is Greg the kind of guy who would light a freaking Bath & Body Works candle in his locker?"

Graham and Greg both blinked at each other, then stared more closely at the candle still cooling in the bottom of the locker. Sure enough, it wasn't the plain grocery store candle most guys would have picked out. It was a pink confection of a candle, with a gingham-style bow for a label and a froufrou name. No guy would have selected it and intended to burn it in public.

"So . . . what? How the hell did it get there?" Graham thought for a moment. "Did someone else . . . shit."

"Yeah," Brad said quietly. Greg's eyes narrowed as he caught on. "I think our vandal has just upgraded to arson."

"And with something that smells like a perfume counter," Greg added with a sneer. "Could the guy not even pick a manly candle to try to burn the locker room with?"

"Who said it's a guy?" Graham waited while they both turned to look at him, stunned expressions on their faces. "What? So far, nothing that's happened has been anything a female couldn't have pulled off. I'm not saying it *is* a woman, but we can't discount it."

"Whoever it is can't be all that brilliant. I mean, I'm no genius, and even I know you can't light wet shit on fire, and those clothes are obviously soaked." Greg scoffed as he toed the shirt, still on the ground.

"There's an entire building full of people. I wonder if they hoped the clothes would dry, and later on, they would catch more fully. After everyone was out of the building. A poor man's long fuse."

Brad's idea made sense. "God. Just . . . God. We have to do something."

"What, check every guy's locker for the matching lotion scent?" Greg rolled his eyes.

"No." With the finality and calmness that made him the team's captain, Brad straightened and shut the locker door. "We handle this as a team. In-house. We don't tell anyone about this. The MPs will get this program shut down. Or we'll lose our practice space. Either way, it's no good for anyone. We all meet here, Monday night, ten o'clock. Tell your squads. Nobody else."

He didn't have to specify the squads were the guys they'd been assigned to watch over during tryouts. Though the squads were no longer in play, it worked as an efficient sort of phone tree. Each younger Marine would trust them, and subsequently would show up when asked.

"I just want to get out of here. I'm done with this shit." Graham slammed his own locker shut, rubbing a towel over his head before chucking it into the laundry bin in the corner by the door.

"And to think, a certain hot yogi and her son came to see you. Guess you won't be finding them after the match, huh?" Greg laughed when Graham growled. "Get over your bad mood. You won. The woman you want came to see you. Her kid's basically president of your fan club. Other than almost getting burned out of the gym, it's been a pretty good night."

"Yeah." Locker room candle aside, it hadn't been a bad day. Maybe he could even convince Kara to let him take them out for a celebratory ice cream . . . if Zach could have any. He'd have to check with Kara on that.

The rest would level itself out. Brad was right. It was time to stop dicking around with the MPs and handle their business in-house.

KARA let Zach greet a few of the boxers, knowing he'd be safe with them while she spoke to Marianne. She didn't know the whole team as well as she did Brad, Greg and Graham, but they were all a decent bunch of guys and didn't mind playing up the superhero card for Zach. Having a young boy idolize them was right up their alley.

"This is insane," Kara said as she hugged Marianne. They were bumped from behind by another hugging duo, and scooted over a bit. "Like high school graduation or something. The crowd is all over the place."

"Welcome to the world of boxing, where first you throw

a punch, and then afterward you grab a beer with the guy you just punched." Her friend grinned, face flushed with excitement, baby-fine blonde hairs sticking to her sweat-dampened temples. "I'm going to need Brad to give me a two-hour-long hand massage, after wrapping so many wrists, fingers and ankles, but this was great."

Marianne was in her element, that was for sure. Caring for athletes, and being a part of the team, had always been her dream. She was living it. "Well, go you."

"Reagan's around here somewhere. The guys will have a team meeting after this dies down a bit. Do you want to grab a drink? Oh wait, you've got Zach."

"Yes, and while I lifted his grounding to attend tonight, he's got to serve the rest of it out, no questions asked." Why was it that nobody told you when you became a mother, your child's punishment was just as much your punishment?

"Understood. We'll do a rain check." Marianne rubbed Kara's arms briefly. "I'm glad you came, though. I saw you cover your face a few times—"

"More than a few," Kara admitted.

"—but you stayed, so that was big. Reagan still battles back nausea half the time."

"Speaking of our professional lady, where is she?"

"I don't know. Somewhere talking to a media person, maybe. Or taking photos to tweet out. Who knows?" Marianne grinned as Brad walked up behind, wrapped his arms around her waist and yanked her back against his chest. "Hey, handsome."

Sensing the couple would want some privacy, she congratulated Brad on his win, then asked if he'd seen Zach.

"I think I saw him with Graham. They were walking toward the parking lot. Probably wanted some fresh air."

"Thanks. Great job," she told them both, then hurried off to catch her son before he conned Graham, or someone else, into helping him extend his day off from grounding.

As she rounded the corner that would lead her to the parking lot, she heard her son's voice. She slowed, wanting to catch him in the act of deception before accusing him.

"But you totally could have kicked his ass," Zach said, deep confusion in his voice. Kara winced at the use of the word "ass," but held her tongue and listened.

"Sometimes, winning early isn't the right choice." There was a pause, then, "There's not always honor in kicking someone who can't keep up. It's a fine line between patronizing the guy—you know what patronizing means, right?"

Zach scoffed, and she could almost see his eyes rolling in the back of his head. "Yeah. I'm ten, not two."

"A wise guy." The amused tone of Graham's deep voice made her smile. "You can't patronize him, 'cause then it's almost worse. But there's no point in coming out and aiming for the knock out. Not when he's got family here to watch him, and he's working his as— sorry, butt off to compete. There's no honor in that. So you use the chance to learn something new. Try out a new technique. Improve your footwork. It's a chance to learn, not to kick someone whose skills aren't up to your level and think that'll make you feel good."

They were both quiet, and she sensed Zach was absorbing the information. Her heart swelled a little at Graham taking the opportunity to give her son an important lesson, and in an age-appropriate way. She rounded the corner and found them both leaning against the wall across from the doors. Graham's back was against the brick, with one knee bent and the foot flat against the wall. Zach's posture mimicked the older man's, and she struggled to not run up and hug him and beg him to not grow up too fast.

"Mom." Straightening, Zach bounced over to her. Still a boy in so many ways. Just not for much longer. "Graham says we can get ice cream, and he'll even drive all the way across town to that place we can eat at." Meaning the one ice cream place locally that managed to cater to all his allergy requirements.

"That's a very sweet offer," she said to both Zach and Graham, resisting the urge to run a hand over his hair. "But you're still grounded, and it's getting late anyway."

It was hard to watch her son's eyes darken as he realized he wouldn't get his way. So she added, "Maybe another day."

"Hey, I'll do ice cream anytime." Graham walked up to them, duffel bag slung over his shoulder. "I'll walk out with you."

Zach filled the three minute walk to Kara's car with enthusiastic retellings of his favorite moments of the night. Up to and including cartoon-esque sound effects as he thrust his fists into thin air. "Bam! Pow!"

As they reached her car, she unlocked it and gave Zach the silent stare that meant, *Get in and don't argue. You're on shaky ground.* He understood at once and got in without another word. Finally.

Then there were two. She rocked back on her heels, clutching her tote as a lifeline. Otherwise, she might embarrass herself by clawing at his chest and trying to rip his T-shirt off. The man shouldn't be allowed to wear clothing. It was criminal to cover up that much perfection. "You, uh . . . you did really . . . good."

Brilliant, Kara. And next, you can make a lackluster comment about the weather.

He grinned slowly, those sinful lips curving to reveal bright white teeth. "Thanks. The competition felt pretty great. Hope we're ready for the All Military games."

"You look ready. You looked amazing." She blinked as his eyes darkened. "I mean, your boxing. You know, your . . . bam. Pow."

Oh, my God. I just said that. Someone please direct me to the nearest hole in which I could crawl into.

He chuckled softly. "I know what you meant. And you

look amazing, too." He stepped closer to her, taking a gentle hold of her elbow. "Pow," he said, leaning in for a kiss.

She turned her head at the last minute, chickening out. Zach was in the car, probably staring. She didn't . . . she couldn't . . .

Oh, hell. She was going to. When he started to pull back, she rose up on her toes and brushed a light kiss across his mouth. He didn't push, didn't press for more. But the way his breath hitched, just a little, told her he was affected.

"We have to get going." When he didn't release her arm, she made a flapping motion. "I need that to drive."

"Right. Sorry." He stepped back, letting go to run a hand over his hair. "Have dinner with me."

"Zach is still grounded," she began, but he cut her off.

"Just us. I need to see you."

"I . . ." Ah, hell. This was not going to end well. "I'll think about it."

"Don't think. Just say yes. Tomorrow night. We've been given Monday morning off, so Sunday's a good night for grilling. Please."

"I'll think about it," she said again, because saying no when he was standing in front of her was impossible. "Congratulations." She ran for the driver's side, opening the door before he could try to do it for her and sliding in. As she closed the door and sighed, Zach leaned forward between the seats from the back.

"Mom? Were you kissing Graham?"

"Adults kiss people they're close to," she said neutrally, watching Graham walk back toward the gym doors.

"How close are you?"

Getting closer every day, whether it was right or not.

CHAPTER

8

Graham settled down in his reclining love seat, a beer in his lap, and handled his phone. The device flipped from hand to hand, rolled over fingers and mesmerized his turned-off brain . . . until he dropped it and it clattered to the floor.

Another super Sunday night for him. He could call friends, though most had lives of their own and would be busy on Sunday. His teammates could possibly make it, but they each had their own women to be home with, or had already made plans to fully utilize their morning off tomorrow. Didn't seem fair to drag them away from their happy cocoons to come wallow with him.

He could call Kara.

That caused him to grimace and take another swig. Yeah. Because punishing himself was a top priority. Why would he call just to get rejected—again—for dinner? He'd asked, and she'd hedged. Because she was too polite to come right out and say "No, now stop asking." The fact that she hadn't called him meant it was a definite no.

Time to move on.

Yeah. Right.

His phone vibrated on the floor, and he nearly pitched himself out of the recliner struggling to pick it up. When he saw Greg's name on the display with the text, he grunted and nearly let it drop again. But he swiped a finger right to read the message.

What are you doing tonight?

Seriously? Greg had a bombshell like Reagan Robilard in his clutches, and he was asking about plans? If his friend was that big of an idiot, Graham couldn't help him. Before he could put the phone away, it buzzed again.

Don't be a chicken shit. Ask her out.

So that was the real reason for the question. Not to join him, but to give him a kick in the ass.

He huffed out a breath, set the beer bottle to the side and texted back.

She's not going to come here alone. Zach's grounded.
It's a SNAFU, all around.

Try anyway.

Drop it.

Try.

Because he wanted to prove Greg wrong, he opened a new message for Kara. Then, thinking better of it, he closed that and called her. When she answered, he blinked in surprise before saying, "Hey."

"Hi," she said, her voice a little breathless.

There was a long pause, then she asked slowly, "Graham? You called me."

"Right. Sorry." *Get it together, man.* "I was wondering about dinner. Tonight. You know, just you and me."

Kara cleared her throat, and he waited in resignation for the no.

"It's funny you should ask." Her voice sounded tight, but he wasn't going to question it when hope soared. "Reagan is here, asking to babysit."

That took him aback. "Reagan is there? What for?"

"To babysit," she said again with what was obviously forced patience. "She just got it into her head to repay me for helping set up the gym the other night before the fight. I guess I'm free."

"She is!" Reagan said cheerfully from the background. "Zach and I are gonna pig out on popcorn and watch romantic comedies."

There was an exaggerated groan from somewhere else in the distance, which made Graham smile. "Okay, so, I'll see you soon?"

"Fifteen or twenty, I'd guess." She hung up without another word.

Thanks, dipshit. Now she thinks I orchestrated the whole thing.

Anytime. You two both need a kick in the ass.

He locked his phone and rolled his eyes, then stood to figure out exactly how much food prep he could accomplish in fifteen minutes.

AS Graham let Kara into the house, she sniffed appreciatively. "Smells . . . wow. Smells great."

He gave her a smile as she left her bag on the love seat and followed him back to the kitchen. "Simple spaghetti. I'd thought about grilling, but when I didn't hear from you, I never marinated the steaks. So it's not as good as it could have been. Nothing to get excited about."

"It's a meal I didn't have to cook. I'm sorry, but I'll get excited and you'll just have to tolerate it." She hopped up onto a stool and watched as he worked, using a spoon to mix something in a bowl. "I see sauce on the stove, so what's in the bowl?"

"Your project." He set it in front of her, taking her fingers and wrapping them gently around the spoon. When she looked down, she saw frothy melted butter. "Italian spices, garlic, salt and pepper. It's for the garlic bread. Season it however you want, and I'll brush it on and toast the bread."

"Trusting. For all you know, I could be a total garlic fiend." Her smile was mischievous as she reached for the powder. "You wouldn't want to be within a hundred yards of me."

"I'll always want to be near you, Kara." He dropped that quiet bombshell like a rapper dropping the mic, then turned to the stove to stir the sauce.

"Oh," she breathed out, then, with shaking hands, picked up the first seasoning and started sprinkling. She tried to speak, but nothing came out so she cleared her throat and tried again. "Reagan told me you didn't know she was coming over."

"I had no clue. Greg and Brad's lives have become almost dangerously boring, so they've taken to meddling with mine." He glanced over his shoulder quickly before turning his attention back to the stove. "I can't complain though, since the result was you coming for dinner."

She'd had a moment of doubt, as Reagan had shown up and insisted she go out for dinner—but not before changing out of her sweats and fixing her hair. Dinner with Graham was bad enough. Dinner at his home, with no servers, other patrons or the bustle of restaurant chatter to act as a buffer was too intimate to think about.

Then she'd realized this was her chance. The opportunity she'd needed to explain exactly why she'd played hard to get on accident. Why he needed to give up the idea of pursuing her and move on to someone he could make a life with.

Whoever that lucky bitch was.

Not very Zen of you, Kara.

Who cares? Thanks to Henry, she was once again missing out on life.

Graham took the bowl back from her and used a brush to coat a loaf of French bread he'd obviously pre-sliced. Sticking that under the broiler, he drained the pasta in the sink. "Should be about five minutes."

"Italian, hmm." Propping her chin on her hands, she watched with appreciation. Just because she couldn't make a meal out of him didn't mean she wasn't allowed to fully consider the menu. "Who taught you to cook?"

"It's boiled pasta and a simple red sauce."

"Which a lot of guys would not be able to handle. And girls. Takeout is too prevalent today. Give yourself a little credit."

He nodded, checked on the bread, then stood again. "My yaya taught me."

"Yaya . . . grandma?"

"Yup, on my dad's side. Born and raised in Greece, then came over here when my dad was about ten. Just her, her six kids—"

"Six," Kara breathed.

"—and the promise of work in her uncle's bakery. Best baklava you could ever hope to taste." He closed his eyes a moment, as if imagining taking a bite from the Greek dessert. That moment of pure delight made her want to reach for him.

"So your very much Greek yaya taught you to cook . . .

Italian food." She smiled as he raised a brow. "Come on, it's funny."

"Much to my yaya's dismay, I actually don't care for Greek food. Or most of it," he added, and she could tell he was thinking of baklava again. "But the basics of cooking remain the same, regardless of the dish's origins. She bakes like a dream, and is a pretty good cook, too. Taught my mother, who is *not* Greek, a few things. They're tight, which is pretty cool since I know what the stereotype about Greek mamas and their sons can be. But Yaya just assumes everyone wants to be a part of the family, and treats them like it. Everyone gets fed until they can't do anything but roll away from the table. If you can eat, you can be family."

"She sounds awesome." The pang of longing hit her harder than she expected. That family connection, his obvious love for them, and the fact that Zachary would never have that with either set of grandparents.

"I'm lucky to have her. We all are. She is the definition of the word 'matriarch.' You'd love her."

He said it casually, but it brought her back to the purpose of the dinner. "Graham—"

"Dinner's ready." Cutting her off, he brought the garlic bread from the oven, and it smelled divine. "Could you set the table? I tossed some silverware and cups over there, but didn't get a chance to make order out of it."

She set it quickly, pleased to see he'd given them simple tumblers instead of wineglasses. No alcohol for her when she'd be driving home soon. Probably none for him, either, given his workout schedule. She filled both their glasses with ice water, and when she returned to the table she found he'd already plated her food and had it waiting. The heaping pile of spaghetti topped with spiced red sauce and a few meatballs was about double what she could really eat. But she didn't complain, merely sat down and waited for him.

"Okay, need anything else?" he asked as he set the salt

and pepper shakers in the middle. "I'm not really used to eating at the table. I'm more of a 'sandwich on the couch with a paper towel' guy."

She tsked, and watched with amusement as he blushed. "I'm kidding, Graham. I get it. When Zach's gone, and I can just get away with eating a bowl of cereal for dinner, I totally do. It's the perk of being an adult."

"Yeah." Nodding in agreement, he twirled some pasta over his fork. "Good point. It's an adult perk. How's Zach today?"

"You ask about him," she said suddenly, leaning an elbow on the table. "It's so new to me that anyone does."

He blinked, letting his fork drop to the plate. "I . . . what?"

"I've dated," she said, deciding to forge on. "I'm not a nun. Well, obviously," she added with a little laugh. "I've tried very hard to not use being a single mother as a reason to push men away. I caught myself trying at the start, but that was more logistical than emotional, because I was just too tired to date. For the simple purpose of survival, men were not on my radar for the first few years."

One had been, and look where that had gotten her . . .

"You don't have to tell me all this." Graham laid a hand on her forearm, thumb rubbing a circle under her wrist, where her pulse beat. "I didn't ask to pry your life story out of you."

"Of course you didn't." She picked up her fork—which forced him to let go—and speared a bite of broccoli. "I'm telling you, so you understand where we stand."

His eyes turned stormy, but he retracted his own hand and nodded. "I have a feeling I'm not going to like this, but go ahead."

Like it or not, here it comes.

GRAHAM listened while Kara explained that dating hadn't been a priority, but she'd tried it on occasion. And how the men she'd dated basically ignored Zach's existence.

Idiots, he thought, but said nothing. When he stabbed a piece of meatball a bit too hard, sending his fork tines screeching against the plate beneath, he winced and looked over at her. Kara's mouth was a little open, garlic bread halfway there, frozen, as she watched him.

"Sorry," he mumbled, popping the bite into his mouth. "Keep going."

"I made the choice to not let Zach meet any of them, at least not at first. My thought was I'd be sure the guy was important before we went there. But they didn't seem to care if it ever happened. It was as if they only wanted me. I never got far enough with any of them to see how they reacted to Zach. Eventually it stopped being an issue."

Because she'd stopped putting herself out there. He could see it.

She set her fork down and leaned back a little, her plate barely half finished. "That was amazing. The sauce . . . you made that from scratch?"

"Cheat-scratch. I didn't have time to start from fresh tomatoes, so I used canned ones. Not as good as from the garden, but it works in a pinch."

She grinned at that. "You're a man of surprising talents, Graham Sweeney."

He took the risk of reaching for her hand and lacing fingers with hers. She didn't pull away, which he took as a good sign. "You've got some surprises, too. But keep going."

The idea that she might be a mystery seemed to faze her, and it took a moment before she could snap out of it. "Uh, where . . ."

"None of the guys took an interest in Zach."

"Right." She cleared her throat, and squeezed his hand. He knew she meant it as a sign to let go. Perversely, he squeezed back and kept on eating with his other hand. She might be finished, but he wasn't nearly done. Not with his food, and sure as hell not with her.

"Henry—that's Zach's father—is not a great guy. He's no evil cartoon villain, or a criminal or anything. Just not a great dad, or that nice of a human. Not someone I should have procreated with. But hey, when you're eighteen . . ." She lifted a shoulder. "He had a cute butt."

That made him smile. "I'm sure a cute butt is very important."

"Of course." Her eyes drifted down to the seat of his chair, and he had a feeling it wasn't meant to be ironic. Did he pass the Cute Butt test?

"He's around just enough to make things miserable when he wants to. It's his favorite card to play. He knows I love Zach, and worry about his allergies. He knows he can use that to his advantage. He plays with people, manipulating them like Claymation to get what he wants with the minimum effort required. It's just what he does. And that's why there can't be anything between us."

Graham played gently with the inside of her wrist, feeling her pulse skip and flutter. "I don't plan on living with the guy, so I don't know what he has to do with this."

"Everything. And nothing. But mostly, everything." She sighed. "It's hard to think when you do that."

"Stop thinking then." His fingers trailed up to the inside of her elbow and back down again. Had he ever felt something as soft as Kara's skin? "For tonight, could you do that?"

Her eyes widened, and he waited for the refusal. The denial. The put-off.

And waited.

"KARA."

Her brain had all but turned off. The way he stroked her arm—just her arm—had her entire body almost shivering in anticipation. Anticipation of what, she couldn't really say. Physical intimacy was—despite having a son for proof—really not something she had much experience in. Sex, maybe. But intimacy . . . that was a whole different story.

And the way Graham looked at her, she had no doubt he wanted to become very intimate with every nook and cranny of her body. God, how she wanted that, too.

"Are you cold?"

She blinked, and realized she'd become mesmerized by the touch of his fingertips, to the point she'd blocked out all conversation. "I'm sorry, my mind just . . ."

He smiled a little, then used the palm of his hands to briskly rub at her upper arms. "You've got goosebumps. I'll get you a sweatshirt."

"No, I—" But he was already up and heading to the back where she knew his bedroom was.

Do not follow him like an eager puppy. Do not follow him.

"Here we go." He handed her the sweatshirt, but when she just stared at it, he rolled it up from the bottom and carefully slid it over her head. He dressed her like she did Zach when he'd still been too little to figure out where the arm holes in his shirts were, guiding her along the process until she was enveloped in fabric that smelled like him, and—if she were being ridiculous—was warm, like him. It was like being wrapped up in his arms, surrounded by him.

Stupid.

"This is the second sweatshirt of mine I've put on you," he said mildly, sitting in his chair again. "You get cold a lot over here. I'm going to have to start keeping the heat on, or else I'll be out a lot of hoodies."

Oh, boy. Might as well be honest. She glanced down at her plate and pushed at her pasta with her fork. Her appetite for food had dried up. "Uh, yeah, I'm sorry about that. I meant to wash it and bring it back."

"I assumed Zach stole it from the hamper. It's no biggie."

"Confession time." If he could be upfront about things, so lacking in mystery, so could she. He liked her son, and he respected her. She could be honest, even if it pinched her heart a little. "He didn't steal it. I've been wearing it around the apartment." At his satisfied look, she narrowed her eyes. "What?"

"You're wearing my clothes. Stealing my stuff and wearing it around your place."

"Not stealing. Just . . . delayed returning." She stabbed at a piece of broccoli, which rolled off her plate. She nudged it back on.

"It's a total girlfriend thing to do."

That made her head snap up. "What is this, high school? I don't need to steal your sweatshirts. I have my own."

"You like mine, apparently," he pointed out, crossing his arms over his chest. "I like it."

"You self-satisfied male."

"Guilty."

"Thanks, counselor." Wanting to get the conversation back on track, she cleared her throat. "Now that we've completely gotten off topic, let's try again. I can't date you."

That took a little wind out of his self-satisfied sails. But he straightened and leaned forward, forearms on the table, a determined glint in his dark eyes. "I know you're a truthful sort of person, Kara. I believe you when you say you're not using Zach as a reason to not date. And I believe you believe you can't date me. But I need you to tell me why."

"Does it matter why?" she asked, feeling miserable now. She'd let this happen, somehow. She hadn't shut down the flirting, the anticipation soon enough. She hadn't prepared Zach enough to not get so attached to the handsome, helpful Marine. Her eyes stung, and to keep from crying she started mentally listing all the reasons she despised Henry.

"Yeah, it does. Because if it's something negotiable, I'm open for it. In fact, I love negotiating."

"Your lawyer's showing."

"I'm not a lawyer right now. I'm a man, who wants a woman, who says not that she doesn't *want* to date me, but that she *can't*. And I'm a determined son of a bitch, so let's find out the 'can't' so we can move on to the 'will.'"

Her mind twisted that around a bit, and she gasped when he grabbed her calves and pulled her feet into his lap. "What—what are you . . . wait, what? That made no sense."

He quickly pulled her sandals off and let them drop to the floor, then started rubbing her ankles. "I'm a big fan of full disclosure, so I'll go first. I want my hands on you, Kara. I want them all over you, and inside you."

Her entire body clenched at that blatant statement. At the heat in his eyes, the tight readiness of his own body. But his hands were gentle as he started to massage. She couldn't quite hold back the pleasured moan when he hit the sweet spot of her arches. Rubbing your own feet was nothing compared to having someone else do it for you.

"Your turn," he added, amusement in his voice.

She glared at him, but didn't want him to stop. "I want you, too."

"Then the rest can wait." His thumbs pressed hard into her instep, and she almost melted into a puddle on the kitchen floor. "There's nothing wrong with living in the moment. We're both adults, right? Both mature, productive members of society. By spending time together, it's not throwing off society's delicate balance. It's simply two adults, getting to know each other better."

He paused, and she sensed he wanted her to say something. Her eyes slid shut. "I hear you speaking words, but all I can hear is my own blood and this vague Charlie Brown teacher sort of voice. I'm in foot rub heaven. Don't kill the buzz."

He went quiet, and she sensed it was difficult for him. But he was the one who started the foot rub in the first place.

His fingertips finally grazed over the tops of her feet, up her calves and back down again for one last squeeze before gently setting her feet down on the floor. Time to stop being an amoeba. But damn if she could open her eyes.

"I want you."

His husky voice was what did it. She cracked one eye open. He watched her with such longing, such hunger, she shivered again. Despite the sweatshirt, despite the fact there was no chill in the house, she couldn't stop her arms and shoulders from shaking a little.

She'd denied herself for so long. Not for Zach's benefit, but for hers. Because she'd been tired, she'd had no time, she'd had no money, or decent prospects. And now here sat a man who wanted her, who was quite possibly the end all, be all of prospects, with plenty of time, a fresh foot rub under her belt, and no need for money.

And she still couldn't have him forever.

Would it be bad to have him for a night?

"You're thinking too much." He reached for her slowly, so slowly, and she could have said no. Instead, when he hooked his hands under her arms and pulled her to sit on his lap, she let him. Her long legs dangled over the side, and her ear rested on his chest, just above his heart. One large hand stroked up and down her sweatshirt-covered arm.

He kissed the tip of her ear. "Will you stop thinking about it so much for tonight?" His phone buzzed, and he grunted and reached for it in his pocket. "Sorry, not trying to be rude but—"

"Work, I get it."

He unlocked the screen, then chuckled a little. "Zach's asleep."

"That's early . . ." She checked her watch. "Normally his bedtime's not for another half hour. And usually he cons a sitter into tacking on another thirty minutes."

"He had some help. Greg ran over and wrestled with him

a bit. Showed him a few takedown moves. And I can hear you doing the mom thing in your head," he added, rubbing a hand down her back. "Reagan says he did great, was happy as a clam, and hit the hay hard. Look."

He held the phone out, and she smiled when she saw the photo of her baby boy sprawled out on his bed, feet where the head should go, in Spiderman boxers and Captain America T-shirt. "He looks happy."

"You can practically see dream bubbles of superhero battles drawn over his head. He's good. And Reagan also says . . ." He navigated away from the photo and back to the text message screen. "'Don't rush home, Greg and I are watching a movie and we're gonna make out for a while. Be a friend, leave us in peace.'"

Kara gasped, then giggled. When Graham stood, her still in his arms, she gasped again and grabbed for his shoulders. "Put me down! I'm too big for this."

"Too big," he scoffed, tossing her a little against his chest. She shrieked—which was probably his number one goal— and held on tighter—a close second. "You're tall, sweetheart, but you're not big. Let's follow in their footsteps and watch a movie. I'll flip through what I've got and yell if you like something."

"Just a movie?" she asked innocently as he settled them down on the couch and turned on the TV for Netflix. "Really."

"I mean, if you wanna throw in some of that making out . . ." He held his hands up in a *what can you do?* gesture. "I won't deny you. I doubt I could deny you anything."

The final sentence had been spoken so softly as he flipped through the instant queue, she wondered if he'd meant for her to hear. But while the movie titles scrolled by, they started to blur. Her skin tingled where it touched his, even through clothing. Her breasts felt heavy, and she fidgeted a little on his lap. In response, she could feel a hard presence making itself known.

"Stop," she croaked out. The movies froze, landing on what looked like a foreign film. She didn't care. She wasn't paying attention.

"See something you want?"

His voice was low, so low, and she knew he was onto her. Just like she knew, if she stood up and walked out, he wouldn't stop her or complain. And would probably just ask her to dinner again tomorrow night.

She shifted, turning and using some creative flexibility until her knees pressed into the couch, straddling him. "Yes, I see something I want."

The remote dropped to the cushion beside him, his hand gripped her waist and pulled her forward, torso to torso, groin to groin. His eyes were gleaming, like black onyx, and his mouth was set in a firm line. She could read him so well, now. He wouldn't move until she made the first one. Wouldn't push another inch until she opened the door and issued the unquestionable invitation.

Wanting to delay, wanting to hurry, she forced herself to calm down and slow down. Kara's hand brushed over his hair, nails scratching lightly in his scalp. It had nearly the same effect as his foot rub had on her. His breathing deepened, and his hands squeezed rhythmically against her hips. Leaning down, she brushed her breasts against his chest to test his response. Even between the layers of the thick sweatshirt, her nipples hardened into points, begging for attention.

"Graham," she said softly by his ear. He uttered a grunt. "Maybe I've been looking at this the wrong way."

Another grunt. He'd gone very quiet for a man who had all the answers earlier.

"Maybe I should be good to myself. I thought being good to myself meant being disciplined, and resisting temptation. But maybe it means treating myself to something, after having waited for so long."

Her throat burned, and her eyes stung a little. She breathed in his scent, just to calm her nerves a bit. Then, pressing her lips to his neck, she whispered, "I've waited for a long time."

He stood again, and she shrieked again. He hoisted her up below the butt, encouraging her to wrap her legs around his waist. He was strong. So, so strong. And without another word, he carried her back to the bedroom.

CHAPTER

9

He'd never been a neat freak. Tidy, for the sake of simplicity and efficiency. Just not a freak about it. But he'd never been so grateful for his natural tendency to put his dirty boxers in the hamper as he was when he carried Kara into his bedroom. It hadn't crossed his mind they would actually make it this far back in the house . . . and not having to shove dirty socks under the bed while she wasn't looking made things much easier.

As he laid Kara out on the bed, he stood and took her in. And had a moment of second-guessing. Was this pushing? Winning the battle but forfeiting the war?

Then she looked up at him, eyes heavy, and reached for him. Any man who could resist the temptation of Kara Smith in his bed reaching for him was destined to be a monk. He quickly stripped his shirt off, just to make things easier on himself, and lay down beside her.

"This skin," she murmured, pressing a kiss to his

sternum, running her hands over his chest. "This skin is amazing to me."

That . . . was a first. "My skin." Skin which was currently tingling with every pass of her hands over it.

"It's so different from mine. That's the real reason why men are attracted to women, isn't it? And vice versa? The differences?"

"And you don't have skin?"

She chuckled, then pressed her cheek to his chest in a way that made him want to hold her close against him, curling around her to act like her shield for all the negativity that might come her way. "I don't have this skin. It's always warm, and this gorgeous golden copper color, and it's hard. Not rough, exactly, but not like mine." She took a testing nip on one of his pecs, and he tensed. "And tasty."

"You're right. Differences are what attract. Time to compare." He pulled until her shirt rolled up and over her head, leaving her in what he supposed could be called a bra . . . in fantasy land. The lace cups held her modest breasts up, barely concealing the areolas from his view. And there was a front clasp. Nothing, to Graham's way of thinking, screamed feminine sexuality more than a lacy, front-clasp bra.

He let his lips wander, reveling in the fact that he finally could. Loving every hitched breath, every little sigh. The way her stomach muscles tightened as he edged close to her nipple, then seemed to shudder when he eased back.

"Graham." Her voice was unsteady. "What are you doing?"

"Getting to know our differences. You're right. You're soft, and your skin is this creamy color that's . . ."

She raised her head, arching one auburn brow at him. "That's what?"

"Never mind." He kissed her stomach and worked on the front clasp to distract her.

"No, what? Now you've got to tell me." When the clasp

sprang free, she scrambled to hold the cups in place. "Tell me, or the girls stay in for the night."

"Kara," he growled.

"Graham," she growled back, sounding like an irate kitten.

"Fine," he bit out. "Your skin reminds me of this antique lace tablecloth my yaya had. Her grandmother made it. And my mom always told me I had to be really careful when we ate at the table, because it was super old and I could hurt it if I wasn't vigilant. So I always thought it was too delicate for me."

She started to speak, but he stretched up to kiss her quiet again.

"Then one day, I spilled juice on it. I was about nine. I freaked out, started crying, and my yaya asked why. I told her I'd ruined it, that it was special and beautiful and I'd ruined it."

"Graham," she began, cupping his cheek. But he shook his head.

"Yaya sat me down and said the tablecloth had survived countless little boys before me, and it would go on to survive countless more after. Because it looked delicate and beautiful, but it was made of stern stuff and wouldn't be ruined so easily. Next time I came over, tablecloth was back on the table. Couldn't even tell where I'd spilled my juice."

"I'm the tablecloth?" she asked slowly.

"You're delicate and beautiful to look at, but I have to keep reminding myself how tough and resilient you are. Your strength isn't easy to see . . . but you've got it."

Her eyes watered, and she blinked rapidly. "Dusty in here."

Graham looked over at his dust-free night stand. "Yeah. Sorry about that. Now, back to where we were . . ." He pulled gently on the cups of her bra, and watched as it fell open for him, revealing more creamy flesh and dusky pink areolas. They furled under his gaze, and he couldn't help but take the closest one into his mouth for a taste.

Kara's hands cupped the back of his head, moaning. He let his free hand move down to unbutton her jeans. Without pushing them down, he reached in, testing her with one finger. Teasing around the entrance to her sex. The tight quarters of her pants gave him little motion, which was exactly what he wanted.

"Take . . . you can take . . . take them off," she said around swallows. She arched her hips up to give him a chance to slide the pants off.

He didn't.

"Graham?" she said, questioning.

"Easy. Just let me do things my way for a while. If you don't like it, we can change it up later." He played more, through the soft hair below, grazing her clit, down to the slick, plump folds that were growing more wet by the minute. "Sometimes, I think we skip past foreplay too quickly."

"We haven't done anything *but* foreplay," she insisted.

"I mean in general. Adults. We spend our teenage years figuring out all the different ways to get off, or simply have fun, without actually having sex. And then we finally have sex"—he grinned when he rubbed the bundle of nerves between two fingers and she cried out—"and we forget all the fun ways we played before we knew what the end result was."

"I like the end result." She gasped. "We could . . . oh my God."

She came then, and he could see it shocked her. Watching her face contort with the pleasure was one of the hottest things he'd ever watched. As she came back down from the high, he stripped her jeans off. She helped, sort of, with languid, heavy-limbed motions. It was like undressing a drunk.

"You're no help," he teased, pulling the final way to get her jeans off the ankle they stubbornly clung to.

"If you wanted help, you should have undressed me before you made me come," she retorted, sort of sing-songy.

"Oh no, you don't," he muttered as he realized she was slipping away. "Come here." He rolled with her, pulling her under, then over, then under him again as he made his way to the other side of the bed where he could grab a condom. "Please, God, tell me you're still awake."

"Let me check." She reached down and cupped him through his own jeans. "Yup, still awake."

He croaked out something, then stood and shucked his jeans as fast as possible. Which, with fumbling fingers and Kara in his line of vision to distract him, took about two minutes longer than it should have.

"Okay, so you're struggling a little." Kara sat up and plucked the condom from his fingers as he finally managed to undo the button to his fly. "I think I should handle this one."

She palmed his ass and urged him to step toward the bed, putting his erection almost at her eye level. With one hand, she wrapped her fingers around the base, squeezing a little.

"Kara," he said, voice hoarse. "You . . . I . . ."

"Shh," she said, licking the head a little before using her teeth to tear the wrapper open and pull out the protection. She rolled it on slowly, so slowly. The sight of her pale, slender fingers working the latex over his penis almost undid him. Then she laid back down, and he couldn't resist anymore. He angled himself, pushing in, sinking deep, sighing with relief.

Her own sigh echoed his.

He needed to go slow. Wanted to go slow. Savor, taste, experience every nuance of being with her, inside her, in her. But she wrapped her legs around his hips, dug her heels into the backs of his thighs and urged him faster.

He couldn't seem to dig up the reserves to resist. He pumped, doing his best to keep to a steady rhythm, until his body was no longer under his own control. He looked down at her, at her face so flushed with pleasure, her eyes filled with it, that he couldn't hold back his release any longer.

And thanked God she climaxed with him, because he was hopeless to do anything more.

KARA'S fingers ruffled through the dark, springy hair on Graham's chest, playing and twirling locks around a fingertip before letting go. When his hand covered hers and flattened it, she smiled and nuzzled closer to him. "That was wonderful."

"'Wonderful' is one word for it." He kissed the top of her head and pulled her in tighter, until she was halfway over him. Her knee slipped in between his thighs and he clamped them tight around so there was no escaping. "I might go a little more bold and say spectacular. That word doesn't get used often enough."

"Spectacular," she mused, grinning in the dark. This part of intimacy had been missing from her life most of all. Yes, the physical portion had been . . . well . . . spectacular. There was no point in discounting the fact that she'd been thoroughly and intensely made love to . . . and wouldn't say no to going back for seconds. But the soft, post-sex whispers, the little touches, the sleepy sounds and heavy-eyed glances . . . this is what she'd truly wanted out of a man. Someone to spend those quiet evenings with, to hold her and make her feel like she wasn't in this life for the long haul alone.

He made a little sound of pure laziness, rolling more toward her to cup her bottom in his hand. The man was going to go for round two, she could tell. She lightly bit down on his pectoral, and had a laugh when he yelped.

"Woman! What was that for?"

He rolled on his back and rubbed at the red mark. "You get punched in the face daily, and you cry about a love bite?" She tsked and sat up, looking for her jeans. "I might have to tell Coach Willis about that."

"I might have to tell Coach Willis what all that yoga

bending actually equates to," he growled and pulled her back into bed just as she'd gotten her jeans up over her butt. "What's with the clothes? Denim and snuggling do not mix."

Her heart melted a little at the thought that he wanted to snuggle—not just have sex—with her. "I have to get home." Cupping his jaw in one hand, loving the scrape of dark bristle, she kissed him long enough that she had to step away before he pulled her under again. The man was a sexual magnet. "I can't abandon Reagan and Greg at my place forever."

"Stay. They deserve it."

"No, they don't. And Zach has school in the morning, and I have a class to teach. Much as I would love to . . . mmm." She couldn't resist nuzzling in for one more kiss before grabbing her bra from the headboard where it had landed. She put it on and located her shirt on the floor, stuck inside the sweatshirt. She pulled and tugged, but it wasn't budging.

"Just put it all back on. I'll get it later."

"At this rate, I'll have more of your clothes at my place than you do here at yours."

"I don't see a problem with that."

She closed her eyes before heading to the door, then looked back. "Graham . . . eventually we have to talk about later. Now is fun. Now is . . . wow."

"Spectacular," he emphasized, getting up to find his own boxers.

Yes, spectacular was the word for it . . . and for him. Lord, he was too delicious for womankind to resist. The navy boxers slid up and over his very fine ass, and she felt a pang of regret she couldn't stay all night.

Being an adult sucked sometimes.

"Nevertheless," she went on as he hunted up his jeans, "eventually, we have to get to the later part of the conversation. There are things you need to know about why later isn't an option. Things that—"

"Oh, hey, look at the time," he said, checking his wrist,

which had no watch. "You did say you had to go, and person-ally I'd love for you to be the one to bust up a Greg-and-Reagan make out session." His smile turned devilish. "In fact, could you be running your video on your camera when you walk in? Just, you know, flip the lights on really fast like it's a raid? I'd love to see how fast Greg's ass hit the floor from the couch."

"You're terrible." She went for her bag, dug out her phone and checked to make sure Reagan hadn't texted with news. Nada. "Thank you for dinner," she began, turning to find him walking behind her. His jeans were only half buttoned, and he hadn't put on a shirt. He was still barefoot.

She was going to go into a coma. A hot guy coma. "I-I-uh . . . thank you."

"You just said that," he pointed out, checking the kitchen. "You have everything?"

"Mm-hmm," she hummed, watching his back muscles strain as he reached into the fridge and pulled out two bottles of water. Carrying them with him, he kissed her once more then walked her to the door, and out to the car.

"For your drive back," he said, handing her one.

"You're a hospitable sort."

"I want you to come back. Often. And stay longer."

She kissed him once more, because he was sexy and shirt-less and considerate and too much for her to resist in the now. The wow now. The spectacular now. Sliding her palm up and down his chest, she pushed firmly so she could open her door all the way and slide behind the wheel. "Get some rest."

"No morning practice. I can stay up as late as I want." He flashed her a sexy smile. "I'll call you."

Normally, she'd have rolled her eyes the moment she hit the main road, because *I'll call you* was typically male code for *Nah, not interested, and no balls to say it to your face.* With Graham, it was code for . . . he'd call. She knew that one down to the bone.

"And next time, bring Zach." With that parting shot, not having a clue how much his simple, unrehearsed acceptance of Zach in her life meant from a man she was interested in, he gently closed her car door and stepped back so she could reverse out of the driveway and head home.

Where she had a couple of babysitters to break apart, and an empty bed to sleep in.

Later sucked. Now was better.

KARA arrived home, parked, and hustled up to her second floor apartment. She debated, just for a moment, getting her phone ready to record, then thought better of it. If she had a cutie boyfriend like Greg, she'd make out with him on any couch she could. No judgment from her.

But when she opened the door, the only one on the couch was Reagan. Her friend's face illuminated in the yellow-blue glow of the TV turned to her. "Hey, stranger. I was about to text Graham to make sure everything was going okay."

"I'm so sorry, I'm way later than I thought."

"I'm not punching a clock. Greg took off a while ago. He was hungry. Again." Reagan rolled her eyes and stood as Kara flipped the lights. Her friend started to take the DVD out of the player. "How'd dinner go?"

"Dinner was nice. Spectacular." That made her grin, though she tried to hide it by turning her back to Reagan. Working to keep her voice neutral, Kara set her purse on the hook by the door. "He's a decent cook. Pasta and home-made garlic bread."

"Hmm. Something cool for dessert?"

Kara cocked her head as she went to the kitchen to toss the empty water bottle in the recycling container. "What?"

"The sweatshirt."

She jolted, realizing she was still wearing his sweatshirt.

Again. She was actually starting a collection of Graham Sweeney sweatshirts. "No, I was just . . ." Shivering with lust. "Cold. No dessert."

"Hmm." Reagan followed her into the kitchen, waited until Kara opened the fridge to get another bottle of water out—despite claiming to be cold, she was suddenly flushed—then slapped her hand over Kara's butt. "You liar! You totally had dessert. You had a Graham Sweeney sundae!"

Kara straightened, face red, eyes wide. "How did you . . . Greg. Did Graham text him? Oh my God, I'm going to kill him!"

"You've got sexy eyes." When Kara leaned back, blinking, Reagan shook her hands at that. "No, not like, 'Hey, sexy eyes, come here often?' You've got that dreamy look in your eyes, like you've had sex. Sexy eyes."

"You failed optometry school, didn't you?"

"Don't deflect. You got some, you hot mama." Reagan hip-checked her, then walked back to the living room to grab her cute clutch. "Zach was fine, which I know you were dying to ask but didn't because you trust me. He kicked Greg's ass in a video game—nice job there, by the way—and chowed down on some snacks. There was some grappling with Greg in there, in which Zach is now sure he is the kung fu master of the universe. We watched a movie, and he basically made it through the opening credits before he was out cold."

Kara's heart swelled at the other woman's rundown of events. She truly had the world's greatest friends. Hugging Reagan tight, she whispered, "Thank you."

"Thank me by giving that man a chance. Don't take the orgasm and run." Tugging gently in a teasing manner on Kara's ponytail, Reagan winked and headed for the door, closing it behind her quietly.

Kara checked on Zach—she was a mom, it was just what she had to do—and was satisfied to find him in nearly the same position as he'd been when Graham had shown her the photo. Still so much a little boy, she thought as she went in to smooth down his hair and kiss his forehead. But growing up fast. Growing up to be a man. She prayed he would be the kind of man who cooked good pasta for a woman, and asked about her own son, who believed in honor instead of taking what he could get and running like hell.

CHAPTER

10

Monday night, Graham sat on the floor, stretching while he waited for the team to show up. They'd passed word, and Marianne had let Brad into the gym before going to her office to work on paperwork. No coaches, no support staff. This was a team meeting, no distractions. He, Brad and Greg had come early, hammering out the meeting before everyone else came in.

"Still sore from practice today?" Brad asked, settling beside him and hissing out a breath as he extended his leg with the knee brace. Then he darted his eyes around the catwalk, as if looking to see if anyone else had witnessed his moment of vulnerability. Practice had ended nearly three hours earlier, but with his injury, he was pushing it to even still be on the team.

"Sore from last night's mattress gymnastics," Greg quipped, then dodged out of range as Graham kicked at him. "Whatever, you gave me shit, too, when I was trying to date Reagan. Turnabout's fair play and all that junk."

"'And all that junk.'" Brad turned to him. "Wise man. Here comes the team. Showtime."

It took a good ten minutes for the guys to all file in up on the catwalk. They'd chosen it because it was the first site of vandalism. The first time they'd sensed trouble. The team quieted down, almost all of them unconsciously standing at parade rest. Tressler, cocky shit that he was, smirked, but when nobody spoke, and the silence grew heavier, his attitude slowly shrank and he found himself mimicking everyone else's pose.

"We've got a problem," Brad started. "It's become very clear to us that whatever this asshole vandal's problem is, it's with the team. And they have access, or have found a way to get access, to wherever we are. They know where we'll be, where we won't. It stands to reason, they're connected to us somehow."

"Last time, someone attempted to set fire to our locker room. It didn't work," Graham added quickly when a few guys shifted and looked enraged. "But Tressler's shorts were in a prime spot to be the fuse for a big ass burn, and it was only luck that we managed to find it when we did and put it out without a problem . . . except for his ruined shirt."

"Someone set my clothes on fire? No shit. That's why I couldn't find them after the match." His face set in stone, Tressler's jaw worked hard as he stared off into a dark corner.

"This building has shitty security." Greg walked a little in a circle around the team, his voice carrying. "And the MPs are shrugging their shoulders. They've got bigger problems to worry about, to their way of thinking. We're on our own. We just get left holding the bag, looking like idiots."

"It stops now." Picking up where they left off, Graham stood. "We close ranks. We watch everyone. We don't turn our backs. It's going to be exhausting. It's going to suck balls. We've got enough shit to worry about, just keeping up with practices, with your life outside the gym. Now we have to add a constant vigilance to our plates. It won't be easy."

Greg grinned over their heads. "Aw, hell, Sweeney. If we wanted it the easy way, we'd have joined the army. Right boys?"

One from the back let out an enthusiastic "Oo-rah!"

Brad snorted. "Pathetic. I'm sorry, I thought this was the Marine Corps boxing team."

"Oo-rah!" three or four responded.

"Son of a bitch. What a weak response. It's like we caught the air force at practice." Graham threw his head back and yelled, *"Who the fuck are we?"*

"OO-RAH!"

The collective war cry echoed off the rafters of the old, dusty gym, settling around them like a comfortable blanket. From the corner of his eye, Graham could see Marianne standing just outside her training room door, looking up at the catwalk and rubbing her arms as if she'd gotten the chills.

He knew the feeling. Knew it well. It was pride, damn it.

Brad nodded once, decisively. "Okay. Bring it in, Marines. Here's how we're going to play it out from here."

"FINAL yoga lesson," Coach Ace said as he greeted Kara at the door. "It's been a pleasure working with you, and watching you work with the Marines."

She smiled at the large man, hoisting her yoga mat beneath her arm as she walked through the door he held open for her. "Playing doorman today, Coach? I didn't see a valet out front for my car."

He barked out a laugh and walked alongside her toward the gym. "I'm not much of one for the stretching and bending myself. But it's been a good time watching the guys twist themselves around. I know it's helped stave off injuries, and improved their flexibility. And I think most of them have enjoyed it, to be honest . . . though I doubt you'd catch them on camera admitting the same."

"I'm glad it's been a benefit to the team. I've had a good time teaching them and getting to know the guys." They entered the gym, where a few early birds were dropping their bags and trading street shoes for their boxing gear. Her eyes immediately found Graham, without even trying.

Yes, she'd definitely enjoyed getting to know them. Including one very special Marine.

"I hope, if you like how things have worked out, you'll consider repeating the experience with next year's team. Maybe mentioning the benefits of weekly yoga to some of the other coaches you know?" Her bank account could use the boost, that was for sure.

"Absolutely. Much as these bones don't like to bend, I know it's a big help. I'll pass your name along."

"I really appreciate it, Coach."

Graham jogged over without another word, waiting patiently while Coach Ace asked how long today's session would run, if she'd make up a few stretching routines for them to use on the road, and gave a few more instructions, including the fact that she would be a welcome guest at the All Military games.

If only she could actually go.

After Coach left—with a curious look at Graham—she smiled shyly. He'd called the night before, as promised, and they'd talked for nearly an hour after Zach's bedtime. He'd had no problem answering questions about his childhood and family, and hadn't pressed when she'd hedged about her own. Most of all, he'd called when he said he would, which was shocking enough as it was, and had let her dictate the conversation.

"Hey." He gave her a big smile, but didn't reach out to touch. In the gym, they were sort of like colleagues. Having seen how Brad and Marianne managed their relationship, she knew he would respect her professional standards the same way. "I liked our conversation last night."

"Me, too." Walking over to the usual corner she led yoga from, she noticed the table where she set up her small speakers for her phone was already set up. They had been for the last several weeks now. "I never think to ask . . . does Marianne have the interns set up my station here? I should thank them. Maybe a gift card."

"It was me." He shrugged when she looked at him. "You struggled setting it up the first day. I saw you while we were being yelled at, so I couldn't help that first time. I figured it would be easier to just get here early on yoga days and do it for you."

She fought back a smile, setting her bag down and pulling out the small travel speakers that would play the soothing mix she'd put together that morning. "Are you a naturally thoughtful man, Graham? Or is this just because you've wanted to get in my yoga pants?"

He snorted a little at that. "I hope I'm a thoughtful person. My mom would be disappointed otherwise."

"Then you can tell her good job from me." She toed off her slides, unrolled her mat and walked across it to flatten it a bit. "I was thinking we could do dinner at my place tonight."

She'd said it casually, hoping he didn't read too much into the gesture. She had ulterior motives, and they had nothing to do with sex. At least, not tonight.

"Yeah, sure. What can I bring?"

A naturally thoughtful man. "Allergies. Don't worry about it, I'll have it all. Just bring yourself."

"Can do." He leaned forward just a little as she scrolled down her phone to bring up the playlist. "Can't wait," he said quietly by her ear, then jogged back toward where his teammates were gathering.

While they stretched and jogged a few laps in miniformation, she did her best to get her body under control before she spent an entire class leading with hard nipples and shaking hands.

KARA held up two different earrings and judged each one in the mirror. She'd worn black tonight, the better to hide small splatters if she made a last minute mess in the kitchen. Not that she'd made a fancy dinner. Her budget didn't run to steak and lobster, nor did her schedule run to three-hour prep time. Chicken, vegetables, and potatoes. But good chicken, veggies and potatoes. It was something. And men liked simple home-cooked meals, didn't they?

Her phone rang, and she glanced down to see Marianne's face grinning up at her. She swiped a finger over the screen and immediately pressed the speaker button. "I'm telling him tonight."

"Telling who what? Oh, wait, is this a guessing game? I'm going with Mr. Plum, in the solarium, with the secret baby."

"No. Colonel Mustard in the kitchen with the long-lost twin brother. Now focus."

Marianne snickered. Kara went with the less dangly earrings. Too dangly looked like she was trying to be fancy. And she was anything *but* fancy. The exact opposite.

"I'm telling him tonight about Henry, and the whole mess I'm in with that. He needs to know that despite the fact that we . . . you know," she added after a moment. Zach was still in his room—or so he should be—cleaning up so he could show Graham a new video on his used laptop, but little ears had a way of popping up just when things got interesting. "Despite that, we still have no actual future."

"Yeah. Okay. And when he ignores you and acts like it's not a big deal, then what?"

"Then . . . I don't know." In exasperation, Kara sighed, laid her palms on the dresser and let her head fall. "I obviously don't know much of anything in this arena. I got pregnant at eighteen. I've had, like, three potential contenders for relationships that never even got off the ground. I'm not built for this sort of dramatic adult relationship."

"It doesn't have to be drama, and you absolutely are built for a relationship. You are the most loving person I know. You should be giving that love to someone else. Besides Zach," she added, reading Kara's mind with the frightening accuracy of a long-time best friend.

She'd have given her parents love. She wanted to, desperately. Hated that her son didn't have grandparents he could spend the night with, grandparents he could call when he thought his mom was being unfair, grandparents who could give him wise advice from well beyond his own mother's years.

Stop that. You can't change their attitude, you can't change their way of thinking. Move on.

"Kara?"

"Sorry." She cleared her throat. "We will figure it out. I don't have a lot of time to devote to a relationship anyway, thanks to Henry threatening to drag me to mediation again."

"Will you do me a favor?"

She grinned, and could only imagine the wide range of ideas that Marianne could come up with. "I won't promise to kick him in the balls for you if and when I see him next. Much as I'd love to."

"That's a close second to my real favor. Lean on Graham. Don't just tell him about the big picture. Ask for his advice on this situation. Don't say you don't want to dump on him. Or burden him. Just do it."

She bit her lip, studying her reflection. Minimal makeup, hair half-braided, then swooped up for a bun, nice black top and a simple pair of capris. She'd be barefoot, because she always was at home. "Maybe."

"Do it."

"Stop pushing, Marianne."

"If you don't want a best friend to push you when you need to be pushed, what the hell good am I to you?"

She thought about that for a moment. "You know how to tape Zach's ankle if he sprains it playing soccer."

Her friend let out a half chuckle, half sigh. "I worry about you. Have fun tonight, regardless. And get yourself a decent good night kiss. Zach won't die if you send him to his room for a few minutes."

"Go get your own good night kiss," Kara instructed. She could have sworn her friend muttered, "I'll get better than that," before hanging up.

After another quick glance in the mirror, she closed her eyes. Pep talk time.

But a knock on the door, and her son's enthusiastic whoop and, "I'll get it!" shout stalled any pep talk she'd hoped for. Time to figure it out on the fly.

No problem there. She had about ten years' worth of practice.

"HEY, kid." Graham held out the small bouquet of flowers. "These are for you."

Zach scrunched up his nose and shook his head. "Why would I want those?"

"Oh, right." Kara rounded the corner, and Graham let out a long breath while Zach shut the door behind him. "Then they must be for you."

She smiled, walking slowly to him on bare feet. She took the flowers, then rose up on her toes and pressed a friendly kiss to his cheek. The skin beneath her lips tingled, and it had nothing to do with his fresh shave. "Thank you. I'll get them in water. Dinner's almost ready."

"Plain chicken," Zach muttered, glancing at Graham in a plea of understanding. "I told her since we were having company, we shoulda had something good, like wings, or pizza . . . or pizza and wings. But instead we just get plain chicken."

"I love plain chicken," he said simply. "I like wings and pizza, too. Okay, no, that's a lie. I love wings and pizza." Zach nodded, as if proving his point. "But I have a feeling if your mom made the chicken, it's going to be good, too."

Zach's face turned a little mutinous, and he froze before entering the kitchen. Graham paused, looked at Kara, who was watching them both carefully without being obvious, and waved her off. She nodded very slightly and turned her back to them, presumably to look for something to put the flowers in. That she trusted him to handle the situation with her son fully hit him like a blow. There was probably no greater compliment a single mother could hand a man.

With that thought ringing through his mind, he said easily, "Let's head to your room while your mom finishes up dinner."

"But I—"

Graham was already steering him with a gentle hand on his shoulder.

"Ten minutes," Kara called behind them. Graham gave her a thumbs-up as he followed Zach into the room.

"You're lucky your mom let you pick your own bedspread," he began, waiting for Zach to join him in his room. "My mom picked mine for me, and it was just a boring navy blue color. I wanted Star Wars, at least until I was about fourteen."

The young boy flopped down on the sloppily made bed, ruffling the Avengers bed covering. His butt covered Tony Stark's face. "Yeah. Well, she lets me pick that, and not dinner."

Graham indicated the spot next to him on the mattress, and Zach lifted one shoulder. Graham sat on the hammer of Thor, considered for a moment, then tried again. "Your mom loves you. It's sort of awesome to watch."

"You want to date her."

That had his head tilting. "Yes, I do."

Zach's eyes blinked in surprise.

"Did you expect me to lie to you about it?"

The young boy extended both feet, let them drop so they banged against the side of the bed with a loud thunk. "No. Maybe. You're supposed to be nice to me."

"I thought I was nice to you. We've hung out before, just us and with Brad and Greg. Maybe I got it wrong, but I thought we had fun."

"We did. I thought you were my friend."

Ah. And welcome to the wonderful world of parenting. "Zach . . . are you upset because I started dating your mom? Or because you think by dating your mom, that means we can't hang out anymore?"

"Maybe some of both," he answered, voice so soft Graham had to strain to hear it. His chin drooped to his chest, and he wouldn't make eye contact. "Now that you're with my mom, you're on her side."

Man up, Sweeney. "Probably." When Zach looked at him again, shock all over his face, he shrugged. "Your mom's a better kisser."

The boy laughed, then slapped a hand over his mouth. "Gross," he muttered from behind the hand. "I don't believe you."

Give it a few years, kid, and you'll understand. "Aside from that, I'm on your mom's side because she's on *your* side. If she's serving something, it's because she thinks it's what is best for you. That means I'm gonna side with her. Sorry, bud. I happen to like you, so I'm on her side. It sounds opposite, but that's how it works."

He mulled that over for a while, then asked quietly, "You weren't being my friend just so you could kiss her, were you?"

Oh, man. "Let's just say, if your mom and I don't work out, I'm still going to check in for video game dates. I've got to have someone who can keep me on my toes, and none of the guys I play with are worth a damn."

His mouth quirked at the last word, and Graham considered the curse he'd let slip worth the price.

"So, we good?"

"You like my mom," Zach said on a sigh. "It's kinda weird."

"I'm kinda weird, so it works out. I like your mom," he agreed. "I like you. We'll see what happens from there. Deal?"

Holding out a hand, he waited for Zach to put his smaller, thinner hand in his, and shook.

CHAPTER

11

Kara stood beside the door, listening without shame as Graham walked through the process with her son. Trusting Graham not to hurt her boy's feelings didn't mean she wasn't curious how he'd work through it. A little awkwardly at first, but they'd gotten around to a place of understanding.

Most of all, she was grateful he hadn't made any promises that couldn't be kept. No mention of forever, or the future. He'd managed to explain the situation on terms her son could understand, without taking a parental role he hadn't yet assumed, but still managing to keep her son in line as an adult who should be respected. It was . . . almost masterful.

When she heard Graham ask if they had a deal, she hustled back to the kitchen, reaching the stove just as they opened Zach's door and came strolling out again. Zach walked up to her, slipped one slim arm around her waist and squeezed.

Her heart in her throat, she simply hugged him back, not

making him say a word. The hug, at his age, was more than enough.

"Go set the table for me," she said when she thought her throat would let her. "Remember the placement I showed you?"

"Fork, plate, knife, spoon." He grinned up at her, and her heart once more caught in her throat. "Got it."

As he gathered the dishes in his hands to take them to the small four-seater kitchen table, Graham walked up behind her and wrapped his arms around her waist. The touch was intimate, though not sexual. And when he rested his chin on top of her head, she leaned back into the embrace, just a little. Then gasped and twisted in his hold to see Zach's reaction.

He stood, watching, one plate still in his hand, head cocked to the side as if still taking it all in.

"We talked," Graham said solemnly. "Right Zach? He's good with it if we kiss and date and stuff."

That forced Kara to muffle a laugh, for her baby's sake. "Oh, did you now?" Her voice was light, but she watched diligently for any sign of problems with her son. "Always good to know the menfolk can come to a decision about such matters and then let the women know."

Graham's quiet laughter was unmistakable, as she was plastered against his chest. But Zach simply shrugged, as if to say *I don't get why you'd wanna kiss, but oh well*. Then he went back to setting the table. The unofficial seal of approval from a ten-year-old.

Kara brought the food to the table, glad she'd splurged for the nice serving bowls for the steamed vegetables and potatoes. The chicken, sadly, sat on a plain plate, ready to be forked up. Couldn't be helped, she had to cut off the spending somewhere.

For all his whining for wings, Zach inhaled his dinner as usual. He took seconds, as did Graham, and cleared his plate without being reminded once. The talk with Graham seemed to have set him in a mood to behave, because he didn't immediately run off to his room. He settled back down when Kara made herself and Graham coffee.

"What, no coffee for you?" Graham asked him when Zach accepted the cup of hot cocoa, made from her own mix. Zach grinned and shook his head.

"The kid and I have a date with destiny for a while," Graham informed her. "Shouldn't take too long, since I plan to whup on him."

"Whatever," Zach said with a worldly snort. "You couldn't whup me if you had an entire platoon holding me down first."

"Good one," Graham murmured, smiling in appreciation at the comeback. "Save that one, it's a keeper."

"I know." He grinned, and her little boy was back again. "Mom, can we be excused?"

She was about to say yes, when Graham said, "We need to help your mother with the dishes first." Zach opened his mouth, but Graham added, "She cooked. We can show some gratitude by cleaning up."

"Okay." Easy with the idea, Zach stood and carried his plate to the sink, returning for hers. "You done, Mom?"

She just stared at Graham in shock. "I'm sorry, do you have wizard powers?"

"Nah. He's got something important to look forward to. And he knows I'm going to make his video game life miserable, so he's just delaying the punishment." Standing, he carried his own plate to the sink, kissing the top of her head as he passed.

Zach made a gagging noise by the sink before turning it on.

"Go sit. Watch TV. Read a book. Something that doesn't involve hovering." With a nudge, Graham pulled her chair out and sent her ambling toward the master bedroom. "We've got it."

Feeling like an intruder for a bit, she watched as Graham and Zach worked in tandem to clean not only the plates, but dump the leftovers into a plastic container—located by Zach—and washed the serving bowls and pots as well.

Okay, then. She'd just go . . . read a book. Or something.

TWO hours later, Graham stretched his neck. Somehow, he was more sore after sitting down and using nothing but his thumbs ninety minutes than he had been after two three-hour-long practices. He was officially getting old when sitting took a toll on his body.

He wandered out into the living room and found Kara, bare feet propped up on the coffee table, typing away at the laptop in her lap. When she looked up at him, he smiled to see dark-rimmed glasses sitting on her face, framing her gorgeous eyes.

"Sexy," he commented, settling beside her as she moved the pillow to make room for him. "How have I not seen those before?"

"Only for reading and computer work. I don't often read in front of other people, so you wouldn't have." She continued typing, so he let her continue. But he did lean back against the cushion and tilt his head so he could watch. Some women might have been annoyed with that. Kara simply kept going. Her fingers—slender, graceful, unadorned by any rings or polish—flew over the keyboard.

"You're fast."

"Gotta be, when you don't have a lot of time to write and your second job depends on it." She clicked on the mouse, sighed, then smiled. "Done."

"What's this all about?"

"An article someone else wrote. I had to write the intro for it, and then do some work to hyperlink it. I'm actually not great at the whole technical blog aspect. It's not my favorite part."

He'd seen the blog, read it, considered it a lifesaver for

when he had Zach over and needed to know if something was okay with his allergies or using her ever-updated list of foods on the OK list so parents didn't have to spend as much time hunting up suggestions for brands to try. And it looked pretty solid to him. "So who runs the blog, then?"

"I do. I just had to teach myself basically everything from scratch. It ate up a lot of time to start with. Eats up more time, now that it's growing—very slowly—and starting to get advertisers. I've had to contract out a few bits and pieces of web design, plus hire a lawyer for the advertising contracts. I'm hoping that breaks even soon, then makes money."

"I could have helped with that. Next time, bring it to me." When she looked at him, from behind slightly smudged lenses, his heart simply stopped for a moment. "What?"

She started to speak, then closed her mouth. Then opened it, and closed it again. She was doing a fantastic job of playing Charades . . . as long as the answer was "fish."

"Kara. What?" He leaned closer and wrapped an arm around her. "What's up?"

"I . . . where's Zach?" She glanced at her watch, confirmed with the time on the laptop screen, then gasped. "Oh my God, it's way past bedtime. He'll be a nightmare tomorrow morning. How long have I been . . . never mind." She closed the laptop and stood so fast he reached out in case the whole thing plummeted to the floor. But she caught it and set it on the coffee table.

"Hey, relax. He's asleep."

"He's . . . what?" That had her frozen halfway to Zach's bedroom door. "No, there's no way. He was so hyped you were coming over. That's impossible."

"That's totally the truth. Check." Smugly, he crossed his arms over his chest and waited while Kara peeked in. She popped back out, mouth hanging open.

"He's asleep." Disbelief laced her words. "He's still fully dressed."

"So? Kids fall asleep in their clothes. Leave him."

She debated for a moment. "He hasn't brushed his teeth. You know what? Never mind. One night won't kill him."

Graham was pleased she could loosen up on the small things a little. Some moms were militant, like his had been. His mother would have marched in there, demanded he brush his teeth, floss, rinse, and comb his hair before putting on pajamas. At the end of it, he wouldn't have even been tired any longer. Kara's natural ability to see the forest for the trees was impressive.

She walked back to the couch and flopped. The natural cushion placement meant she rolled a bit toward him. He gave the couch some help by scooting over enough that she was tucked in against his side, knees bent and nudging against his thigh, head resting on his shoulder. In a word: perfect.

"We have to talk." Her voice was quiet, but firm. "When you mentioned asking you for help . . ." She trailed off, but he knew she wasn't falling asleep. He gave her time, letting his fingers run up and down her arm. If it took all night, he'd let her make the next move. "When you mentioned asking you for help with the contracts, it made me wonder if I could ask you for help with something else. Not that you'd be doing work, exactly. Just, maybe, advising?"

He was used to people asking for free advice. Friends, family, even people from high school he barely remembered but found him on Facebook. Everyone wanted to know what a lawyer thought, nobody wanted to pay for the privilege. With Kara, it felt different. He sensed asking was hard, and not her first choice. It only made him more determined to assist. "Hit me."

"It's about my ex, Henry. Zach's father." His fingers tightened a little on her arm, and he quickly forced himself to relax it again. But she'd noticed, and she rubbed the heel of her hand over his chest, soothing. "He's not in our lives, either of us. Which is exactly how we like it, honestly. But sometimes, when he's feeling the pinch of child support, he likes to threaten that he'll takes us back to court or mediation to lower the amount. Usually giving some bullshit reasoning, having to do with taking him for more visitation to justify the amount he pays in support. It's a threat, really, and not a new one. He's been using it for years."

"Does he see Zach often?"

"He hasn't seen Zach in years. He took Zach for what was supposed to be a full day visit, and brought him back at lunchtime claiming there was nothing he could feed him and I'd set him up to fail. I'd given him a list of foods Zach could eat because we were still going through the allergy testing phase and he also was going through a picky phase."

"As any kid tends to do," Graham murmured.

"Exactly. He survived on bread, butter and a few other staples for about eighteen months back then because we were so limited on what we could add into his diet, and again by what he would actually eat. Henry accused me of making up a lot of his allergies—but thank God he didn't try to test that theory out. And that was the end of him giving enough of a shit to come see his son."

"Bastard," was Graham's quick and unequivocal judgment. "The guy is scum."

"I'm not arguing. But he's pulling it again, this whole 'if I'm paying for being the kid's dad, I should see him' junk. Henry doesn't want to see him. He just knows that I don't want him to take Zach alone. He's old enough to know what he should and shouldn't eat—Zach, obviously, not Henry— but that doesn't mean I want to trust him with an adult who has shown zero respect for his medical issues in the past, and uses his son's feelings as a weapon."

"Of course not." She was so calm about it, so collected. No hysterics, no sobs, and no real anger either. The anger, she'd have earned. But she kept it down, and he sensed it was only because it was more efficient to be able to talk without using curse words that she did so. "How can I help?"

"The lawyers think it's going to come to a head. He can't keep coming back and demanding we lower support on paper, because even the state has its own standards that he can't go below. But he might be more tempted to lower the payments made directly to me, and for me to keep my mouth shut about it, if I knew it meant he would abide by this unspoken agreement he leaves us alone and doesn't push his right for visitation."

"I'm not really up on family law," Graham began, and he could feel her slump against him. "But the law is the law. I can give you suggestions, I just can't represent you."

"I have a lawyer," she said quickly. "I pay for her, it's not like, court appointed or anything. She's just expensive."

"The good ones usually are."

"No kidding," Kara said with a puff of air that stirred her bangs. "I had a court-appointed lawyer back in the day, when I was still a teenager. I remember sitting in court before our time to go in front of the judge, and Tasha was representing the mom ahead of me. She ripped into the deadbeat father like a shark on a bucket of frozen chum. It was . . . a little terrifying to watch, actually. She's scary in the court room. I knew then and there, if I ever had enough money to hire a lawyer, I'd do whatever I could to make her mine."

Graham smiled, but said nothing.

"I'd rather not waste my hourly rate asking simple questions that could be answered if I just knew where to look."

"Research, basically. Someone to bounce ideas off of."

"Exactly. I'm sure you get asked this sort of thing all the time." Sadness tinged her voice now, and she rolled and shifted until she perched on her knees, facing him. One hand came up and cupped his cheek. "I hate to be another person to ask."

"You're not 'another person,' Kara." He held her hand in place, then eased forward to kiss her long, deep and slow. When her other hand came up to play in his hair, then slide down and pull him against her more, he called it a win. He broke the kiss. "You're not 'another person.' You mean a lot to me. You and Zach both. It's for both of you. I'll do whatever I can, however I can."

She kissed him this time, peppering his face with tiny, playful pecks in between gasping "thank you, thank you, thank you."

"I'm sorry," he said, holding her a bit away from him. "I'm going to require a bit more of a thank-you than that."

"Oh." Her lips twitched, and she threw a leg over him to straddle his lap. Her soft center pressed against his hardness, and he wanted nothing more than to be the wizard she'd accused him of, cast a spell and watch their clothing disappear so he could slide his erection deep into her. "So that's how it'll be, hmm? Am I paying for your very lawyerly services with free rein of my body?"

"No, never that. But," he added, nipping her bottom lip when she raised a brow in surprise, "but, I am more than willing to accept generous donations of gratitude in the form of, shall we say, physical demonstrations."

She laughed, kissed him again, and gasped when his hand slid under her shirt. "Graham." Her voice was unsteady. "Zach . . ."

He froze. Damn. He'd forgotten entirely where they were. "Sorry."

"No." She gripped his wrist hard, keeping his hand in place. "Don't stop. Just . . . be careful."

The idea turned in his mind a moment. Staying quiet, being careful, the element of discretion . . . his blood fired and his hips twerked up just a little in response. "So, you're saying, if I do this, you can't say a word." His hand moved slowly across her soft skin to cup her breast through her bra.

"And maybe if this happened"— he used touch alone to pull and roll the lacy edge of the cup down to free her breast, still under her shirt—"then you wouldn't moan."

Biting her lip, she shook her head. Resolute, this woman.

"So then this won't make you gasp," he said low, pinching her nipple between his thumb and forefinger, pulling gently. He heard it, actually saw the gasp form in her chest, then stop with a convulsion like a trapped hiccup. Her face was red, but her expression said, *Try again, buddy.*

"You're good," he admitted, then pulled up the hem of her shirt over her breasts. "I guess if I want any sort of reaction out of you, I'll have to try harder." Then he closed his mouth over her breast.

She made a sound then, as he rhythmically pulled and sucked, running his tongue over the peak. It was something like a keening cry, but only heard through the vibration of her chest. He placed his hand flat against her sternum to feel it again, chuckling when he felt it. The soft, plush skin of her breast fit perfectly in the U-shaped hold of his hand. He could die happily after spending an hour worshiping them.

Her fingers worked hard to pull the other cup down, and he took that as the invitation it was meant and transferred over to the second. Her back arched to press more firmly against his mouth, which pressed her center harder against his cock. He wanted so much to release his belt, pull out his cock and press into her. But not tonight.

He worried for a moment his mind had blocked out the action of his own hand when he felt a tug on his belt loop. Looking down, it wasn't his own hand, but Kara's, pulling restlessly, and futilely at his buckle and the first button of his pants. At this angle, nothing would happen but make him harder and frustrate them both. "Shh," he soothed, and reclined back when she pressed her lips to his.

She'd been hungry for him on Sunday, in his bed. She'd wanted him, and participated fully in their bedroom activities.

But now she was ravenous. A totally different beast, and one he'd like to explore later. Now, however, when stealth and quiet were required, ravenous hunger would do nothing but wake up Zach and end the shenanigans before they got really interesting.

CHAPTER

12

Graham stood, holding onto her and swallowing her gasps of shock with another kiss. Then he walked back toward the bedroom—or what he assumed was her bedroom, pausing only to open the door and walk through before shutting it behind them.

Then laid her down on the bed, straightening to admire the picture she presented. A sexy woman, her shirt rolled up over her breasts, legs opened wide in a butterfly pose, eyes hot and a little wild for him . . .

Yeah. He could get used to this.

"Why are we here?" she asked.

"Because I fully intend to do what I want with you, and while making out and fooling around on second base is amusing, and easy to hide quickly, I'd rather not force you to reschedule the birds and the bees talk for Zach if he wandered out looking for a cup of water and found us doing what we're about to be doing."

Ignoring her reaching hands, he unbuttoned her pants

and tugged, leaving her slip of underwear behind. He had plans, and none of them involved his pants being off. "Here's the thing though. These apartments, they usually don't have the best soundproofing. As in, none. You start making noise? He'll hear you. I'm not sure you can stay quiet. Are you?"

She bit her lip, then nodded. Pulling at her ankle until her butt was at the edge of the bed, he knelt down on the floor and pressed a kiss to the inside of one thigh, then the other.

And managed, just barely, to put up a block when she tried to close her thighs and push him out. Not happening. He raised his brows at her, questioning if she wanted him to stop. The blush that covered her throat and cheeks was adorable, but she simply closed her eyes and laid back.

He let his tongue work along the seam of her panties, dipping under every so often, then back out again. Her thigh muscles quivered with every wet pass of his tongue, but she stayed silent. When his fingers pulled back the edge to reveal her core, the quivering upgraded to shaking. He blew cool air against her hot flesh, and smiled as her entire body jerked.

But, she didn't make a sound. Damn, she was good.

The first long lick changed things. It was a soundless sound, if that made any sense. As if the entire scream had lost steam while she breathed heavily. A sound only a dog could hear, but he knew existed. He took another leisurely lap, and she clamped a hand over her mouth.

Yes, she was good. But he was better.

He focused on her clit, and that made her thrash her head around the bedspread like a fish on dry land. One hand clutched the bedspread as if it were the only thing keeping her grounded. While he circled, sucked and nibbled, she bucked and rolled beneath him.

He inserted one, then two fingers into her warm heat, groaning himself when he felt how hot she was, how wet, how undeniably ready for him inside her. The knowledge that he wouldn't get more than this taste tonight made him want to beat his head against the bed rail. This was about her, though, and he could resist. He'd been resisting for weeks. He wouldn't lose his mind over a night of delayed pleasure.

Crooking his fingers, he stroked her inside and out, watching her body, listening for the hitches of her breath. He forced himself to examine every vibration, every twitch. Focus on how warm her skin was beneath his palm while he held her stomach down. Notice the clenching of her muscles beneath his hand, the way she grew even more wet around his fingers, tightening in pulses. Every nuance of her existence was a clue that told him without any words exactly what she liked, what she liked more, and what was the best of all. When he found that *best of all*, he gave it everything he had.

And then she came, with the most gloriously silent orgasm he had ever had the privilege of watching. Her long, slender body writhed and moved with such grace, even under the power of a climax, that she took his breath away. Her face was a study of pain, though he knew she felt nothing remotely negative. It was the price of holding back vocally that twisted her face.

Kara's body finally relaxed, and she sprawled on the bed like a woman who had run a marathon. Replete, sweaty, utterly exhausted but with a sense of true accomplishment. The satisfied smile that tilted the corners of her mouth made him ache with the longing to crawl under the covers with her and hold her all night long.

Not now. Not yet. Sometime soon.

He kissed her once more, had the pleasure of watching her twitch in response, then settled her lacy underwear back in place. He laid down beside her, taking in the way her creamy skin was still flushed and a little splotchy, but in a cute way. Her eyes were closed, with those blond lashes spiky against her cheeks. But he was surprised to see a silvery trail of what had been tears that led from the corner of her eye down into her hair.

"Hey." He kissed the wetness, then brushed another over her cheek. "You okay?"

"No," she whispered, smile fading. "Not really."

Worried, he wrapped his arms around her and pulled her tightly against him. She didn't sob, didn't heave. But he felt more dampness against his neck. "I . . . I didn't hurt you, did I? If I did something, I'm sorry. I'm so sorry, I—"

"No, of course not." Her voice was low, but strong enough. "It's just how you . . . you know. How I didn't say a word and you still managed to . . . you know."

"Make you come?" he said, laughing a little when she winced. "You can say it, I won't tell anyone."

"Not just that. But how you . . . I don't know. I'm being stupid." She rolled back on her back and wiped at her face, hiding her eyes. "Ignore me. I'm just having a moment of stupidity."

"No, you're not. If you feel something, it's not stupid." But she seemed to need to grapple with whatever it was solo. He hoped that changed in the future. "I should get going. I'll call you tomorrow." He kissed her forehead and stood, shaking out one leg a little and adjusting the front of his jeans. This would make for an uncomfortable drive home.

She glared at him from bed. "You're leaving? We're not finished."

They were for now. "Tonight was yours." When she just stared at him, he grinned. "I believe the phrase you are searching for is, 'Thank you, Graham. I'll miss you.'"

She rolled her eyes, then rolled up and out of bed, pulling off her shirt and bra fully as she did so.

"I'm sorry, I couldn't hear that." He pinched the top of her thigh as she bent over to pick up her pants. She shrieked and jumped. That made him laugh. "Oh, now we can't stay quiet."

"You!" She swatted at him, but he darted out of reach.

When she threw her clothes in the hamper in the corner and opened a drawer, he crossed his arms to watch. She pulled out what he assumed were her pajamas—an oversized T-shirt and a tiny pair of booty shorts—and started to pull them on.

Looking supremely annoyed, with mussed up hair and a blush that seemed permanent around him, she yanked the shirt on over her head. "What's the deal? You come in here and you eat dinner and you play video games and you make me . . . you know. And then you leave?"

He thought for a moment about that. "Sounds like a decent Tuesday night . . . minus the leaving." When she narrowed her eyes at him, he caught her around the waist, hauled her against him so she could feel his erection, and kissed her with enough passion she wouldn't doubt for a moment he wanted to stay. "If I could, I'd stay. But you don't want me to, because of the circumstances. I don't blame you a bit. So I'm not going to make you kick me out. I'm going to leave myself, before things go farther."

"At least . . . just lie with me for a bit?" She held out a hand to him, sitting down on the bed as she did so. "Please. This is the part I like the most. When we were quiet on Sunday night, after . . . you know. Afterward, just laying together."

How the hell did he say no to that? "Fine. A few minutes." He toed off his shoes, thought for a moment about his cargo shorts and shirt, then decided they were sufficient enough. He crawled into her bed, surrounded by fluffy white pillows, then sighed in contentment as she curled up beside him, humming with pleasure.

"It doesn't feel right," she admitted softly, tracing the hem of his T-shirt with her fingertip. "That I got so much and you got nothing."

"Oh, sweetheart." He kissed her again, tenderly. "Don't you know watching you get what you want is exactly what I want?"

* * *

KARA woke to the alarm, as she did every morning. She purposefully set it ten minutes early so she had one snooze button's worth of extra time before she had no choice but to leave the warm comfort of the covers and the softness of her pillow.

Except her pillow was hard this morning. It was firm, barely yielding as she pushed her hand to it to gain leverage to roll over and hit her snooze button. And it grunted.

Her pillow grunted . . .

Oh, sweet Jesus.

"Graham!" she hissed, bolting up straight. "Graham. Oh my God, we fell asleep!"

"Yeah," he said, not opening his eyes. "You made me lay down."

"You have to wake up!" She pushed at his torso. It was as effective as shoving at a boulder.

"I will, chill out." He stretched his hands above his head, which made the shirt ride up his stomach. All that golden skin, warm and inviting and . . .

"Zach will wake up in ten minutes. *Getupgetupgetup!*"

"No, we just . . . no." One dark eye cracked open, glanced around. "We were out for five minutes. Ten, max."

"We were out for almost eight *hours*. Up."

"Damn. Okay, I'm up. Where are my shoes?" he asked, rolling out of bed. "They're, okay, here."

She walked with him to the living room, then stood gaping when he paused long enough to sit on the couch. "What are you doing?"

"Shoes. I don't think I should walk barefoot out of here. Gross. Can I hit the head before I go?"

"No, I . . . oh God," she whispered as she heard Zach's door open, then the door to the bathroom. "Throw your shoes down."

He looked up, bewildered, from tying the first shoelace. "I just got it on. Wha—okay!" he said when she glared. "What now?"

"Sun salutation. Now. Now!" she whispered harshly as he stared at her dumbly. Were all men this stupid in the morning, or just him? "Get up and salute the sun or so help me, God . . ."

"Okay, okay." A smile pulled at his lips, but he managed to roll it back before standing and following her lead. They were in the first lunge when Zach walked in, scratching his belly, a confused look on his face.

"Graham?"

"Hey, bud." He rolled up from the first lunge, moving as Kara did into the second. "Ready for school?"

Bewildered, Zach looked down at himself, still dressed in the clothes from the night before. "No?"

"Ah. Better get a move on." His voice muffled as they worked into a back arch.

"Mom?"

"Graham's just getting a little extra yoga in this morning before practice," she said, feeling breathless.

Her son seemed to take that at face value, with a shrug. "Okay. See ya for breakfast then," he told Graham, then went back to his room and shut the door to change.

Kara collapsed on the carpet, covering her face with her hands. "I can't believe that just happened."

Graham chuckled and rolled over to her, kissing her gently on the cheek. "C'mon, it's funny."

"Says you."

"Yup, says me. And look at the bright side."

When she looked at him through her fingers, he was grinning down at her. The shadow of growth covering his face, combined with his naturally swarthy skin and white teeth, gave him the look of a pirate. "What bright side?"

"I'm getting a home-cooked breakfast out of the deal."

She punched his arm and rolled out of reach.

* * *

"MUFFIN me," Reagan demanded as she walked into the training room that morning. At Marianne's narrowed gaze, she sighed and retreated back a few steps to kick off her heels and slip her feet into the fuzzy blue slippers by the door. "I need the energy. I had quite the rude awakening this morning."

"Is that what Greg calls his penis? The Rude Awakening?" Marianne snickered when Reagan rolled her eyes. "Come on, it was funny. But shush, we're not talking about your Rude Awakening. Kara has a muffin-worthy story."

"Not just muffins. Chocolate muffins," Reagan said, inspecting the baked good she'd stolen from the basket on Marianne's desk as she sat on the second table. Unlike Kara, who was stretching—oh God, felt so good—Reagan sat primly in her sharp pencil skirt and tailored shirt. The effect of a high-powered businesswoman was ruined only by the blue slippers, which she wore under silent protest, but in accordance with the training room rules set by Marianne. "You have a chocolate muffin story. Do tell."

"I was just waiting on you to stop primping and get your fabulously dressed ass in here." Kara took a breath, then stopped. "Nobody is out there, right?"

"One Marine is. It's weird though," Reagan said thoughtfully. "He's just sort of sitting in the middle of the gym, reading a book. Nobody else is here yet because we're the only two crazy enough to get here this early. Now spill."

"He can't hear us?" Reagan and Marianne both shook their heads. "Okay then. Graham came over last night for dinner, just the three of us."

"Aww," Reagan interrupted. "That's so cute." When Marianne sent her an evil glare, she shrugged. "What? It is."

"He's great with Zach. He really is. And then he forced me to go off and do something for myself instead of cleaning the kitchen. He made Zach help, but not in a super conde-scending sort of way. Total hero worship. He's great with him." Just thinking of the private conversation she'd eaves-dropped on in Zach's room made her warm.

Marianne sighed and covered her heart with her hand. "He's so hot, and good with kids, and seriously has a body to die for. On top of that, he does dishes? I can see red flags everywhere."

"Shut up. So after dishes and a few rounds of video games with Zach, he gets Zach in bed—"

"Hold on. He tucked the kid into bed, too? Jesus, what does this guy have to do, cure cancer? Marry him!" Reagan demanded.

"Shut up," Marianne and Kara said together. "Let her finish," Marianne added.

Reagan shot her the finger, but waved for Kara to continue.

"So we're on the couch, and it sort of comes out how I could use the help with Henry and the child support. No hesitation, he offers to help. Not that he can represent me, but just with research and stuff. To save me some money."

"Perfect," Marianne said.

"I'll take him if you don't want him," Reagan added.

"You have a boyfriend, Greedy McGreederson."

Reagan shot Marianne the finger again. "Continue."

"So in my gratitude, I sort of started making out with him. Which led to . . . stuff."

"She's been through childbirth, but can't say the word 'sex.' Sex. They had sex." Marianne spun in her chair. "Hot mama alert!"

"No, not really."

That caused Marianne to grab ahold of the desk to stop the spin midflight. "What? You've got that man on your couch and you didn't have sex?"

"I would have! He didn't want to. Or something. He gave me the most intense orgasm of my life—even including the ones he gave me on Sunday—"

"Show-off," her best friend grumbled.

"We're going to have to interrupt this program here and get some details. Come on. Most intense orgasm . . . how? Something. Anything."

"He . . ." She felt the tips of her ears burning, and she double-checked the door leading to the training room. Empty. "He went down on me."

Both friends watched her expectantly.

"And he wouldn't let me make a noise."

Reagan cocked her head to the side.

She sighed. "So all that normal tension-burning stuff, the moans and the groans and the sighs, it had nowhere to go. Everything felt three times as intense because it was all bottled up beneath my skin waiting to burst out. When the orgasm actually hit, and I still couldn't make a sound . . ." She sighed and shivered a little. "I can't really explain it except to say . . . wow. That's the best I can do. Wow."

"That," Marianne said after a full ten seconds of silence, "I might have to try."

"Yeah, no kidding. My muffin melted a little just thinking about it. You may continue," Reagan said.

"And that was it. I offered to return the favor, but then he talked about how it was just for me and that was fun for him, and it doesn't always have to be an even trade-off and whatever." Kara waved that away. "I don't get it. I was willing. I was basically putty in his hands. He knows I want him. And it's not like we haven't already done it. What happened?"

"Kid factor?" Reagan guessed, taking a bite out of her muffin and kicking her heels a little in delight. "I really don't get how you make these muffins without all the normal ingredients and they're still so good."

"In an effort to avoid the expensive boxed mix, I experimented a lot. And no, he clearly had no problem with the oral part in the same apartment as Zach. He just . . . stopped everything."

"He stopped himself. Because he wanted to give you a special moment. It's sweet. Stop overthinking it. Be grateful for what sounds like a mind-blowing orgasm and call it a win."

"A man who can give you an orgasm and leave without pushing for sex is definitely scoring points," Reagan agreed.

"He didn't leave. I mean, not right away." She blushed, then told them about falling asleep, only to scramble to make it appear as though they were having a morning yoga private.

Both Marianne and Reagan spent several minutes laughing at the mental image Kara painted. "So he's there doing sun salutations, wearing the same thing he wore last night, and Zach had no clue?" Marianne asked through gasps.

"He's ten, and a boy. They don't tend to make the fashion connection."

"And he let you put him through morning yoga to appease your son. Extra bonus points," was Reagan's comment.

Marianne added, "Go back over there tonight and screw his brains out as a thank-you."

Kara stared at Marianne. "I can't. Zach. I can't afford to keep hiring a babysitter so I can get laid."

"What's your schedule like today?"

"Class at nine, class at ten, class at one, private at—"

"Aha!" Reagan pointed at her with the muffin. "Lunch nookie. They have a three-hour break for lunch, from eleven to two today. Be at his house, waiting for him, after you get done with your second class. You've got two hours for a nooner. Make them count."

Kara looked to her friend to confirm. Marianne nodded with a smile. "You deserve this happiness. Don't let future junk get in the way."

"I haven't told him. About not being able to leave, about the reality of no future."

"You will. And something tells me Graham isn't about to take that as an answer. But either way, you'll get there. Now before we leave, let's—damn," Marianne muttered under her breath as she heard voices. "Here come . . . hey, Levi. Hey, Nikki."

The two walked hand in hand, shocking all three women. Nikki quickly pulled her hand from Levi's, blushing and turning away to store her bag in a drawer. Levi looked supremely pleased with himself. Maybe Kara wasn't the only one who'd gotten some the night before.

"Okay, I'm heading out. Levi, Nikki, would you like a muffin before I go?"

Levi took one and gave her a smile. "Thank you."

He was such a shy boy, and she worried about his heart when Nikki inevitably broke it. "You're welcome. Nikki?"

"Too much fat," the young woman said, wrinkling her nose at the basket Kara held out. "Nope."

Uh-huh. "I'm out. I'll, uh, keep you updated on the events as they unfold."

Both her friends grinned at her as she walked out.

CHAPTER
13

"I'll bring Simpson some food during lunch, since he's taking the shift here between practices." Greg nodded at the youngest of the team, who had changed into street clothes and was now settling against the folded-in bleachers with a tablet to watch a movie. "Probably get something for myself, too, and just eat here with him. Reagan's got a meeting so she's not available for me to bug."

"You're getting fast food, aren't you?" When Greg scowled, Brad shook his head. "Nasty. Your body—"

"Is a temple. I know, Grandpa." Greg clapped Graham on the shoulder. "How are we friends with this guy?"

"He's got the hot trainer hookup."

"Ah, right," Greg mused as Marianne exited the training room and waved to Brad. He followed without another word for them. "He's toast. If they're not married in a year, I'll eat my boots."

"I doubt it happens that fast." Graham watched as the two interns followed Marianne out. The young blonde paused, looking back toward the gym and the solo Simpson sitting there, then kept walking.

Were they being too obvious with guard duty? If people started noticing the guys hanging around the gym for a purpose, it could backfire.

"I'm heading home. I could use a nap."

Greg wiggled his eyebrows in a crude gesture. "Yeah? Late night?"

"Yeah. I got my ass handed to me. Twice."

That had his friend's brows lifting in surprise. "What?"

"Oh, yeah. Rough all around. He really let me have it on that second round of Minecraft. That kid knows how to build."

Greg rolled his eyes and bumped against him. "You suck. Fine. I'll ask. How are things with Kara?"

Though he knew his friend would never spread rumors or gossip, he decided to keep Kara's troubles to himself. If she wanted others to know about her issues with her ex, she would tell them. Maybe already had. "Good. Moving slow." Probably should have moved slower, but that was over and done now.

"Slow is good when you've got a kid to consider. Great kid, though."

"You're not kidding." They parted ways in the parking lot. "See you at two."

Greg waved, and Graham drove the fifteen minutes home through the back gate. When he turned down his street, he squinted. There was another car parked in his driveway.

As he pulled closer, he realized whose it was, and he grinned. Kara had come to visit.

She got out of her car as he pulled into his garage. She wore skintight pants that capped at her ankle and a racerback tank, showing off her svelte body to perfection. Her feet were in running shoes and her hair, in a high, messy bun. A few strands of hair were stuck to her temple, as if she'd been sweating earlier, and it had dried that way.

"Hey, you." He opened his arms and she walked right into them, as if it were an everyday occurrence to meet for lunch at home. The idea appealed. "What brings you to my neck of the woods at this time of day?"

"I had time, and a little birdie told me you did, too."

"Is the little birdie about yea tall, with Nordic goddess coloring and can wrap an ankle in under a minute?"

Kara laughed at that, wrapping one arm around him and walking with him into the house. "She would love that description. But no, this birdie likes impractical heels and business suits."

"Reagan." *Thank you, Reagan.* "I admit I don't have a lot to eat here. I was just going to sort of scrounge around for something. Not very healthy, I know, but it works." He opened the fridge and passed her a bottle of water without looking behind him. She took it, and he heard the top crack open. "I see my leftover salad from yesterday, which I could eat but you probably wouldn't want. Maybe a sandwich? I've always got bread and peanut butter and jelly. Some lunch meat, but that's probably not safe, so—Whoa."

Kara's hand slipped below the waistband of his shorts and yanked hard enough to send him stumbling back a step. The refrigerator door snapped closed.

He leaned back against the counter by the sink, watching as she set the water bottle down on the table. Something had shifted in her gaze. Gone was the easygoing yogi happy to spend the lunch hour relaxing on his couch with a sandwich. In her place was a woman who had an obvious hunger nothing in his fridge would satisfy.

"I've been thinking," she said slowly, walking to him. One step, she toed off her running shoe and let it drop. Then another step, toed off the other. Left them where they landed. "Thinking about last night."

He knew a moment of panic, then realized no. This wasn't regret. This was a continuation. "Yeah? Are you going to ask for a repeat performance? Just to make sure I haven't lost my skills overnight?"

"Mmm." Threading her fingers through his hair, she shook her head. "Another time. But right now, I need some practice."

He wanted to ask what kind of practice, but she sealed her lips over his and kissed the question out of his mind. When he grabbed her hips to pull her into him, she stood on her toes, bringing their groins together. With a groan, he reached for the waistband of her yoga pants. She did the same with his shorts.

Thanks to the modern invention of the elastic waistband, she had his shorts around his ass before he could blink, his hardening cock in her hand and she was stroking him fast. At this rate, he'd last maybe a dozen seconds before shooting off in her hand and ruining the entire lunch break. When he managed to get her pants over her butt and down to her knees, he grabbed her ass, twirled her around and deposited her on the counter.

"Ohmygod, that's cold!" She shrieked it, hissing in a breath and shifting her weight from cheek to cheek. He pulled and tugged until one of her pant legs came free; the other, he abandoned entirely to dangle from her calf. Then she stopped shifting as he thrust her thighs apart. Yoga had definitely done her well, when they split wide, giving him easy access. She no longer could reach him, but her core was open and perfectly displayed for him.

He bent down and gave her a few testing licks, inserting two fingers quickly to pump. If he didn't speed her up to where he was, he'd embarrass the hell out of himself in three quick thrusts. He wouldn't—couldn't—leave her hanging behind.

Her hips pistoned up and into his hands while he licked and circled her clit with his tongue. Gone was the hope of staying quiet, and she moaned and muttered his name, clutching at his head, the counter edge, the cabinets behind her head. "Graham, Gra—oh! Stop! You ha-have to st-st-stop or I'll—"

He straightened, positioned his cock at her entrance, and thrust hard into her. She closed around his erection with tight heat. His six-foot-two height gave him just enough leverage to ease in and out of her snug opening. She clawed at his back through his shirt. He might carry marks later, and he'd wear them proudly.

The sound beside his ear was nearly a scream when she fluttered inside, around him, then came. He followed her over the edge of the climax, all but draped over her and the countertop.

WHAT a lunch break.

The thought made her giggle, then send a silent thank-you to Reagan for insisting she give noontime nookie as try.

"Laughing while a man is still inside you isn't very kind," Graham admonished, nipping at her shoulder. He was still half on top of her, breathing heavily. She patted his sweaty back in a *there, there* gesture.

"Just thinking about how I'll never be able to think about a lunch hour the same way again."

"No kidding. I think I—fuck."

She blinked at the ceiling. "Well, okay, but do you think we could take a five minute break first?"

"No, I . . . damn." He pulled from her in a wet slide, then quickly grabbed the roll of paper towels and handed her a few. "I forgot the condom. Kara—"

"We're good. I'm covered and clean. Which you would have known if I'd mentioned it, and I hadn't. That's on me."

"Same. I mean, clean. Not covered, because, well . . ." He indicated where he was wiping at his half-erect penis. "Not covered, as they don't yet make male birth control pills. That was irresponsible of me. I'm an asshole."

"You're not an asshole. It was wonderful to be wanted that much." It had been like two animals mating, not two mature adults. Fantastic. Refreshing. Needed. "Don't be hard on yourself," she demanded, cupping his cheek. When he fixed his shorts, took their paper towels and tossed them at the kitchen trash can—two points—she noticed he wouldn't look at her. "Graham."

"I should have been more careful. Especially with you. When you know what—damn," he muttered again when she felt a cold chill sweep through her. "That wasn't right, either. Kara, I'm fucking up all over the place today. I'm sorry. I'm so sorry."

Maybe with another man, she could have read it differently. But with Graham, she believed his apology sincerely. He would never insult her, insult her son purposefully. "You're right, I do know what the repercussions are. At eighteen, I didn't. Or, maybe intellectually, I did, because hello, health class. But what eighteen-year-old can know that for sure? I'm an adult. I trust you. I know you respect me. It's different."

He let his forehead drop to hers, and he simply waited. Breathing with her, until she couldn't tell if her rhythm had matched his, or his matched hers. They were simply in tandem now. "You humble me with your faith. I should be more careful with you. You're too important to be careless."

"Have a little faith in yourself, please. I do. You're not careless. It was unbelievable to be wanted like that. Hell, Graham, you couldn't even get my pants off."

"Or mine. God, you do something to me." He hugged her gently, as if she were a precious, fragile thing to him and he wanted to surround and protect her. Insulate her from all things. The thought made her eyes sting, so she buried her nose in his neck and breathed in. "We're combustible."

That got a laugh out of him. "Can we take this back to the bedroom, or do you need to go?"

She looked over his shoulder at the kitchen clock. Judging travel time, plus traffic, she said, "I don't think my lunch hour is quite over yet. I could be persuaded to look at the dessert menu before I go."

That made him laugh harder. Standing up straight, he gripped the backs of her thighs so she had to wrap her legs around his hips. "You've got a habit of carrying me to bedrooms."

"They don't make a patch for that. Guess I'm stuck with the habit."

"Such a shame," she said, drawing a pattern on his back while he walked.

She had to tell him the rest. Had to tell him not to get attached. To apologize for letting things get this far, letting things evolve so much that two hearts could easily be broken when it ended.

Maybe three hearts.

But the illusion of a happy couple with nothing but bright skies ahead was too tempting. When he laid her down on his bed and finished stripping her properly, she decided the storm clouds could stay on the horizon. At least until tomorrow.

FEELING good about life, Graham headed back to the gym a little early. Kara had needed to be at her next class an hour earlier than he did, but his home, with the reminder of her and of their wild romp, felt too empty after she'd left. As he pulled up, finishing up the last of the sandwich he'd hastily thrown together and wrapped in a paper towel for the drive back, he realized Greg's car was nowhere to be found. Hadn't the other man said he'd be bringing Simpson back something to eat since he was doing guard duty between practices? He checked his watch as he climbed out of the car. He had plenty of time to double-check with

Simpson, then run out and grab the guy something from the MCX if Greg had forgotten.

As he walked into the gym, he heard nothing but the low hum of the florescent lights suspended far above. The building was old, and the lights probably predated the Second World War. Okay, maybe not that old, but the majority of the place was pretty ancient, which was why the boxing team was the only one who used it 90 percent of the time. The maintenance crew was constantly putting Band-Aids on the building. Patch job here, quick fix there. Soon enough, Graham figured they'd raze the thing and start fresh. Just not before the end of the season.

When he rounded the corner of the folded-in bleachers, he found Simpson and—surprisingly—Nikki sitting side by side against the bleachers. They spoke in low tones, so he hadn't heard them before.

As he got closer, he realized Simpson was doing almost no talking. It was all Nikki. And Simpson looked supremely uncomfortable with the whole thing. Most of the guys had wised up to the intern's game early on. Tag chaser, all the way. Even as he watched, he saw Nikki lean forward emphatically, and Simpson inch back.

Poor kid. He was probably twenty or twenty-one, and had no clue how to let a woman down gently. Everything in his body language screamed *I'm uncomfortable!* But Nikki was either clueless as clueless could get, or she was deliberately misreading the situation in order to advance her own agenda.

Graham feared the latter, but couldn't discount the former.

"Simpson!" he barked, wanting to save the kid. "Get over here."

Eyes wild, the younger Marine jumped up, startling Nikki back a bit, and ran over to him. "Sir, I—"

"Don't speak," he ordered, biting back a smile when Simpson immediately went to attention. He was a good

Marine, and a good boxer. The kid had a future for sure. "Simpson, have you eaten lunch?"

"Yes, sir."

He didn't care for the "sir" when on boxing time. Together, they were a team, no one man higher in rank than the other once they stepped into the ring. No uniforms, no insignia. Their leader was their coach, and that was the end of it. But for the moment, the military hierarchy served a purpose.

"Where is Higgs?"

"He went for a quick jog, sir. Wanted to stay limber, sir."

Nikki stood, sauntering over in khaki shorts that were an inch or so too short for comfort. Her polo seemed too tight, though he'd seen her twist a knot at the small of her back before when she thought she could get away with it. Marianne wouldn't approve, and made her unroll it whenever she noticed. "Hey there. We were just talking. I hope he's not in any trouble."

From the pleading look in Simpson's dark eyes, Graham knew exactly what the Marine was thinking. *Help me. Punish me. Make me run laps in the sweltering heat. Just get me out of here.*

"Simpson knows what he's done wrong. Chat time's over."

There was an infinitesimal relaxing of the younger man's shoulders. Relief, in droves, shone in his eyes, along with gratitude.

"You're not in practice yet," Nikki pointed out, hands on her hips. "That's not fair. He shouldn't be punished for—"

"Thank you, Nikki." Shutting her down, however rude it was, would be the fastest, easiest track for them all to take. "We will see you later."

Somewhere else in the building, a door opened and shut. One of the coaches, most likely. Or a maintenance guy coming to look at the busted light. Best to end this quickly, without an audience.

She looked at him, then at Simpson's profile. Simpson didn't look back. Then she blew out a breath. "You're not the coach, you know. This is rude. We were talking." Wrapping an arm around the other man's bicep, she tugged gently. "Come back and sit with me. I'm bored."

"Nikki, please excuse us," Graham said through clenched teeth. God, the woman was a barnacle.

"I'm not in the military, you can't tell me what to do. And you can't tell him, either. Come on, Alex." She tugged harder, and Simpson actually jerked a little off balance before correcting. "We'll—"

"Nikki, *stop!*"

She froze, mouth open. "You can't speak to me like that!"

"I just did. Leave us alone for the moment, please."

She just stared at him.

"*Now.* I'll be discussing your behavior with Ms. Cook when she comes back. You're out of line, so far out you can't even *see* the line anymore. Get your stuff and stay out of the gym until you're due to report back to the training room this evening, and not a minute sooner."

"You can't—"

"I just did." He gave her his iciest stare, the one he reserved for court when cross-examining a witness. It was rare he needed it, but he knew it was effective. Her hand shook a little as she pulled away, and her eyes swam with unshed tears. The second she hit the parking lot, she'd be a sobbing mess, he bet.

Oh, well. He'd tried subtlety. Simpson had tried subtlety. They'd *all* tried to quietly and kindly brush off her advances. When that didn't work, it was time for plan B.

Huffing her way to her large pink tote bag, she grabbed it and threw it over her shoulder, stomping her way to the gym entrance and up the stairs before shoving her way through the door to the parking lot. The second it closed behind her, Simpson heaved a sigh and slumped a bit.

"Thanks, man." He rubbed at the back of his neck, his

dark face flushed with embarrassment. "She just . . . wouldn't leave."

Graham clapped the man on the shoulder and shook a little. "I know you wanted to be nice about it, and you're not the kind of guy who takes pleasure in hurting someone's feelings. But with that one, you can't be subtle. We've all tried it, and it doesn't work. Be firm next time. 'Sorry, Nikki, I don't want to lead you on. I'm not interested.'"

"Easy for you to say," he muttered, looking down at shoes. "She doesn't hit on you."

Probably because she realized from the start it was a lost cause. She'd chosen the younger guys to work on more. She was a viper.

"You've done your duty, so you won't be in the gym alone again anytime soon. Stick in groups. Do as the antelope do and form a herd against the lion." Or rather, lioness.

That made the younger man laugh, and he went back to sit down. Graham sat nearby, playing on his phone a little, debating texting Kara and leaving her a message for when she checked her phone between classes.

When Coach Cartwright entered fifteen minutes later, he walked straight for them instead of heading to the coaching office. "Either of you boys drive a blue Camry?"

"Yeah, me." Graham reached for his bag, automatically digging for his keys. "I didn't do something stupid like leave my dome light on, did I?"

"No . . . that's not the problem." The man's grim face said it all. "Better come check it out."

Simpson jumped up beside him. "How bad could it be? You haven't even been here an hour. What . . . oh, shit."

Yeah. Oh, shit just about covered it.

Wainwright stood, thumbs tucked in the hooks of his jeans. "I'm guessing you didn't drive here with that brick through your windshield."

"Son of a bitch." Graham stood for a moment, shocked

to see the brick sticking half in, half out of his windshield. The glass had spiderwebbed across the entire width, but the shatterproof material had kept the brick from going through completely. He looked around, but what the hell did he expect to find? A crazy brick-wielding cartoon villain dancing around the parking lot, waiting to be found and cackling maniacally? Whoever did this threw it and ran like hell. No questions asked.

Even as he scanned the parking lot, he noted his car had been the only one to be nailed. Everyone else's was safe. He walked up to the car, carefully watching his step to avoid stepping on any glass, if there was any. But it looked as though the windshield had done its job.

"Why didn't it go all the way through? Even with the type of glass it's made of, you throw a brick hard enough, it would go through. They're shatter resistant, but not shatterproof."

"Maybe they lost their grip throwing it," Simpson suggested.

"Maybe they're huge pussies and throw like a three-year-old," Cartwright muttered. "Call the MPs, son," he told Simpson. "Get in there and grab your personals, Sweeney. Documents and all that junk. Anything you don't want heading to the mechanic when this bad boy gets towed."

It was still locked, so he had to use his key fob to unlock it. As he reached for the door handle, he froze. Not only had the fucker tossed a brick at his car, but he'd been keyed as well. Jagged scrapes ran down the driver's side. "Son of a bitch. If it's not one thing . . ."

He gingerly picked around the few shards of glass that had come loose from the now-flimsy window, opening compartments and searching for anything he wouldn't want to lose. Who the fuck was crazy enough to throw a brick through—or mostly through—his window? And had it been aimed directly at him, or simply another bit of vandalism for the team in general, with his car being the unlucky one?

The MPs showed up ten minutes later, and Graham resigned himself to missing most of the practice to an interview.

The warmth and happiness from his lunch hour with Kara bled out, and when he was finally able to return to practice, he found himself with anger to burn. It fueled him, kept him fierce, and sent him home to take a cold shower after a ride from Greg.

That ruination of his lunch hour with Kara was the worst of it. Not the cost of a new windshield, not the expense of having to rent a car for a few days while they got around to fixing his windshield. The fact that his day had been tainted with something so stupid, so unproductive, so childish . . . after his perfect moment with her.

CHAPTER

14

Kara stared at her phone, willing it to ring. Then willing herself to stop staring at the phone. This was absolutely pathetic.

But he'd said he would call her later. She knew for a fact the guys were done with practice, as Marianne had posted a selfie of her and Brad at the movie theater, seeing the new romantic comedy, an hour ago.

#truelove.

She scoffed at herself. Now she was thinking in hashtags. Her life was going off the rails.

Zach wandered into the kitchen and started poking around the snack shelf in the pantry. Though she hated the expense, she stocked pre-made, pre-packaged snacks for him there, and he knew he could have what he wanted from that shelf without question. She'd prefer him to grab an apple, but when your son was as skinny as hers, and his diet as limited as his, you accepted calories where you could get them.

"Didn't you just have dinner an hour ago?"

"Fractions make me hangry," he grumbled.

"Hangry?" She smiled when he sat down beside her at the kitchen table. He did that so infrequently anymore, willingly sitting with her. He was growing up, and Mom was no longer the coolest person in his life.

"Yeah. Hungry and angry. Hangry. It's a portmanteau. We learned about them yesterday." He beamed at her.

"Grammar and math all wrapped up in one night. Very nice." She wanted so badly to run a hand over his hair, but she knew he would duck away and make an aggravated sound. So she let him open his snack and went back to reviewing a blog advertising request. But she felt his stare on her, so after another moment, she looked back his way.

"Mom?" He glanced down at the wrapper of the granola bar he was eating, fiddling with it between his fingers.

"Yeah, honey?"

"Is Graham coming back sometime?"

"I'm sure he is. Why? Did you want to invite him to dinner again?"

"No. I mean, yeah, sure. Just, I mean I wondered . . . is he . . . are you . . ."

Oh, boy. She nudged her chair out a little to better face him. "Are you wondering if we're dating?"

"Sort of. I guess you are, since I've seen him kiss you."
Thank God that's all you've seen.

"But then you guys don't go out a lot, and I don't know." He sounded miserable, as if talking about this was the last thing he wanted to be doing, but couldn't resist knowing.

"Honey . . ." She sighed. Giving false hope would be pointless. "Graham and I are friends. We like hanging out. I hang out with a lot of adults, like Marianne and Reagan."

"You don't kiss them," he said defiantly, then the corners of his mouth twitched as if the idea was funny.

"No . . . it's a complicated thing, adult friendships. It's—"

"Why don't you want to date him? He wants to date you. I like him. What's wrong?"

She fought hard not to cry. This part was the worst. She'd vowed early on she would never say anything negative about her son's father, or her parents, in front of Zach. It served no purpose to poison the well. But it was moments like these—moments when she longed to explain why she couldn't move on with her life—when she could cheerfully murder Henry six different ways with her bare hands and not think twice about it.

"Nothing is wrong. It's just not . . . the timing . . . it's . . . not going to work. Graham is a great guy. And I'm so glad you two have become friends. I hope that continues. But he and I . . ." She lifted her hands, let them fall back into her lap again. Fought hard against the tears. "It won't work."

"You won't let it work," he accused, his hand fisting hard around the wrapper. The crinkle of the foil sounded harsh in the kitchen. "You won't let it. He could have been my dad, and you won't let it work. I hate you."

He stood back so fast the chair tipped over, clattering to the linoleum floor. He flung the wrapper at the trash—missing by a mile—and ran back to his room where he slammed the door.

Some mothers might have stormed after him and demanded he apologize. It was tempting. But Kara knew far too well what that would do . . . push him further away. He was a pre-teen, and going through changes that must confuse him daily. Given his normally sunny nature, she knew it would soon pass. Giving him time alone before approaching him would be the best option. Everyone was entitled to feel their own emotions. Kids just didn't know how to hide them like adults.

A tear escaped before she could stop it. She used the heel of her hand to wipe it away. Stupid, pointless tears would do nothing to make the situation better.

She wanted Graham to call now more than ever. She wanted him to never call again. She wanted . . . so much. Too much.

Almost as if by design, her phone rang. Graham's smiling face appeared on the screen. It would be better to let it go to voice mail, especially when she was this upset. He didn't deserve to be burdened with her emotional junk.

The phone stopped ringing before she could make up her mind. And then it started back again. She'd missed calls from him before, and she knew his score. He'd try twice, then text and say he'd try back later. Graham wasn't one for playing games when it came to following through.

So she answered, because what else was she supposed to do?

"Hey, you."

"Hey, beautiful." He groaned, and she pictured him sitting on the couch or stretching out in bed. She wanted so, so badly to be there with him. Curling up beside him on the couch, or tucked against his shoulder in bed. "How was your day?"

"Boring. Busy. The usual." She wiped another tear away. Maybe she should give herself a break. Like Zach's ever-changing hormones, she couldn't forever battle back her emotions and walk around like ice.

There was a long silence, then, "Kara? Everything okay?"

"Fine, yeah. Everything's fine. We're all . . . fine." Lame, so very lame.

Graham must have agreed because she heard the squeak of his bed rails—a sound she was intimately familiar with after their lunch hour rendezvous—and he obviously got back out of bed. "I'm coming over."

"Graham, no. I just had a fight with Zach, that's all. I'm sad about that. Please, don't worry about anything."

Don't come over here. I'll lose my everlovin' mind. I can't resist you.

"I'm coming. Fifteen minutes." He hung up before she

could argue further. She could send a text, but that wouldn't matter. He would ignore it.

She got up, shaky yet on her legs, and closed her laptop. Even without Graham coming over, her productivity was shot for the night. She got a bottle of water and stood beside the door, waiting for his text that he was there. At this time of night, she knew he wouldn't knock in case Zach went to bed early.

She was proved right when the text came ten minutes later.

I'm here. Please let me in. Don't turn me away.

She opened the door and stood, watching him. He looked tired. Exhausted, actually. "Is everything okay?"

"I was going to ask you the same thing." He stepped in as she widened the door, shut it behind him, then enveloped her in a strong, unbreakable hug. She wanted to be resistant, but couldn't, and her arms came around him, seeking comfort.

"Hey, hey." He cupped the back of her head as she nuzzled in, whispering softly and swaying as if they were on the dance floor instead of in her apartment. "What's wrong? Tell me what's wrong."

"I . . ." She fought back the tears, fought so hard, then decided now was as good a time as any to let some release. "I'm sorry but I'm about to—" She hiccuped, and that was the end of holding back. She burst into tears.

WORRIED, Graham held Kara while she cried. She'd mentioned a fight with Zach—natural enough for most parent-child relationships, but not for theirs—yet this crying jag seemed disproportionate for a simple fight with her son.

"Let's . . . okay, then." He held her tighter when she sobbed. "Let's sit on the couch for a bit."

She shook her head vigorously against his chest, but didn't say more, just kept crying.

So he stood and held her, knowing it would eventually pass, wondering what in the world had set her off. Kara was a practical, intelligent woman. She wouldn't break down into tears over something silly. It had to be real, and it had to be important.

Zach peeked around the corner, his eyes wide with surprise. "Mom?" he mouthed.

Graham shook his head, giving him a hand signal that said, *Give it a minute.*

The boy took another few cautious steps toward them. He was completely out of Kara's line of sight—though everything was, with her face buried against his shirt like that—and he seemed to want to stay that way. His eyes watched his mother's shoulders shake, sadness and regret clear in them. "I made her cry," he whispered.

"She'll be okay. Can you put yourself to bed tonight?"

He nodded rapidly, ready to prove himself worthy of the task. He tried one more step forward, then turned and ran back to his room, shutting the door quietly.

They'd be alone for the night, Graham knew. Nothing turned a boy's blood cold faster than his own mother's tears.

They were doing a number on him, and he was nearly thirty.

When she didn't seem to slow down, Graham took matters into his own hands and picked her up, carrying her to her bedroom. The couch might have been closer, but he sensed they needed privacy for whatever was bothering her. Because, while he had no problem letting her cry on his shoulder, giving her some space to get the worst of the emotions out, there was no way he was leaving without hearing the issue so he could help. He had to help her, damn it.

Settling back against her headboard, he cuddled her in

his lap and let the tears run their course. After another five minutes, she sniffled and sighed, hand clenching in his shirt.

He smoothed back a few strands of hair stuck to her temple. "Better?"

"Sorry," was her watery, muffled reply.

"Never be sorry. You're allowed to cry when you need to. If you don't let it go sometimes, it makes you sick. I have a feeling you haven't been letting it go for some time now."

"Who has the time for a weep session when you've got a son to raise?" Though they could have been, the words weren't spoken bitterly. Simply said with the practical curtness he knew she took on when attacking a task at hand. "I'll be better in the morning. Thanks for letting me cry on you."

"No way. We're not done." When she lifted her head to glare at him, he smiled and kissed her between her brows. "The whole mean mug loses its effectiveness when you do it with red, puffy eyes."

She gasped at him, then slapped at his chest and hopped down. He watched while she walked to the tiny attached half bath and closed the door. He'd give her another few minutes to pull it together, and then they were going to discuss what the hell was going on with her. And because he didn't believe in keeping people he loved in the dark— and hell, yes, he loved her, and Zach—he'd tell her about the brick. She might have insight on who could have done it.

When she opened the door a few moments later, Kara was pulled together. Or as pulled together as she could be in sweats with dried paint flecks, red eyes and a red nose. Her hair had been tamed though, and her jaw was firm.

"Don't even try to send me away," he warned before she could speak. "I'm here, and I'm going to hear your problems, then you're going to hear mine. That's what people in a relationship do. Then we'll talk about what I'd wanted to discuss with you this evening before all the other shit went down."

That pulled her up short, and she sat on the edge of the bed, not touching him. "Was that part good?"

"Yes. So let's take our medicine now so we can have our treat as a reward after. You first."

She shook her head, and he sensed she might need a little more distance before she was ready to go into it. "You first, please. I'm . . . I need a minute."

"Okay." Lacing his hands behind his head, he settled back. If he had his way, she'd ask him to stay the night. Had, in fact, packed a bag so he could run straight to practice in the morning. But being the smart man he was, he'd left it in his car. "My car was vandalized today. No, not quite right. My car was attacked."

She stilled, all motion halted, not even a blink. Then she was beside him like a shot, cupping his cheeks in her palms. "Oh my God. Graham. Please tell me you're okay. Are you okay?" She ran her hands down his shoulders, his arms, his torso. "How fast were you going? Where was this? Was anyone else hurt?"

"Not a wreck, I wasn't driving. I'm not hurt." He didn't mind her stroking and searching hands, though. She could keep that up all night. "It was in the gym parking lot. Someone heaved a brick through my windshield. Badly, at that."

That made her rear her head back to stare at him funny. "How does one throw a brick through a windshield badly? Isn't it always bad?"

"It didn't go through. The result is the same, I guess, in that I had to have my car towed so the damn thing could be replaced, but overall the interior was saved."

"Who would do something like that?" Fire heated her eyes, and her hands fisted against his chest. Gone from memory was the woman fighting to maintain composure. "What kind of sick person throws a brick?"

"Good question. We're still trying to figure that out. Any ideas?"

"It fits with the same profile of the vandalism from the gym." She tapped her lip a moment, then scooted around to sit beside him. "Was yours the only one hit?"

"Yes, which only adds to the confusion. When the guys' tires were punctured, it was everyone's car who was parked at the barracks. Why only mine? Simpson's car was there, too. Was it an attack on me, personally? Or was it another act of vandalism by the same person or people who have had it out for the boxing team from the start?"

"Pissed anyone off lately?" she teased.

"No, I—damn." He beat his head against the headboard a few times. "Nikki."

"Nikki's a child. And I thought she gave you three team captains a wide berth."

"She does. But I caught her making another teammate uncomfortable, and she wouldn't stop. Even after I gave her a quick, not-so-friendly hint to move along, she kept after it. So I gave her a set down, and talked to Marianne about it. She needs to be disciplined, though I'm not sure that falls under Marianne's jurisdiction."

"She'll handle it."

"She will. She also had a mouthful to say about my car being bricked and keyed."

"Keyed?" At that, Kara straightened. "That's different. You didn't mention that part."

Graham shrugged. "Sort of seemed like a distant second to the whole brick bit. Doesn't tell us anymore than what we already know."

Kara's smile was slow, and a little devilish. "I beg to differ. The brick? Anyone can pick up a brick and toss it somewhere."

"Anyone can pick up a set of keys and scrape it down paint."

"They can. But would they? Think about it. What would you want to bet that ninety percent of cars that get keyed like that are by females? It's such a petty, sissy thing to do. That might be an assault on my own gender, but I think the odds are probably in favor of my theory. A guy might slash tires, or do the brick thing. But I'd bet dollars to doughnuts it was a female who keyed your car."

That had him thinking. "Huh. I guess I didn't think of it like that. So you think, what, it's a pack of teenage girls doing the vandalism?"

"I think, at least as far as this specific instance goes, you're looking at a female. And though she might not be a teen any longer, age-wise, her maturity hasn't quite caught up with her yet."

"Nikki," he breathed out. "You think she left the gym after I gave her the set-down, found the brick by the pile of construction materials in the back, tossed it at the windshield, and when it didn't do as much damage as she thought—because she's got chicken arms—she keyed it and took off."

Kara's arms crossed over her chest, and she nodded with a self-satisfied smile. "How did she look when she came for afternoon practice?"

"She didn't," Graham said slowly. "She was a no-show. I didn't have time to ask Marianne what happened, since I had to haul ass to the shop and my ride was leaving ASAP after practice. I just figured Marianne gave her the afternoon off to think about things. Or maybe asked her to not come back. I don't know."

"I think she was scared after her little hissy fit, and knew it couldn't be undone, and now she's hiding like a three-year-old who spilled grape juice on the white carpet." Her smile wobbled a little, as if the reminder of something a child might do brought back the problems she had with Zach.

"Hey. C'mere." He waited for her to sit next to him again and kissed her temple. "You'll figure it out. Whatever it was."

"He asked about you," she said weakly. "About us. It's the first time he's ever . . . first time it's ever been an issue."

Graham swallowed hard. This could go one of two ways. "Was he worried about me being around so much?"

"Opposite," she mumbled, as if not pleased with it. "He worried I was pushing you away."

An ally. Perfect. "Yeah, you should cut that out."

She poked him in the ribs with a finger.

"This might cheer you up. We've got the All Military games next week, and we leave this weekend to get there early for practice and setup. So I'll be out of town for a while."

"I know," she said absently. Her fingers worked and worried at the hem of his T-shirt absently. "Not sure why that would cheer me up, though."

"Because I wanted to give you and Zach tickets to come see us compete."

Her head snapped up so fast he nearly took a header in his nose. "What? That's in Texas. Marianne said it was in Texas. She's been freaking out for a week about packing so she doesn't have to pay for an extra bag on the flight."

"It is in Texas. I meant, I wanted to give you and Zach tickets to fly out and see us. We might not have the home court advantage, but seeing friendly faces in the crowd makes it easier."

She just stared at him. Her face was horrified, as if he'd just told her he enjoyed slaughtering puppies in his free time instead of offering her a trip to Texas.

"What? Jesus, what, Kara? If it's the money, don't—"

"No," she said quietly. "It's not. I mean, it is. That's an extravagant gift, Graham, even for a girlfriend."

How about the woman I love, and want to marry?

"It's not, when I want it. It's a selfish thing, what I'm asking you to do. It's a gift for myself more than anything. Having you there . . ." He took her hand, held it firmly in his when she tugged. "Having you and Zach there to watch our scrimmage? It was incredible. It made me want it ten times harder. Made me want to make you both proud."

There was so much in her eyes, he couldn't read her at all.

"Please."

CHAPTER

15

"Graham," she said on a sigh. "Zach adores you. Of course he was proud of you, and not just because you won."

"Good. So consider coming out to watch me in a bigger match. When the stakes are as high as they'll get for me. Come watch. It might mean taking Zach out of school for a day," he went on quickly, "but he's a bright kid. I can't see that being an issue for him."

Academically, no. But he missed so many days due to doctor's appointments and minor reactions, that she didn't like to risk taking him out for frivolous days here and there.

Graham competing in the All Military games is not frivolous.

And it didn't matter, anyway.

"Let me stop you there." *Be firm, Kara.* "We can't come."

His spirit drooped. There was no other way to put it. It was as if something inside him deflated. "Yeah, okay. It's last minute anyway."

"Not because of that. Because of . . . things. The main

reason I've been pushing back when you've been fighting to get closer to us. The reason there's no future for us."

His face turned mutinous, just like Zach's did when he was fighting a battle of wills against her. "That's bullshit, but fine. Whatever it is, put it on the table, let's come up with a way to fix it, and move ahead."

"You're so sure we can fix it." It made her smile, the determination in his eyes, in the hardness of his jaw. He would tackle the world to make her happy. She felt it. This was a man a woman would be lucky to have in her life, in her corner, in her everything.

"You're amazing, and resilient and resourceful and sexy as hell. And I can punch stuff. Together, we're the Dream Team."

That made her laugh, which was a gift after all the crying she'd done that evening. And all the crying she might still do yet. "Why do you have to make it difficult to not love you?"

He was quiet at that, as if thinking about the answer. Then finally, quietly, he said, "Because I love you, and sort of want the same thing in return."

Her heart stopped. Her blood chilled. Her fingers pricked and tingled with the loss of feeling. Somehow, despite her best intentions, she'd screwed up again.

"Let me tell you a story," she began, sitting across from him now, not touching. If she touched him—or he touched her—she might collapse and they'd accomplish nothing. "I got pregnant when I was eighteen."

"Young," he murmured, but with no accusation in his tone.

"Yes. Very. Barely eighteen, but still a child in too many ways. I was several months along when I graduated high school. The first time I felt Zach kick, I was sitting in my cap and gown, listening to our principal drone on about the wonders of our future lives, reaching for our dreams, never giving up, all that cliché stuff you hear at a graduation." Graham's eyes slid down her torso to her stomach, and she looked down, realizing she'd cupped her belly as if she could once again feel that tiny life fluttering around inside of her. "It's a feeling you don't forget."

"I can imagine."

"I joked with myself later that Zach literally kicked me across the stage to take my diploma. He was the reason I graduated at all."

"What did your parents think?"

"They didn't know, at the time. I hadn't told anyone, even Marianne. I was determined to make it through high school before telling anyone. Fortunately, those tops that are sort of tight around the bust and then flow out around your waist were in style at the time, so I was able to carry it off the last few weeks of school."

"And once you told your parents? You never really talk about them. Do they not live around?"

Her hand shook as she reached up to redo her hair into another messy bun. "They do. They haven't seen Zach since he was about five, except for one time maybe two years ago when he and I ran into my mother in Target by complete accident. She . . ." Kara took a deep breath, and let it out again on a shudder. "She looked at me, with this shocked sort of horror, then turned and walked away. Like I was a stranger. Nothing to her."

Graham simply rubbed her shoulder.

"They . . . don't agree with the life I've set up for myself."

His hand tightened, just a little, on her shoulder. "What, being an awesome mother who provides for her kid even when his father won't? Being a smart entrepreneur with a mind on growing that small business? Being healthy and keeping her son's allergies in check, which is a daily battle, while helping other people who are facing the same challenges? Yeah. I can see where the disappointment comes into play." His voice was full of scorn, and anger.

She patted his knee gently, then took her hand back. "It

used to matter. It doesn't anymore. But thanks for that. I've never considered myself an entrepreneur before."

"Of course you are. Your blog earns money. It's a small business. You gain and maintain private yoga clients. Give yourself some credit, Kara."

I love you. I love you so much.

It would hurt them both, deeply, if she admitted it out loud.

"Anyway, it doesn't matter. I eventually told them I was pregnant, well past the time for an abortion—"

"Would they have wanted you to get one?"

"Maybe, if they'd known right away. My gut says they would have pressured me, intensely, to get one, but who knows? I just knew I didn't want to give them the option. But when they did find out, they went straight into adoption mode. Save Kara's future. Save the family's reputation. Nobody needs to know. Kara can go live with an aunt in Missouri until the baby is born. We'll say she went on an internship and will start college in the spring." She squeezed her eyes shut at the memory. "They'd written him off before even meeting him. It was painful. So painful. I had this little person inside me, clinging to my heart it felt like daily, and they were going to take him and hand him to someone else and expect me to just move on."

"Oh, baby." He reached for her, and because of the pain, she let him hold her. When he kissed the corners of her eyes, she realized she'd been crying. "Maybe they were just in over their heads, trying to figure out how to help you."

"They didn't even ask. When I told them I wanted to keep him, they wrote me off. Told me to get out. I stayed with Henry for three days. He was older, by almost four years. Had his own apartment—with a roommate—and I thought this would be it. This would be our new normal. Come to find out, the roommate was a female, and it was not a strictly platonic roommate situation."

He hissed out a breath, the sound harsh in her ears.

"Doesn't matter. He saved me the effort of waiting around for him to step up. I had been working part time, and they kicked it up to full time for me. Slept in the guest room at Marianne's parents' house for a while. They're wonderful people. They warned me I couldn't stay past the summer, and that was fine. But then every night, Frank—that's Marianne's dad—would sit down with me and go over plans for the future. He'd work on a budget with me, help me figure out which apartments I could afford . . . dad stuff."

"I've never met the guy, but I could kiss him."

"Save that for Mary, her mom. That woman saw exactly what I was, under the bravado and the *I'm fine, it's fine, we're all fine* answers I gave. She knew I was terrified of being a mom, and with zero guidance from my own mother. She helped, a little, picking out maternity clothes. She'd bring something home for me and lay it on the bed, telling me don't worry about it. It was on sale, she couldn't resist. Probably wasn't, now that I think back. I love them."

He made a sound of agreement and held her tighter.

"Basically, they gave me a safety net, but didn't let me rest on my ass. They coached me into adulthood. So I started on my journey to independence. We had nothing for a long time, surviving on welfare . . ." She hadn't told anyone besides the Cooks that before. It embarrassed her.

"Don't. Don't you dare feel bad for using assistance when you obviously needed it. That's bullshit, Kara. It gave you and Zach a head start. Don't ever regret it."

"You're right." Shaky breath in, shaky breath out. "Anyway, the rest of it is pretty clear. Henry helps as little as legally possible, and often less than that. He finds things here and there to hold over our heads to keep us from taking him back to court for nonpayment."

"Let me at the asshole. One time, Kara. One time."

The fury burned in him; she could feel it vibrating in his chest. She sat back and watched him a moment, then cupped his cheek. "I can't go to Texas with you. I can't take Zach out of state. It's part of the agreement. Neither of us can take him out of state without the other's written consent. And basically, that means me. Not him. Because he's never got him."

"How can he get away without seeing his own kid?"

Kara shrugged. "Not showing up for his scheduled visitation, mostly. He knows I'm never going to argue, and if I do, he'll threaten court again. He has money, I don't. I need it to survive. I can make it on my own, but it would require a third job, or moving into a tiny apartment." She wanted to choke down the tears, so she reached for anger instead. "Any idea how expensive allergy-friendly food is? How expensive it is to buy another EpiPen so he's got one wherever he goes? I can't do these things alone."

"Okay," he said slowly. "Your ex is an asshole, who uses child support like a leash, and tugs whenever he wants to. You can't leave the state with Zach. But what does that have to do with a future for us?"

"Graham." She sighed, then brought her legs up, wrapped her arms around her shins and let her forehead fall to her knees. "You're in the military. How much longer are you going to be here, in Jacksonville?"

"I don't know, maybe another year or so. Needs of the Corps, and all that. Oh." As if the truth just hit him in the face, he stopped.

The clock from the family room ticked incessantly in the dead quiet, marking the awkwardly passing seconds. She wondered for a moment if Zach had gone to sleep, if he was waiting for her to tuck him in. If he was listening at the door. She'd done her best to never breathe a negative word about his father, or her parents, in his presence. Easy enough, as they never were involved in their lives. But now, it was all being churned to the surface.

"Makes sense now, doesn't it?"

"But that's only until he's eighteen, right?" She nodded. "Not forever."

"Sure, not forever. And would you like to have a long-distance relationship for that long? What about when you want to get married? Have kids? You want the family you create to deliberately be across the country?"

"I could get out. The military isn't permanent. I could start a civilian life here."

"And I would wonder forever, if you gave up something better because I had no other options. If my past life ruined your potential future. Plus, even that's not a guarantee. What if you can't find a position around here? What if you find a job you like, and they want to transfer you to another firm elsewhere? What if you get an amazing opportunity and it's in Maine, or Colorado?"

His fists balled, but he said nothing.

"Putting your life on hold for eight years is insanity, when you don't have to. My life is Zach, so nothing is on hold. It's unfair of me to expect that from you. So, I don't. There's no future."

He started to speak, but she leaned forward and pressed two fingers to his lips.

"I don't want to hurt you. I . . . I really enjoy spending time with you. You're the best man I've known . . . outside of Frank Cook. But I can't have him. Mary would kill me."

That made his eyes smile a little, and he pressed a kiss to those two fingers before leaning in to drop his forehead to hers.

"I get it."

Her heart sank, which was completely unreasonable. She'd just told the man there was no future for them. He was taking her at her word. She had no right to be upset.

"And I understand why you wanted to protect me, and yourself, and probably Zach, too, from getting too far into the idea of tomorrow. But, Kara . . ." He kissed her then, taking her by surprise. His lips captured hers, tongue invading to mingle around hers, hands palming her head to keep her where he wanted her. "Kara," he said again, pulling back with obvious reluctance. "I can't let that go."

Oh God. It was up to her to do it. "Then we have to stop now."

"No."

No? Kara blinked. "You can't block me breaking up with you. That's not how this works."

"It is, when the reason for breaking up is bullshit. I'm not asking you to marry me tomorrow."

Her heart sank again. Traitorous organ.

"I'm asking you to take it a day at a time. There might be other ways. I'm here now, and you're here now, and that's all we need . . . for now. One day at a time."

She'd used up all her strength for the night arguing. She shook her head sadly, but he seemed to only take that as resignation, not a denial. Pulling her against him, he settled them back against the headboard.

"Now, you could always ask me to stay the night. But I won't, because I'm a gentleman and I know you'd only be doing it because you're too exhausted to walk me to the door and kick me out. I'll do it for you. But promise me one thing."

When she lifted one shoulder and let it fall again, he understood she was too wiped out to talk anymore.

"Call your lawyer in the morning and put me on the approved list for access to your files, and so she can discuss the case with me. She wouldn't do it otherwise. Then I can give you a hand. Can you do that for me?"

She nodded, feeling her eyelids droop. It was as if she'd run an emotional marathon that had taken its toll on her whole body, and she had nothing more to give. Vaguely, she was aware of him scooting and rolling her until she landed under the covers, tucked high below her chin. He pressed a kiss to her forehead, said he would lock the door on his way out, and was gone.

CHAPTER

16

The next morning, Graham's first stop was at the MPs office. He filled them in on Kara's theory, telling them about how it might not be related to the vandalism at all, but rather an isolated incident. They agreed to come talk with her at some point in the day. It was the best he could do. His car being keyed was hardly a priority for them, especially if it wasn't linked to a serial vandal.

Stop number two was to pick up Brad from the BOQ, who went with him to pick up his car, now fixed, and turn in the rental. It still heated his blood to see the key marks on his door. The windshield had been a quick fix. To get the paint redone would be longer than he wanted to be with a rental car. For now, he'd live with it.

While waiting at the rental place, he received Kara's text telling him she'd spoken to the lawyer and gotten his name approved for the file and information on the situation. She also sent the lawyer's contact information.

He decided to take this as a positive sign from last night.

It had been touch and go for a while, emotionally. But this sealed the deal for him. They were on the other side of it. Her worst fears were out in the open. Now they could start taming them.

And lastly, to the gym for the last day of workout before they flew down to Texas. When he stopped into the training room first to get two fingers wrapped as a precaution, he was surprised to see Nikki filling one of the large water jugs with ice. He raised a brow at Marianne, who shook her head and rolled her eyes, mouthing, "Later," while she taped him up. He took that to mean she would explain later. That should be interesting.

Coach Ace led them through the first circuit, explaining every station before they broke into groups of four to work and rotate around. Graham was as surprised as everyone else when they found the circuit to be lighter than anticipated. They'd all assumed the sadistic man would take the final day to kill them, as they would have three days off before their first practice in Texas. But he'd surprised them all.

Twenty minutes into his second circuit, Graham caught movement from the corner of his eye. Two Marines in uniform—MPs from what he could tell—walked into the gym and headed straight for the training room. Two of his group members stopped working the heavy bags entirely to stare, and he growled.

"Get back to it, lazy asses. We get on a plane in forty-eight freaking hours. Don't waste what time we've got."

Another minute later, Marianne stepped out of the room, and the door closed behind her. She sat against the wall, her laptop on her thighs, seemingly uninterested in the proceedings behind closed doors.

Levi wheeled the water jug to its place beside their station. Graham paused long enough to grab a cup and some water. "Thanks, man."

The younger kid—probably twenty or twenty-one,

max—just stared at him as if he'd busted out his limited Greek instead of speaking plain English. Okay, then.

After another few minutes, the gym quieted as they all heard a shout from the training room. Marianne jumped up, setting her laptop aside. Levi sprinted for the door, but she held him back with a palm on the chest. He tried to knock her hands away, but she pushed back with both hands. They started to argue, and Coach Cartwright ran over to give her help. Graham felt someone walk by him, and he reached out to snag Brad's shirt before he went over and made it worse.

"Leave it alone, Brad."

"Fuck off, she needs some help."

"And she's got Cartwright. Let her handle it." He winced when Marianne had to knock Levi back from the door again. "She's holding her own. She'll skin you raw if you step in and handle it for her. Cartwright's there, and he won't let her get hurt."

His friend sagged a little. Graham couldn't blame him for wanting to run over and step between Marianne and trouble, even the mild kind a kid like Levi might give her. He'd want the exact same thing if it were Kara there.

Graham realized the entire team was watching now, with nobody even giving the pretense of working out a shot anymore. Coach Ace, normally a hard-ass about distractions, was as riveted as the rest of them at the scene unfolding in their gym.

Levi thrust his hands in his shaggy hair and paced away, then back again. "She needs someone!"

His voice rang out clearly now, with nothing and no one else to compete with the sound.

"They're just asking her questions. If she has nothing to hide, then she's fine. Leave it. *Leave it!*" she barked again, shouldering him back. The kid, though on the slender side, towered over the athletic trainer. But she was sturdy, strong and determined, and wasn't about to take any bullshit.

It was no wonder Brad was head over heels crazy for her. If he hadn't fallen for Kara, he might have been just as enamored. Marianne, pissed and in charge, was quite a sight.

The door opened behind her, bumping her in the back. Marianne jumped away as one of the MPs walked out, holding a sobbing Nikki by the upper arm. Her hands were at her sides, except when she reached up to her face to wipe at the mascara-tinted tears running down her cheeks.

The second MP held Levi back as he rushed at her. "What the hell is going on? Nikki. Nikki!"

"I'm sorry. I said I'm sorry! Please don't. Please. I'm sorry!"

"Nikki, tell me what happened. Please. God damn it, let me go!" The younger man shoved at the MP, but the Marine held firm until his partner had the young woman out the door. Levi's head drooped, then the MP leaned forward and whispered something to him. He jerked from the Marine's hold and stalked out the door himself.

"What the hell is going on?" Brad murmured, echoing exactly Graham's thoughts.

But he had a good idea exactly what the hell was going on. And his suspicions were confirmed when the remaining MP approached him a minute later.

"Captain Sweeney, can we speak privately for a moment?"

"Uh, let me check with—"

A large hand landed on his shoulder, and he heard Coach Ace's deep, rumbling voice behind him. "You can use my office, if it's quick. I need him back to finish up this last workout. We've got the games to get ready for. Marine pride and all that."

The MP smiled briefly. "Understand, sir. Just a few minutes and he's all yours again." They followed Coach Ace, who opened the door to his office and closed it behind him when they were situated.

"She did it," he surmised quietly while the MP pulled out a notebook from his pocket. "She admitted it, I guess?"

"Not at first. We mentioned the partial print we pulled from the brick, and that was enough to get her to say it was an 'accident.'" He scoffed at that. "You always hope one of them will get a little more creative . . . never happens."

"I didn't realize the brick came with prints."

"It didn't. Or none that were helpful. You're in JAG. You know how it goes. We can mislead all we want, long as we don't coerce. She confessed, said you yelled at her—"

"I did."

"Which you already told us, so no problems there. Then she said the brick was just sitting there, in a pile, where they've got the construction materials for the repair on the back wall. And suddenly it was just in her hand, flying at your car. 'Couldn't be helped,'" he added, using quote fingers on the last with a smirk.

Graham groaned and covered his face with his hands. "Couldn't be helped. Right. So, now what?"

"You know the drill from here. We need to determine if she was behind the rest of the vandalism on the building and the team's tires. My gut, though, says no. I just need to hear it from her."

His gut said the same thing. "She might be part of it. A small cog in a large group. Herd mentality or something."

"Doubtful. I'm still hanging onto the cut teammate theory. But we'll see. It's just too damn expensive to put up security cameras. We don't have that kind of a budget. And your season is almost over. If it's got to do with the team, and not just boxing in general, then it's almost over. Come back next year with a fresh team, and hopefully no troubles."

Graham didn't point out that with all the trouble they'd run into, the team could be disbanded entirely. No point. He stood, shook the MPs hand and headed back out to rejoin his group, who had moved onto the third circuit.

He reached for a jump rope, realized people were staring at him, and he shrugged. "What?"

"Jesus Christ walking on the moon, it's a team practice, not the set of a telenovela. Get to work, you assholes!" Coach Ace bellowed.

Ah, there it was. Grinning at Greg across the gym, Graham started to practice on his footwork.

KARA sat with Zach, both staring at Graham's house from her car. Her grip on the wheel tightened.

"Are, uh, we going in?" Zach shook the shoebox he held in his hands. The contents rattled around.

"Just give me a minute." She breathed in, then out, much as she had before the barbeque two weeks earlier. The only difference this time was . . . oh, hell. There were a thousand differences now. She'd kissed him. Slept with him. Heard him say he loved her. Fallen in love with him in return.

Nothing would ever be like it was before.

"Zach, about Graham . . ."

"I know, don't get attached." He rolled his eyes. Though her son had apologized that morning for his outburst the night before, she sensed he was more sorry for how he'd said it, not what he had said. And thought that she was holding back from letting them both get closer to Graham for "some stupid adult reason."

Wasn't that the truth . . .

She got out of the car and walked to the front door, which was already open thanks to Zach walking in without knocking. "Zachary!"

"He told me I could, Mom." Toeing off his shoes, he sprinted to the kitchen where Graham stood by the oven, a large red oven mitt on one hand. "Hey, Graham! I made you this box."

He took it with the non-mitt hand, smiling a little puzzled. "Looks like Nike made it, bud."

Zach rolled his eyes at the lame joke. Then watched

curiously as Graham pulled her in for a sweet kiss. "Are you guys going to do that all night?"

"How would we eat, then?" Kissing her again, he nudged her toward the fridge. "Grab a drink. Dinner's almost finished."

"Can I eat it?"

Kara watched, stepping back a little to let Graham handle this one on his own. She knew what he'd made—he'd called her twice to be positive it was okay—but Zach didn't.

He hooked an arm around Zach's neck and pulled him in for a side hug. "Kid, I'm going to make you a promise. I will never invite you over for a meal you can't eat. If I'm serving it to you, you know you can eat it. Deal?"

"I still have to check," he said slowly, as if unsure it was okay to correct an adult. "Because it's important."

"Smart. Then that's two promises. I promise to serve food you can eat, and also promise to not get offended if you double-check." Rubbing a hand over his head briskly, Graham let him go to get a drink. "And we're having pizza."

Kara smiled when Zach looked at her and she nodded. He'd gotten the specific brand of frozen pizza she'd pointed out, and rarely bought, because of how expensive it was.

Zach whooped, then went to get himself a drink from the fridge. Kara kissed Graham's cheek. "Thanks," she whispered.

"Thank me again later, when we send the midget into the living room to start up the Xbox," he suggested.

She smiled at that, then set the table.

They ate and talked, and laughed more than once. Kara had the heart-panging realization that this could have been their life, if things had been different.

Stop that. Not your fault, not worth picking at the scab.

After she'd collected the dishes—"You cooked, I'll wash"—she nudged Zach. "Get the box."

"Oh, right!" He ran to the living room where he'd left it,

and brought it back to the table. When Graham shot her a look, she shrugged. Zach had told her what he was doing, but she had no clue what was actually in the box.

"This," he said proudly, sitting beside Graham and scooting the box over to him, "is your Good Luck box. Mom said we probably won't see you again before you go, and this tournament is important for you, so I made you this."

Graham stared at it for a moment. Then he reached over and tugged Zach's chair closer, letting his arm fall across the young boy's shoulders. "Well, let's open it."

Kara started to wash the plates to give them a chance for some privacy . . . sort of. She heard her son explain he'd written a letter, but he couldn't read it until the night before his match. A lucky penny, a picture of a gold medal he'd colored in and written Graham's name on, a few other assorted items a boy likes to grab and consider good luck. Smooth sticks, cool pebbles, the various flotsam and jetsam that appeals to kids.

"And this is me and mom. Because I figure you're good for us, so we might be good luck for you."

Kara whipped around, dish towel dropping from her hands.

Graham held the photograph carefully at the edges. She knew that photograph. Had seen it thousands of times, framed on her wall. Zach had taken it from the frame and given it to the man she was dating. The man he wanted to keep in their lives.

"I'm, like, an hour old. Right, Mom?" Zach's smiling face turned to her. She nodded, unable to speak. "The nurse took it and gave it to Mom. I guess that's just something the nurses do when you have a baby."

It is when you have nobody else there to do it for you.

"It's just a picture I like, so . . ." Zach's voice trailed off as he realized Graham still hadn't said anything. The lump in Kara's throat grew, until she wanted to claw at it. "I didn't ask Mom. I should have, but I really wanted you to have it, because Mom looks really, really happy and I look funny."

Graham cleared his own throat, then gently bumped his temple against Zach's. "Thanks, kid. That's . . . that's some serious luck right there. I can't lose now."

Zach threw up his fists and yelled out, then jumped up and ran for the living room. "I'm gonna set the Xbox up. When you're ready for a beat down, come on in!"

Kara finished the last dish and set it on the drainer to dry, wiping her hands on the dish towel. Graham's large hands settled on her hips, drawing her back against him with a soft gasp. For the first time in a while, he wasn't hard as stone. His hands slid around to rest on her stomach, his chin resting on her head. His heartbeat was steady against her ear when she turned a little.

"I'll make a copy of the photo and get you the original back."

"Thank you."

"I love you," he said quietly as they both stared out the window over the kitchen sink. "Don't say anything back. Just hear the words and know I mean them. I love you. I love you both."

She cried silently, because there was too much built up inside her to do anything else. It hurt so much, so very much. But he simply held her and let the tears fall without trying to stop them. He understood even that . . . that she needed to release some of the sadness and tears were the only way to get the job done.

After a few minutes, she patted his top forearm. "Better go knock my kid down a peg. He's too cocky for his own good."

"Consider it done." He kissed her cheek, where the tears were still damp, and squeezed her once more before letting go.

*   *   *

HOURS after Kara and Zach had gone home, Graham laid on the floor of the gym with Brad and Greg. They'd each taken about five yoga mats from the stash kept for Yoga Tuesdays and piled them up to form the world's worst cots.

"We leave in less than two days for the games, and instead of relaxing with our women, we're hanging out here, alone, in the freaking gym. What's wrong with us?" Greg rolled over on his back and stared at the rafters, poking at Brad, who lay closest to him. "I'm really curious about this. What's wrong with us?"

"We didn't want anything to happen to our equipment, or to psych our guys out before we leave, and so we are taking the overnight shift tonight at the gym. Nothing more than that. Plus, we have tomorrow off completely, so you can go home and sleep in your nice, comfortable bed after this. God, all this bitching and whining about sleeping indoors on cushy mats. And y'all call me the grandpa."

"But they took Nikki away. I mean, I doubt she's still in jail. She posted bail, or her parents did, then took her back to Wilmington with them. They're not going to let her back around here to screw with us anymore."

"And if it wasn't all her? What if she had a friend? What if she actually only did the windshield brick routine?" Brad shot back.

They both went quiet.

"You're a chatterbox," Greg said after a minute, kicking at Graham.

He rolled onto his stomach, palms flat on the mat, resting his chin on top of them. "What is there to say? She confessed to the windshield and keying my car, but swears the rest wasn't her."

"She confessed because it clearly *was* her. Probably

hoped if she was honest about one thing, it would look less like she was lying about something else. Twisted logic."

"I thought that was my department."

"Figure it out then, counselor," Greg said with a grin. "Court will seem like child's play after all this."

"Please. I'm hardly ever in court. It's all reviewing rental agreements and separation papers and document junk. Mediation and giving advice to people who won't take it anyway."

"Try not to make your job sound so exciting," Brad said dryly. "It makes the rest of us jealous."

"Noted. All I am saying is that we shouldn't let down our guard."

"Hmm," was all Greg said. Brad remained silent.

After another five minutes of quiet, Graham said, "I'm going to ask Kara to marry me."

Brad and Greg jackknifed up simultaneously. "What?"

"Not tomorrow. Calm down," he said evenly, still staring straight up. "But she's it for me. When you know, you know. It's as simple as that."

"Simple as that," Greg said in a disbelieving tone.

"You're getting a two-for-one special there," Brad reminded him.

"I know." The grin spread; he couldn't help it. "Zach's basically the best bonus you could ask for."

"He's a pretty cool little twerp," Greg agreed, laying back down. "I think if I asked Reagan to marry me now, she'd throw a shoe at me. Not that I would, but hypothetically."

"Marianne would probably throw up," Brad put in, chuckling under his breath. "It might be worth it just to watch her turn a little green. She's way too involved in her career to think about marriage. Thinking about asking her to move in with me, though."

"You live in California. That's not across town, that's across the country."

Brad shrugged and settled back on his pile of mats. "So?"

"So," Greg repeated, again disbelieving. "You are both crazy. Reagan might look for jobs on the west coast after this, but she'd never agree to move in with me."

"She's also several years younger than Cook and Kara," Brad pointed out. "She might want a little more freedom before considering tying herself to someone—namely, you—forever."

"Crazy," was Greg's pronouncement. "Just crazy."

"Or maybe we just know what we want," Graham said softly. "Why waste time?"

Time, he knew, was the problem. Eight years of it. After debating a moment, he told his friends about the situation involving Kara's ex and the custody issue with Zach's father.

"Sounds like the worst piece of shit," Brad said, rolling over better to see them. "He doesn't want them, but he makes it impossible for them to be with anyone else."

"Not entirely, but true enough." Realizing Greg had been quiet awhile, Graham turned and looked at him. "Thoughts?"

"I knew guys like him. Usually a foster brother or sister's mom or dad. They'd dance in when it was convenient, talk a big game, then dance right back out again when they smelled responsibility. Played huge mind games with the kids when they'd do it. Kids, up to a certain age, are naturally hopeful." Greg shook his head. "Fucker."

"I have to figure out how to handle this. If I thought beating the shit out of him would solve problems, I'd be damn tempted."

Neither man spoke.

"But that won't work. It has to be done through the legal channels. Kara's too scared to talk to him about it and ask him straight out. Scared it might poke him enough to take Zach for a weekend when he technically has rights . . . just to piss her off."

"Might," Brad agreed. "I could see it. Guys like that live off people being intimidated by the *what if*."

"So it has to be done precisely in a way that won't have any blowback on them."

"Before or after we leave?" Greg wondered, shifting slightly on his mat.

"After." Maybe. "I asked them to come watch us. I was going to fly them down to Texas to watch. That's how this whole thing came out. She had to explain why they wouldn't be able to come."

"She still could, couldn't she?" Greg sat up a little on his elbows. "Oh. Right. The kid. Can't leave him home alone. Well, damn."

"Go to sleep," Brad grumbled. "In less than two days, we'll be on the way to Texas. You can chitchat and gossip all you want on the way there."

"It's like he doesn't even know us," Greg said on an exaggerated sigh. "Nighty night, fellas."

Graham smiled in the dark, thankful he had two friends who got where he was coming from, and who didn't judge him—okay, only a little—for knowing his own mind and his heart where Kara and Zach were concerned.

Now to figure out the rest of the puzzle.

CHAPTER

17

Kara twisted her fingers together, then forced her palms to smooth out over the conference table. Nerves fluttered in her belly, and she knew they were only more so because every fifteen minutes she sat in this room, she was paying through the nose.

"Kara, hi." Tasha Williams, dressed as always in a sharply tailored suit in ivory with a silk maroon blouse under that made her dark skin look gorgeous, walked into the conference room. All of her outfits made her curves look equally alluring and dangerous, like the femme fatale of the courtroom. She closed the door behind her and extended her hand, as always, while she pulled out a chair to sit down. "Sorry to keep you waiting. Let's get started." Pen in hand, she opened the folder with Kara's past records. "Based on our history with Zach's father, we—"

"I need to get out of this," Kara blurted out, then closed her eyes. Yup, that was definitely the mature way to handle that.

Tasha set her pen down and settled back in her chair. Her dark eyes were kind, even understanding, as she motioned for Kara to continue.

"I met a man. And . . ." Biting her lip, she forced herself to go on. "He's just . . . amazing. He makes me realize I could have more. And even if we didn't work out, he makes me want more than just a single life with Zach. I . . . I deserve more."

"Finally." Leaning forward, Tasha took both hands and grabbed Kara's shoulders, shaking gently. "Finally, girl. You've been playing defense for way too long. You've seen the light! Let's get on the offense. But first, this man wouldn't happen to be the same one you had me add to my list of approved contacts, would it? One . . ." She checked her file. "Graham Sweeney?"

Kara felt the flush move up to the roots of her hair. "Maybe."

"Girl, bump that 'maybe' up to a 'yes, ma'am.'" Tasha's tight, dark curls bounced as she shook her head in appreciation. "He was something to look at."

That took her back a step. "What? He was in here?"

Tasha nodded and picked her pen back up. "You bet. This morning, in fact. We had a quick chat so I could catch him up on the situation, gave him my honest opinion, answered a few of his questions, gave him some counsel, and that was that."

"How did he . . . I mean, what did he ask?"

Her attorney looked regretful at that. "Unfortunately, I can't say. Captain Sweeney was here officially as a client."

"But . . . it's my case."

"Mmm, yes and no." Looking caught between a rock and a hard place, Tasha shrugged. "He was more consulting with me on a matter related to, but not directly in line with your specific custody battle. He paid for my services. He's sharp, that one. He's got the client-attorney privilege. If you want to know more, you'll have to ask him. Sorry."

She blew out a breath and nodded once. "Fine. I'd like

to find a way to get my son into my full custody. If I want to move to another state, or if I want to marry a man and have Zach take his name . . . or if I want to take him to freaking Disney World, I want that option, without the threat of his support being 'forgotten' for a month. It will be tight. I have to start budgeting my life around only my salary. But I'll make it work." It had to work. She was so tired of letting a negligent, careless, pitiful excuse for a man dictate what she could and could not do with herself.

"Let's see what we can do here." Tasha clicked her pen back on and grinned. "Time to get to work."

GRAHAM checked the address once more, then got out of his car. This wasn't what he expected when he'd taken the contact information for Henry Theodore James . . . but then again, he had no clue what else he could have expected. The home was a simple, well-maintained single family dwelling in a lower middle-class neighborhood. Not the best area, but a decent part of Jacksonville.

Maybe in his mind, he'd seen something rundown, bordering on a hovel. A home to match the kind of man that neglected his son and that son's mother for a decade.

Or maybe that's just what he *wished* Henry James lived in.

No car in the driveway, though it could have been pulled into the single-car garage. The odds were he was at work. But Graham walked up the narrow walkway, lined by well-groomed shrubs, and knocked on the door anyway. He took another step back when the inside door opened.

"Yeah?" The man standing in front of him was about his age, with a dark goatee and Zach's hazel eyes. He wore a T-shirt that had dried paint on it, jeans with the same splatters, and bare feet. His hands were clutched around a rag, as if he'd just finished drying his hands. "Can I help you?"

"Uh, yeah." He looked down once more at the small scrap

of paper he'd jotted the address down on. "I'm looking for Henry James."

"Are you a process server?"

That made Graham blink. "No, no, I'm not."

The other man shrugged and stepped onto the porch, letting the screen door slam in his wake. "That's me. What do you want?"

Here was the man standing between a future with Kara. Flesh and bone, not a ghost. And blissfully unaware—or uncaring—of the shitstorm he left in his wake. Graham's hand tightened around the address and let it fall to his side. Too tempting.

"I'm here about Zach. Zach and Kara."

Henry made a little sound in his throat, then leaned one shoulder against the front doorjamb. "New lawyer, huh. Let me save you some time, buddy. You're supposed to call my lawyer, not come to me directly. This is a sort of violation of privacy, I think. I'll have to check with mine." His grin was all teeth, and completely unfriendly.

Graham sent him a matching smile of his own. "Not Kara's lawyer, *buddy*. Just a guy who cares. You've been dicking around with being a nonexistent father for long enough. Cut the cord. When she comes to you asking you to terminate your parental rights, you go along with it."

"Ha!" Rolling his eyes, Henry kicked at the leg of a rocking chair on the small front porch and sat down with a thud. He propped his feet up on the railing, looking very comfortable with his asshole-ness. "Yeah, okay. I'm not sure who you think you are, but that's not going to happen. That's my son." He jabbed at his chest in an imitation of a macho move. "My. Son."

"Who you never see. Ever."

"I'm a busy guy. I pay support."

"Which you threaten constantly to take away. What is it, Henry? There's some reason you keep holding onto the thread, using it to yank them back when you sense they're leaving you behind. Pride? Ego? Maybe you like having a sob story for the ladies you meet at bars. Wah, my ex won't let me see my kid. Please comfort my emotional wounds in bed."

Henry's eyes went steely. Finally, Graham had his attention.

"Maybe not. You like claiming him on taxes, perhaps. Do you list him on angel trees at Christmastime and take all the stuff well-meaning families donate to your son that you never see?"

The tick in his jaw told him to keep hammering.

"Maybe it's a little closer to home." Leaning in, he said in a low voice, "Don't want to disappoint your own mom and dad by permanently giving up their grandkid."

Henry leaped out of the rocking chair, knocking Graham back several steps. Graham could have easily defended himself, and chose not to. "Fuck you, asshole. Who the fuck do you think you are, coming here and insulting me? If you're not their lawyer, you've got no business—"

"But I do," he said softly, glad when Henry quieted down to listen. "It is my business, because *they* are my business."

"Oh, that's how it is. You're fucking Kara. Shoulda figured. Now we're talking." Looking pleased, Henry sat again, elbows on his knees. "Surprised it took this long. So what, you want rights or something? Want the kid to take your name? You have any clue how expensive that kid's medical junk is?"

That kid's medical junk. It took everything in him to keep from plowing his fist straight into Henry James' face until the man was spitting out teeth.

Trust the system. Use the system. So when you go to court, you can say under oath, "No, Your Honor, I never once punched him . . . even if he would have deserved it."

Graham fought to sound reasonable. "What does it matter? You don't want the responsibility, and I do. That should be enough. A little paperwork and you're done."

"Paperwork is pretty boring. And, you know, lawyers are

expensive." Henry glanced at the rag in his hand. "I might need another incentive to bother."

And there it was. Finally. The real, true, no-bullshit reason he'd been holding on for so long. Money. "You want a payout. A bribe to actually do the best thing for your son."

"I figured someone would have come by long before now. Kara's still a hot piece of ass, from what I can see. Oh, I check in from time to time. Still teaching yoga. Nothing changes for good old Kara." His smile turned secretive and a bit lurid, as if he were mentally reliving what she'd looked like naked a decade ago. "But maybe she was just picky. Either way, looks like you're the winner. You wanna keep her happy, sweep her away from it all, make all her single mama dreams come true . . . go right ahead. But that's my son." He sniffled a little, and his eyes watered up. "My only son. My flesh and blood. I couldn't . . . couldn't let him go unless I knew it was for the right reason."

Henry sized him up visually. Graham could all but feel the scan. Though Graham hadn't worn his uniform, he knew everything about him, from his posture to his haircut to the clothes he wore—an iron-pressed button-down shirt, clean khakis with a leather belt and simple brown shoes— screamed *I'm a Marine*.

"You military guys . . . you make decent money. Good benefits and shit. It would help to see a good faith offering of how you'll be able to care for my boy." He blinked slowly, as if holding back the manufactured tears.

Oh, you unbelievable, disgusting asshole. Graham pulled deep and used a few yoga breaths. It calmed his system, and reminded him why he was doing it the right way in the first place.

Kara. Zach.

"Let me be clear." He leaned forward, bracing his elbows on the porch railing, face-to-face with the jackass. "I'm not *her* lawyer. But I am *a* lawyer. Know what that means? I have connections, and knowledge on my side. And what I have is money."

There was a gleam there now, Graham noted. He'd said the M word, and Henry scented a payout like a shark scenting blood on the surface.

"What I also have is patience. It took me a long time to find Kara, and I couldn't be more happy she comes with a son I can love, too. That means I'm doing this the right way. I can afford to drag your ass to court so often, your employers might start wondering why you're gone all the time. They might check in on your court appearances. That's public record, did you know that? When they see all the things Kara will be putting in that court case—the honest, truthful, proven things, with such delightful phrases as 'deadbeat' and 'irresponsible' and 'negligent'—they might start asking questions. You might lose your job. You do have a job, don't you, Henry?"

He clenched his jaw, but said nothing.

"After a while, your friends might wonder why you aren't working anymore. Family, too. That mom and dad you want to keep disillusioned about why they never see their grand-kid . . . they might see the court papers, too. All those things—totally true things—Kara can drag in front of a judge to prove you're not just an unfit parent, but true human scum. You want people to know all about that?"

"Fuck you," Henry hissed.

But Graham was just getting started. "I know why you've gotten away with this shit up to now. You've been dealing with a single mom with limited resources, who has a kid with high-cost medical needs. A mom who has to debate between using up precious resources fighting against her kid's father, or living in terror daily he'll flip the switch and demand time again with his kid, when he's not capable of caring for a goldfish."

Henry said nothing.

"That's changing. See, the thing is, I'm just a single guy

right now. I can live pretty simply. Not into cars, or guns, or expensive hobbies. Know what happens when you make money and don't spend it? It sort of piles up. So I've got this interesting pile of cash, and no clue what to do with it right now. I might rename that fund Henry. I'll rename it the Kick Henry's Ass Fund. And its sole purpose will be to drag you to court so often, and so regularly, that you are smothered with court fees and law office bills." He paused for a moment. "How long do you think you can hold that up, Henry? One month? Two? A year? The law taught me patience. The Corps taught me perseverance. And my parents taught me not to be a disgusting human being. You're toast. It's just a matter of how soon you admit it to yourself, so we can all move on."

"You can't threaten me," Henry said, standing so he towered over Graham from the porch. "You don't have the right."

"Threaten?" Graham looked around theatrically. "Who said I threatened you? I was simply explaining one potential outcome of fighting back against terminating parental rights." He pointed as he stepped back toward his car. "Zach's going to be mine, just like Kara is, because I care about them both. If you're smart, when Kara comes at you with the papers, you'll sign them and move on. Because I'll be damned if you get a penny out of me, or Kara, to make this stop."

As he got in his car, the front door slammed shut. And Graham let his hands shake, as they'd wanted to for the last ten minutes.

He'd seen arrogance, and ego in the man's face, then triumph. But it was what Graham saw last that told him half the battle was already won.

Fear.

Now to tell Kara what had happened, and pray she didn't lose her shit on him.

CHAPTER

18

I t had been a struggle to make the choice to get a babysitter for Zach at the last minute. Especially when she'd spent way more time than she'd anticipated talking to Tasha, and had to brace herself for the inevitable battle that would come along with taking a stand—finally—against Henry and his reign of parental terror. But for tonight, and tonight only, she was going to be frivolous and do it.

Zach had, of course, begged to come along. Knowing she got to see Graham one last time before he left, and Zach didn't, burned her son's biscuits. But when she had explained they still had adult things to work out, he'd seen reason and worked on his homework so he could watch an extra movie with the sitter.

Some battles weren't worth fighting in a ten-year-old's mind.

She pulled into Graham's driveway and soothed her nerves along with her skirt front. The dress had a full skirt that wrapped around her legs when she walked, and a tight bodice that she'd worn a sweater over when leaving the apartment . . . because it was almost indecent without one.

Perfect for what she wanted to accomplish now. She'd ditched the sweater the minute she'd pulled out of her apartment's parking lot.

She knocked on the door, then rang the bell when nothing happened. Not a sound. She rang again, just in case, and waited for two minutes before she heard a muffled thump and a curse. The pause told her Graham was looking out the peephole seconds before the front door flew open.

"Kara!"

He stood there in a towel, dripping wet and covered in nothing but a towel hanging low on his hips, held up by one hand fisted in the fabric at his side.

"Well." She chewed on her lip a moment, giving herself the chance to really take in the whole picture. "And what if I'd been the Avon lady?"

"I wouldn't have opened the door for the Avon lady. I wouldn't have opened the door for anyone but you. Get in here." He reached out with his other hand and pulled her in, shutting the door behind her and kissing her senseless. "God, I missed you."

"It's been less than twenty-four hours," she reminded him, ridiculously pleased. Her fingertip traced down one pec, following the line of a drop of water as it rolled over his smooth skin.

"Sorry, I'm getting you wet."

"Yes, you are." Her voice was husky, unintentionally, but he caught the note of lust.

His hand came down to pull at the skirt a little, baring her thigh. "You look gorgeous. Edible, almost."

"Graham?"

"Hmm?" He busied himself with nuzzling at her neck. The scent of warm, damp male mixed with his body wash and filled her with longing. As his teeth scraped over her tendons, she shivered, and her nipples puckered painfully beneath the bodice.

"This is a new dress."

"And I'm getting it wet," he said again, though he didn't move away from her. Just slid his lips along the underside of her jaw and chin to reach the other side of her neck.

"No. I mean, yes, but that's not what I was going . . . oh, don't stop." He bit gently on her earlobe.

"What?" he whispered. "What were you going to say?"

"Only that . . ." She took a shaky breath. She was the same woman who'd had insane, wild animal sex on his kitchen counter not long ago. She could say this. "Only that, I bought it without trying it on. And as it turns out, it was too tight to wear anything underneath."

Her skin burned with embarrassment when he froze, taken aback.

"You're . . ." He cleared his throat, then held her at arm's length with one hand. "You're not wearing a bra."

"Or panties." She swished the skirt around a little and did her best to look irritated. "The darn thing was too tight to get them on."

"Yeah, I can see that," he said dryly. "Shame."

"I'm assuming you're also naked under your, uh, outfit." She dipped a fingertip between the towel and his skin, loving the power she seemed to hold over him. "We're a matching set."

"Not yet," he muttered, pulling and tugging at the zipper behind her. "But we will be." And with that, he abandoned any pretense of holding the towel in place and used both hands to unzip her dress. The towel fell to their feet, along with the dress as he roughly shoved it down her breasts, over her hips and off to pool around her ankles.

"Matching set," he said with satisfaction, then gripped her butt and lifted.

"Shoes," she gasped as he kissed her and walked her over to the couch. "My shoes . . ."

"Should stay on. Because I'm sexist enough to admit I've got this amazing fantasy about you, with these legs of yours, and some sexy heels, and nothing else. Gorgeous," he muttered as he rested her on the couch lengthwise. "You're just too damn gorgeous."

She felt more than gorgeous as he worshipped her with his mouth. She felt powerful. She'd taken her future into her own hands, no longer a victim of circumstance. No longer powerless. Formidable.

He covered her, his erection pressing into her thigh. Because it pleased her, she wrapped her legs around his waist and let the heels dig, just a little, into his backside.

Graham growled and covered her breast with his mouth, sucking hard on the tip while his hand massaged the other breast. His cock prodded and ran down her slit, seeking entrance without guidance. She reached down to help, but he shook his head.

"No, wait."

A small part of her wanted to argue back. Assert the dominance she'd so newly discovered. Be the force. But the other, wiser part of her whispered, *It's okay . . . because he's going to make it good. So good. So very, very good . . .*

Not weak to give in to pleasure. Just smart.

So she let the torment continue. The thick, fat head of his penis glided through her folds, almost without purpose as he licked and sucked and nipped at her breasts. The occasional, infrequent contact with her clit left her guessing, then experiencing zingers when she least expected it.

When she didn't think she could last any longer—couldn't take the madness another second—he arched his hips up and drove into her.

Her eyelids burst with a cacophony of color. Arching into him, pushing hard with the heels of her feet, she urged him into a fast pace to keep up with her growing climax. It was a snowball rolling down the mountain, too long ignored, and was immediately upon her.

A few more thrusts and she burst, screaming his name and loving the harsh way her own name fell from his lips before he collapsed with her. As spent, as exhausted, as completely used as she.

Power. It was a beautiful thing to take back one's own power.

"WHAT made you decide to come over?" Graham combed through Kara's hair with his fingers, watching as the silky red and gold strands flowed between them like water.

She'd jumped back in the shower with him after their romp on the couch. He'd been sticky with sweat, and after he'd just gotten clean, he'd needed to start over. She'd volunteered to join him. He wasn't about to argue.

Now she lay with him, naked but for the sheet that covered her in the cool bedroom. Her makeup was long gone, but her hair was dry, thanks to piling it on top of her head in the steamy shower. It fanned across her pillow—and he thought of it as hers, officially, now—to create a beautiful auburn backdrop to the woman he loved.

"I just . . . I felt good, and I wanted to share it with someone." Her smile was soft, as were her eyes. "You know that feeling? When you've got so much hope, so much positivity in you, and you can't sit still another second, because it's wrong not to let others in on that sort of thing?"

He kissed her forehead. "Sort of. Hearing you explain it is fun though. What's the good news?"

"Not yet." Mouth firm, she shook her head. "Let's get you through the All Military games first, and then when you get back, we can lay it all out on the table."

"I wish you were coming," he said, and regretted it

instantly. Her face fell, and her eyes started to shine with unshed tears. "I understand though," he added quickly. "I do. I'm not mad. Just . . . you know. You're important to me. Zach, too, but of course I get why he can't come."

"We're a set." The words were quiet. "That's just how it is, for now."

The fact that she'd mentioned sharing positive news with him after the All Military games gave him hope she would be open to the next bit he was going to share with her. "I want to tell you something. And the reason I'm telling you is because I don't believe in keeping things from you. I was going to tell you when I came back, but you're here now, so . . ."

She sat up a little, pulling the sheet higher around her breasts. "You're scaring me, Graham."

"Nothing to be scared about. I saw Henry today."

"You . . . what?" He could tell he'd shocked her. Not just a surprise, but a total shock. "How did you even . . . what did you . . . ho-how?"

"I got his contact info from Tasha. Good lawyer, by the way. On top of it. I can tell she wants to rip the guy in two, legally speaking . . . she's just waiting for your say-so."

"I haven't had the ability to do it before," she mumbled, scrubbing her hands over her face. "You went to his house? To, what, confront him? Yell at him? Oh my God." Her eyes grew wide, a little frightened. "Graham, tell me you didn't beat him up."

"No." Offended, he sat back. "Why the hell would I beat him up?"

"I don't know . . . you spend half your day lately throwing punches and practicing how to dodge a punch . . . muscle memory?" She rubbed her eyes. "I don't . . . I don't understand. Why did you do that?"

"It was a strategy. I wanted to cut him out at the knees before he could cause any more trouble. Because I think you should file to terminate his parental rights, completely."

"I . . ." She shook her head, and he wasn't sure if that was in exasperation, or confusion, or what. "I don't . . . I can't believe you did that."

She hadn't yelled at him yet, so he went on. "I just gave him the logistics of the process"—*sort of*—"and told him it was really in his best interest to go along without fighting."

She sat in silence, staring at her hands, trembling on top of the sheet in her lap. Was it the mention of him seeing her ex that bothered her? That he'd stepped in the situation without permission?

"I wish you hadn't done that," she finally whispered.

It was an uppercut to the ego, but he did his best to mask any reaction. "Why?"

"So, so many reasons. The first being you didn't even ask, you just did. I gave you permission to see the files and discuss strategy with Tasha. Advice, guidance, moral support . . . that's all I hoped for. I didn't intend for you to make this something you got involved in personally."

"I just had sex with you on my couch. My ass still has dents from your heels, and you want to tell me this isn't something I should be personally involved in? Kara, I love you. I love Zach. How the hell am I not personally involved?"

He hated that the word "love" made her flinch.

She stood, as regal as a queen, and walked out of the room. He stood and sighed, grabbing a pair of boxers from the dresser. After hopping in, he followed her out, finding her struggling with the zipper to her dress.

"I wish you'd stay a little longer."

"Zip me up, please." She moved her hair to one side to give him access to the back. "I need to get home. I used my backup babysitter and she charges three dollars an hour more than the regular."

The implied, *And now I'm regretting it,* was left unspoken.

As he finished zipping her up, he ran his fingertips over her neck, down her shoulders and arms to pull her elbows until her back landed against his front. "Don't leave like this."

"You don't know what you could have done. My life right now is so precarious." She glanced over her shoulder at him, sadness in her eyes. "If he decides to slap out at me because he's insulted you got involved? What then? It's a delicate balance, and I'm terrified you upset it."

"I did it because I love you. Because I hate that you feel dependent on that asshole for money to live. And because I want you to depend on me instead."

That made her turn around fully. Her face was flushed. With anger? With shock? "What?"

"You heard me." He took her hands, ignoring that they trembled. "I love you. I know this is fast. I know you haven't said it yourself yet. I tell myself you love me, too, and you're just cautious because you've got so much on your plate to worry about. But I know, without a doubt, that I want to spend the rest of my life with you."

Her bottom lip trembled, and she bit it before looking away. He caught her chin in one hand and forced her eyes back to his.

"I want to marry you. I want you and Zach to live here. I want you to keep teaching yoga if you want, or quit and run the blog and help other allergy moms advocate for their kids. I want you to know you never have to worry about that scumbag again for money. Because I have you, and you're precious to me. You both are. And what's precious to me, I protect."

"God," she croaked out, taking a step back. "Now? Right now? You're getting on a plane in, like, eight hours."

"I won't, if you ask me not to." He meant it. If she asked him to stay, he would. Boxing was his hobby, and competing at this level was a dream. But Kara was his future. Her needs, her wants, her everything came first.

That made her gasp a little. "I would never do that. Stop," she said with more bite to her tone when he took a step toward her. "I can't do this right now. You . . . you need to get on that plane and go to Texas and have your space and figure . . ." She waved at the space between them. "Figure this out more concretely with space between us. It's too hard when we're still high from the pheromones and I have your body wash on my skin and . . ."

She was near tears now. He'd made her cry, and he couldn't figure out how so he could stop doing it and never do it again. "Baby, please don't."

"No. This is going to stop for tonight. You need distance and I need clarity." She backed away toward the door, as if not wanting to turn her back on him. "I want you to kick some ass in Texas, okay?"

She wiped away a tear, and it broke his heart. "I'll call you when I land."

Kara nodded, but didn't say good-bye as she closed the door behind her.

He'd royally fucked that up. Something about the best intentions made him a total sucker.

She wanted him to have distance? It was the last thing he wanted. The last thing he believed either of them needed. But fine. He'd compete. He'd go to Texas and kick ass, as she'd requested.

But when he returned, he wasn't going to take no for an answer.

CHAPTER

19

"If we were real ballers," Tressler said, settling down in the seat in front of Graham, "we would be flying private."

"We're not *ballers*," Brad said, sounding disgusted. "And the day the military has the money to fly us private anywhere is the day we know something has gone very, very wrong in Congress."

"Isn't something always wrong in Congress?" Greg asked.

"Stop talking politics," Graham muttered. He just wanted to wait for takeoff, take his motion sickness medication and pass the fuck out and not listen to these idiots anymore.

"Grumpy." Tressler, He of Little Sense, leaned over the back of his seat. "What crawled up your ass and died? We're finally going. It's our time, baby."

"Did you get more stupid in the last week, or am I just that much more annoyed with you?" Graham wondered out loud.

"Both," Greg and Brad said together.

Tressler flopped back down with a huff, grumbling about old men who couldn't take a damn joke.

"Okay, but really, what crawled up your ass and died?" Brad asked across the aisle, leaning back for someone to pass through. "You said you hate flying, and you're clutching that packet of Dramamine like it's a gold nugget. But that's not all, is it?"

"Maybe I had a rough day off yesterday. Maybe I don't want to talk about it. Maybe," he said through his teeth, "I want everyone to mind their business."

Greg snorted. "Bullshit. The day we mind our own business is the day we stop caring. And we love you, man."

"I'm going to hit you."

Greg settled against the window of their two-seat row. "Did you have a fight with Kara?"

"Drop it."

"You both had so much to say when I was doing battle with Cook, and now you can't take the heat yourself." Brad's self-satisfied smirk made Graham want to reach across the aisle and choke him. His teammate's saving grace was the numerous people filing through, preventing him from doing so. Also, he'd have to let go of his Dramamine, and that wasn't happening.

Greg reached in his bag under the seat in front of him and pulled out a thick book. Brad reached in front of Graham— which made him want to slam his hand down on the tray and lock it upright—and asked, "Did you take my book?"

Greg glanced at the cover, then shrugged. "Probably. You weren't reading it. You're never at our rooms anyway. You're always with Cook."

"So you just took my book? Jackass, hand it back. I wasn't finished with it."

"Oh my God, stop it, both of you. You're like freaking

two-year-old twin brothers. What fucking book could even be so important you're going to bicker like babies about it?"

Greg held up the front cover. "*Sandbox Seven*. Military thriller. Marines, natch, given we are the best. Guy who wrote it was a Marine, too, I think." He flipped to the back cover jacket. "Yup. Jeremy C. Phillips.

"I read that." Tressler popped his head up again, like a fucking groundhog who was begging to be exterminated. "It's good, especially because the guy actually knows his terminology. I met his wife once last year. She's a Navy nurse." He grinned. "And hot."

"Go away, Tressler."

He rolled his eyes and flopped down again.

Another few minutes passed, with less and less people walking past, and then Marianne approached. "Hey, boys. Sorry I don't get to sit with y'all."

Brad grabbed her hand and pulled her down for a quick kiss before she passed by. "Don't have too much fun back there with the coaches."

"Oh, it'll be a challenge," she said, then looked behind her with a sigh. "If Levi doesn't get on this plane soon, I'm going to lose my second intern. That can't look good for future employers, can it? Hi, I'm Marianne Cook, the intern slayer."

"He's a big boy. If he can't figure out how to time his potty breaks like an adult, that's on him, not you. He done being pissed about Nikki yet?"

"He doesn't seem to be mad at me specifically, just the world in general. He really liked her. I'm sure it was puppy love, not the real thing. But in the throes of it, puppy love feels just as real."

"If he has bad taste, there's not a whole lot that you can do about it," Greg pointed out.

Graham just grunted and did his best not to moan when

he felt something shift under them. Closing the cargo door, likely.

"Wow, you're really looking raw, Graham." Marianne crouched down beside him, then felt his forehead. "You okay?"

He let his eyes close and held up the packet. Currently, he wasn't sick. This was simply the anticipation. His body's instinctive reaction to knowing what was going to happen next.

"Oh. Sorry. Water, small sips, something dry without a lot of flavoring to keep in your stomach. It's counterintuitive but keeping something in there makes you retch less than an empty stomach."

"God, you're actually going to throw up? I thought you just got a headache or something." Greg looked panicked at Brad. "Trade me seats."

"Fuck no." Staring straight ahead with a smirk, Brad shrugged. "You wanted a window seat."

"I want one that will smell less like barf."

"I'm not going to throw up," Graham said through clenched teeth. "Unless you annoy me so much I decide to make myself, just for spite."

"Keep your head back, and—oh, thank God. Levi, you made it. We're all the way in the back."

He slitted his eyes and saw the lanky male intern walking—more like stomping—up the aisle as if he were storming the castle. He waited for Marianne to move aside—which she did by scooting in front of Brad and sitting on his lap for a moment, then kept walking back.

"This will be a fun plane ride," she muttered, then rubbed Graham's upper arm. "Let me know if you need anything, okay?"

He waved without talking. *Make the plane move so I can take the pills.*

"Why don't you take them now?" Greg wondered.

"Because if something happens at the last minute and we have to deplane and wait—like mechanical problems or weather—I'm passed out cold and can't do it. If I wait until takeoff then we're set and it's safe."

"Makes sense. Just . . . here." He dug through his front seat pocket and handed Graham the air sick bag. "Have a second one in case. And make sure you aim that way."

Brad simply flipped him off.

THREE days. Three days without seeing or hearing from Graham, and she was ready to scream. She sat in her lawyer's conference room, drumming her nails and staring at her silent, dark phone.

Okay, fine, so she'd *heard* him, but only in text. He'd called once, but she'd been teaching a class, so it had gone to voice mail. Plenty of chances to return the call later in the evening, but she hadn't. Even when Zach had begged her to call Graham to wish him luck "just one more time." He was busy, she rationalized, and a distraction could hurt his chances. He needed his space.

She needed hers.

She still couldn't escape the idea that he'd gone behind her back and approached Henry without telling her. Oh, sure, he'd told her soon afterward. And he'd done it with the best intentions. But he'd still tried to save the day, when she didn't need saving. This had been her battle to fight. Her battle to wage. She'd wanted support, not a shield.

Now she'd never know if she could have won without him. She'd never know if she were strong enough, powerful enough. It was as if he'd taken that feeling of power she'd carried with her into his home in a tight dress and pricked it with a needle. *Pop.*

Tasha entered, a black pencil skirt hugging her curves and a wine red shell tank showing off her dark, toned arms.

When she settled down in the seat beside Kara, she crossed her legs, leaned back, and just shook her head.

"What?" Oh God . . . had his visit to Henry made things worse? "Tell me."

"It's almost too easy. Anticlimactic, when I was looking forward to skewering that little prick." Tasha shrugged and scooted a file folder over to her. "This is the paperwork to get started. I reached out to his lawyers, and they say he's willing to go through the processes, as long as you pick up the tab for the court fees and any other potential financial issues that come along. Filing fees and such."

"That's . . ." She stared at the file, dumbfounded. "That's it?"

"That's it. I didn't want to push our good fortune because, well, I'm no fool. But I have a feeling there might be more to it than just a man who came to his senses and had a moment of clarity. Don't you?" With a small smile, Tasha leaned forward. "You deserve this happiness, Kara."

"I wanted to make the move," she murmured, flipping through the paperwork without seeing any of it. "I had plans, strategies . . . I'd started looking for more private clients to make extra money for the attorney fees."

"Don't tell the partners, but I'm perfectly happy you won't be requiring our services much longer, at least not for this. Girl, you can't be upset about this, can you?"

"No, not at all. It's just a little . . . I don't know. Am I wrong? Is this stupid?"

Tasha leaned her chin on her hand. "Stupid, no. Wrong, no. What you feel is what you feel, and feelings are never wrong. But maybe . . . maybe a little prideful. That's up to you to figure out if that is a benefit or a curse."

Prideful. The word bounced around her mind as she listened to Tasha explain the process of terminating Henry's parental rights. Could her pride be the thing standing in the way of her happiness? Zach's happiness?

It ate at her, and she knew she wouldn't sleep until she figured it out.

"HEY, you. What's up back in J-ville?"

"Am I too prideful?" Kara asked without preamble.

Marianne laughed a little. "And hello to you, too. Sure, yes, Texas is fine. A little dry, a lot hot, but what can you expect?"

Kara blew out a breath. "Marianne. Am I too prideful?"

"Yes."

Wow. Well, you didn't go to your best friend for a sugar-coated answer.

"But that's not a bad thing."

"Pride isn't a virtue."

"It should be," her friend shot back. "You've been raising your son alone for ten years, without even the benefit of your parents for guidance or help. You've scraped together enough to keep your son happy and healthy—no small feat when you look at the billions of foods he can't eat—and you still work with your passion instead of some mindless job you do just for the paycheck. You're independent, you're stable, and you've raised a kid who, at the age of ten, is already a better person than some fully grown men I know. Why the hell wouldn't you be proud of that?"

"But do I let it get in the way? Am I letting pride act as a sort of, I don't know, wall from life?"

"Yes."

"Jeez, could you ease up a little? I don't think my ego can take much more."

"Good for you. Yes, you are letting the fact that Graham stepped in to help you—help, not control—get in the way. You've been doing it for so long on your own you aren't entirely sure what a cooperative relationship looks like. That's okay, because it's understandable. Now you know, and now you know what the goal is. So get the damn goal. Don't be a nincompoop. Show him you love him, too."

Kara brushed away the tears coursing down her cheeks. "I never said I loved him."

"I'm going to pretend I'm not insulted you said that. Hold on!" she yelled, then let out an exasperated sigh. "I swear, these men are all babies. If you don't get them their ice five seconds after they ask, suddenly they're dying and it's all your fault."

"How's it going?"

"Oh, *now* you wanna know." She could hear the grin in her best friend's voice. "Practice has been going well. Competition starts tomorrow. Should be pretty fierce, from what I'm seeing." There was a bit of a pause, and Kara heard the sound of ice and a metal scoop. She knew the sound well, having hung around Marianne's training room. Another few seconds later, she heard, "Here. Tie it off and ice for twenty. And go away. I'm on the phone. No, Simpson, sit there. Right there. Good boy. Children," she muttered. "They're all children. If you don't literally walk them to the spot you want them at, they're clueless."

Kara laughed. "I guess I'll have to wait until you come back to hear about most of it. I wish . . ."

"Come out here."

Kara rolled her eyes and stared at the ceiling of her bedroom. "You've forgotten, like, seven details in that statement."

"You said he emailed you the flight information for the tickets he bought. Your plane ticket is for tomorrow morning. So . . . come out."

"Just because things seem to be going the right direction for terminating Henry's parental rights doesn't mean it's happened yet. I still can't take Zach across state lines. And besides that, he can't miss school."

"So take him to my parents' house."

Kara sat up for a moment. "I can't ask your parents to do that."

"Look, I'm not giving them grandbabies for a few years,

at least. I'm sure they'd love having Zach over there. It's just for a few days, and Mom can run him to and from school. They'll be careful with his diet. You'd trust them, right?"

"Yes, of course, but—"

"I'll call Mom to double-check, but I bet they'll be all over it."

"Marianne, I—"

"Gotta go!" There was a click, and the phone's screen blanked away.

Kara sighed and flopped back down. She still had work to consider. Though really, the middle of the week was her slowest time. If she called around, surely a few people could take some of her classes, then . . .

No, this was ridiculous. Nobody would just up and take a ten-year-old boy who wasn't their own flesh and blood for several days. Watching grandkids was one thing, and most normal grandparents leapt at the chance to have their grandchildren come visit. Watching your daughter's friend's son who came with a host of allergy needs was another thing entirely. They wouldn't . . .

Her phone beeped, and she looked at the incoming text.

Mom said yes, and not to dare think about backing out after this. She is thrilled about the idea of having Zach over. You don't argue with Mary Cook. Pack a bag, drop it off at Mom's tomorrow morning after Zach is in school, and she will get him from school in the afternoon.

She rolled onto her side and hugged her pillow tight to her chest. God, her friends were amazing. "Zach? Zach! Come get this duffle bag. We've got a few clothes to pack."

CHAPTER

20

When Marianne ran at her, nearly plowing her over at the airport, Kara knew she'd made the right decision.

"Oh my God, I can't believe you did it! You came! This is insane!" Jumping a little, she looked like a loon, with her bright blond hair fluttering around her face like feathers. "You're here!"

"Yes, I'm here. Now, how the heck did you manage to get out to come get me?"

"I stole Reagan's car and came over." She grinned. "Reagan gets a rental, thanks to the travel work order, but I didn't. So I took it. She's busy all day, anyway. First matches are tonight. Baggage?"

"No, just this." She held up her small bag—her gym bag, because she didn't have luggage—and smiled weakly. "I haven't really had a need for luggage, and it seemed like an impractical purchase for this one trip, so . . ."

"Who cares? If it holds your stuff, then it's good enough. Whoops, rhymed. I'm just so jazzed!"

"No kidding," Kara said dryly as they walked arm in arm toward the parking lot. "It's like talking to a five-year-old before their ADHD meds kick in in the morning."

Marianne's steps bounced as she walked along, keeping up with Kara's longer strides. "Maybe. The competition is getting to me. I can't help it. The scrimmages were fun and exciting, but nothing compared to this. The teams are all looking good, and we're ready, but once you get in the ring it's anyone's match. It's an intense atmosphere in practices, with everyone sort of side-eyeing each other, and—"

"Okay, you have to stop." Kara pulled up short, pulling Marianne to a stop beside her. "You're making me nervous along with you. I can't do what I need to do if I'm nervous."

"What are you doing? What's there to be nervous about? Oh, Zach? He's totally fine. My mom texted me to say she'd picked him up and they were making cookies using that recipe on your blog. I sent her the link," Marianne added.

"Yes, I know. Mary texted me the same thing. I mean you're making me nervous about seeing Graham."

"Oh, that." Marianne waved it off and started walking once more toward temporary parking. "Don't worry about it. He's golden. The man has strategy like nobody's business. Probably why he's so good at his normal job. You know, that whole 'knowing your opponent's next move' bit has to work well in court. Here we are!" She stopped by a midsized sedan in a light tan color, unlocking it with the key fob. "Just toss your stuff in the back."

"I meant seeing him and dealing with the fact that he proposed to me."

"He . . ." Marianne opened the driver side door and stared at her over the top of the car. "He proposed? You're kidding me."

"Right, because I find marriage humor to be the best sort." Sliding in, Kara hissed as the backs of her thighs hit scorching hot plastic. "Jesus!" she yelled, hopping back out again. Her legs were on fire. Actually melting. She was melting from her ass down to the backs of her knees.

"Yeah . . . I was going to warn you, but you sort of stupefied me with that whole proposal thing." Without getting in, Marianne reached in and started the car, then closed the door again. "It has to cool down for about five minutes before it's safe to get in. Texas is no joke with the heat, man."

They stood in silence a minute. "So, we just stand here and wait?"

"Yeah. It'll be okay, just give it a minute." Her best friend watched her speculatively. "Are you going to say yes? Did you already say yes?"

"I said nothing yet."

"And what are you going to say?"

"I'm going to say it to him first, Marianne. Whatever *it* is."

"You don't know?" Marianne's eyes widened. "How do you not know? Isn't that one of those instinctive gut things?"

"Not when you've got a kid to worry about. Jumping with your gut isn't usually a good choice."

"Right. Forgot." She waited another few seconds. "He'd make a good dad."

"Yes, he would. That's not reason enough, though. I've known the man two months. We've only been together, like that, for two weeks. It's so fast . . ." Kara nibbled on her lip. "How soon did you know with Brad?"

"That I loved him? Couple weeks . . . we sort of jumped into bed a little faster than you and Graham though." She opened her door and laid a palm on the seat. "We're safe."

"The fact that you have to feel a car's interior before you get in is scary. Texas is scary."

"Kara, you haven't seen anything yet. Just wait."

GRAHAM flexed his hands once more before sliding his boxing gloves on. After they were secured, he wouldn't be able to move them freely until after the match. He savored the last minute of flexibility before he lost it.

"How you feeling?" Brad sat down beside him in the locker room. By Graham's estimation, they had another five minutes or so.

"Good. I'm good. Really good."

Brad glanced around the locker room. "We're alone. Nobody else here."

"Fucked up. I'm fucked up." He held out his hand, which shook, glove and all. "I'm almost thirty years old. What am I doing this for?"

"Because getting punched is fun?" Brad smiled and bumped his shoulder gently. "Calm down. You've got this."

Graham said nothing.

After another minute, Brad asked slowly, "Did it help, when you had Kara and Zach in the stands at the scrimmage?"

"Marianne's here, so you don't have to worry about that."

"I know. I'm just asking you. Were your nerves better or worse then?"

"I wasn't nearly as nervous for that match from the start. It was just a scrimmage. But," he added with a sigh, "yeah. Them being there . . . I don't know. It grounded me. Made me remember at the end of it, I would walk away and leave it behind, and have something more important to focus on."

Brad nodded in agreement, staring at the wall ahead. "She's here."

Graham assumed he meant Marianne, so said nothing.

"Kara. She's here."

Every electric synapse in his body zapped at once. "Here? In Texas? *Here* here? In the crowd? I need to see her."

"Sit down, you idiot." Brad shoved him back down on the bench. "I didn't tell you so you could go hopping off to see her like an antelope frolicking in the meadow. I told you so you'd have something out there to ground you."

"You lied."

"No, I didn't. She came. Marianne picked her up at the airport nearly three hours ago."

She'd been nearby, within touching distance, for hours. Why hadn't she come to see him?

Because she'd think she was a distraction. Of course.

"I told you because you know that's going to help you get in there and do your job. You've got something to look forward to when you climb out of the ring. So when you're inside, you get in, you get out. You kick that Army boy's ass, and go hug your woman. Deal?"

"Deal."

Coach Willis poked his head in. "Sweeney, you're on deck. Let's go."

Graham picked up his mouth guard and stood with Brad. "If I'd said having Kara here would have distracted me, would you still have told me she was here?"

Brad's face was nearly comical. "Hell no, you idiot. I came here to win. You can kiss the girl later. Beat someone up first."

He laughed, then walked out ready for his first match.

KARA sat in the stands, wishing she had someone beside her to talk to. Even Zach had been a good boxing buddy, for the sake of company. But Marianne and Reagan both had work to do. Important work. So she would sit down and be quiet and watch in amazement. The last few fights had been interesting. Some were men she knew from the team, and others pitted Army against Air Force, meaning both competitors were strangers to her. She couldn't help but become excited every time one of the Marines took to the mat, though she had no clue what was going on. During Tressler's match, she'd actually found herself on her feet, screaming along with everyone else, for him to kick some ass.

It was exhausting just to watch. She also had no clue how the scoring worked, but was relieved when the referee—judge? in-charge person?—held up Tressler's gloved hand as the victor. Maybe to an experienced spectator, that would have been obvious. To her, it was thrilling.

She watched as Brad walked beside Graham, wearing a silky red robe trimmed with gold. Marine Corps colors. Brad took the robe as he walked to the corner where Coach Willis and Cartwright stood, then settled down in a seat on the front row with the rest of the team.

God, Graham was gorgeous to look at. A Greek god come to life. She wanted to touch him now. Give him a hug, whisper something encouraging in his ear. Stroke her hand down his back, feeling every ripple of muscle under her fingertips as she did so . . .

Okay, so maybe that last one was more for her pleasure than his. Who cared? The man was magnificent.

Unlike his teammates before him, he looked to be scanning the crowd. Had Brad told him she was here? She'd had enough time before his match to find him and tell him good luck. But in her mind, that would have distracted him from the purpose. They had so much to talk about, so much to discuss. Too much to cram into one before-match conversation. Better he have his full attention on the task at hand so he could escape from this round unscathed, then talk later.

Those dark eyes seemed to take in the crowd in quick sections, even as Coach Willis started talking to him. He nearly missed her; she felt his eyes actually rake over her as they kept scanning, then they zeroed back in on her.

She was in a crowd of five hundred plus—on her side of the stands, anyway—and he'd still managed to find her. He must be a champion Where's Waldo? player.

Raising her hand a little, she smiled and gave a tiny wave.

His grin broke out, a little distorted from the mouth guard, but she knew that was what he meant. He didn't wave, just sent her a wink—at least, she thought it was a wink, hard to tell from this distance—and nodded once. She understood it was an acknowledgment there would be more to come, but now, he had a job to do.

Go get 'em, baby.

The first bell rang to indicate the start of round one, and she covered her eyes. His Army opponent came out swinging, and Graham instantly went on the defense, using footwork and an innate understanding of where each punch would be thrown before it was to dodge and weave around the barrage of punches and jabs. If she knew more . . . she could have given him mental instructions. As if that would have helped . . . but it would have made her feel more productive than just watching him work his ass off to keep from being hit.

When a blow from Mr. Army connected, glancing off his jaw, she looked down and sat. As everyone around her stood, she had no view of the ring. And probably for the best. No wonder Reagan had said before she'd nearly thrown up at her first match. How did someone watch the man she loved intentionally step into the ring and get punched?

When the bell sounded for the end of round one, a few people sat, but not enough to see. She jumped back up and saw Graham walking to the corner and the tiny stool set there by Coach Cartwright. His back was to her, and he didn't look behind him. Good idea. Keep focused. There was no way to know how it had gone. No way to know if he'd been hit in the face, or the stomach . . . God, this stupid, violent sport! If Zach ever decided to take up boxing, she'd just have to kill him.

So instead, she focused on Graham's opponent. His chest heaved as he sucked in wind, and it was shiny with sweat, but he appeared untouched. As if they'd spent the entire first round doing nothing but practicing their Zumba moves around each other instead of trying to punch and jab each other's eyes out.

This sport made no sense to her at all.

When the bell for round two started, she sat back down. Wuss. Total wuss. This was just something they would have to come to grips with. He would have his boxing hobby, and she would encourage him from a distance. A long distance away. Like, from home.

After the last round, she stood and watched as Graham and his opponent came to stand in the middle, not looking at each other, an arm's length apart. Graham's head was bowed, as if he didn't want to look up. Or maybe because he was exhausted. Or possibly hurt? Kara's heart raced at the thought. She wanted nothing more than to throw herself down the bleachers and crowd surf to the floor, run to him and hold him until he recovered.

Overreaction much, Kara?

After conferring with the judges at their table on the main floor—who Kara knew based their scoring on connected punches—the referee climbed back into the ring. He stood between the two men, pausing for effect. The rumble of the gym grew quiet as they waited, like a classroom full of students whose teacher was about to hand out either a reward or a punishment, and they didn't know which . . . then grabbed Graham's hand and lifted it high.

She screamed. She screamed so loud the person in front of her covered her ears and turned to give her a bitchy look. Kara couldn't have cared less. He'd won. He *won!* Grabbing her purse, she made her way quickly out of the row—apologizing profusely along the way as she was sure she knocked into more than one set of knees in her haste—and worked her way through the people leaving during the break to hit the restrooms or concession stands to run at the main floor. But she couldn't get to it. The area for the team and staff was roped off this time, with security standing guard.

Graham had shrugged back into his robe and was heading back toward the exit that would lead him into the locker rooms. She wanted him to turn around, to notice her. To come for her.

"Graham!" She jumped and waved like a lunatic, but he either didn't hear her, or wasn't ready yet to talk. He kept walking.

"Hey, girl."

She shrieked and jumped a mile high. Hand over her racing heart, she turned to find Reagan standing behind her . . . or rather, towering over her. "How freaking tall are your heels today?"

"A mile. The more stressful the situation, the higher the heel. It's my coping mechanism. You must be excited. He won!"

He won. She breathed in, then out, then out some more as Reagan squished her with a big hug. Kara hugged back. "Thanks for letting Marianne borrow your car."

"She borrowed my car?" Reagan pulled back, a look of confusion on her face. "What?"

"Uh, never mind. I'm going to hit the restroom while I can. See you later!"

Sorry, Marianne.

GRAHAM shook a little as Brad yanked off his gloves. He could have done it himself, with a little effort, but his hands were still cramped, and the shaking wouldn't help.

Grabbing a pair of scissors from the supply table, Brad waited. "You gonna stop shaking so I can cut your tape off? Otherwise you might lose a finger."

"I'm trying," he said through clenched teeth, then growled when he flexed his fingers wide and they only shook more violently. "God damn it."

"Adrenaline. Just give it a minute." Brad set the scissors down. "Shake it off, walk it out, whatever you need to. No big."

It was embarrassing the match had affected him this

much, but then again, it was the biggest match he'd ever competed in. That in itself made it a bit of an anomaly.

Also an anomaly . . . having his future wife in the stands. Because there was no way he'd let Kara tell him she flew down to watch him compete as a friend. She and Zach were his, end of story.

The door opened and Greg sauntered in, looking supremely pleased with himself. And he should be . . . he'd trounced his Air Force opponent earlier in the day. "Winner winner, chicken dinner. Congrats, man." He gave Graham a slap on the back. "Way to keep it up. So far, in the points, we're ahead. Close margin with Army, but we're holding strong. Long as this pansy-ass grandpa's knee keeps him upright, we should be good to go."

"This pansy-ass grandpa still needs to cut some tape," Brad said mildly, holding out his hand for Graham's first wrist. "Your parents come down to watch, Sweeney?"

"No, they couldn't make it. They'll be watching online though, as the matches get uploaded to streaming. I'll call them later. Your mom and stepdad come?"

"Yup. First time they met Marianne, too. Big week for everyone." Brad's grin turned smug. "Marianne was all worried about it, though God knows why. My mom practically wanted to adopt her after she watched Cook ream some Army yokel for messing with her rolls of tape. You know how Cook is about her athletic tape."

"She loves it almost as much as her pamphlets. Ow," he grumbled as Brad pulled off the tape, and a little wrist hair.

"Sorry, if your arms weren't so damn hairy," Brad muttered.

"Consider waxing?" Greg asked with a grin.

"Bite me."

"He's just anxious to get out there and run to Kara. It's going to be like watching two lovers run in slow motion across a field of flowers, arms wide open."

Brad scoffed at Greg's imagery. "Don't make me throw up."

"You two have lived together for too long," Graham said thoughtfully. "Remember back when you hated each other? Those were the good days. Let's go back to that."

"Done," Brad said, pulling the last of the tape off. "You know the coaches aren't going to let you leave yet. You'll have to stay and watch the rest of the matches before we head out to dinner."

"No group dinner tonight," Greg reminded him. "Remember? Coach Ace said we could mingle with friends and family tonight, long as we're back in our rooms by twenty-one hundred hours."

He considered a moment, then nodded. "That's enough time."

Both Greg and Brad grinned at him. "Go, before you gross me out. I've got to start getting ready for my own match."

"Good luck, man." Graham gripped both of his shoulders and looked him dead in the eyes. "You've got this, grandpa."

"Fuck off," he replied mildly. "Go kiss your girl."

"Don't have to tell me twice."

CHAPTER

21

Kara found Marianne wrapping a Marine's ankle in a small room that served as the training room. From the looks of it, she was sharing the space with two other trainers. Levi was nowhere to be found. When she asked, Marianne rolled her eyes and slapped the Marine on the arm. "Off you go. I sent him out for lunch. He was annoying the shit out of me. Nothing but moping from that kid, combined with evil looks at any Marine who walks in here. It's like he blames them all for Nikki's stupidity, not her. I don't get it."

"He's young, and infatuated. The young and infatuated aren't always rational." Hadn't she been the same way with Henry eleven years ago? Though she loved Zach with all her heart, it wasn't untrue to say he had been the result of an irrational, hormonal teenage choice.

"No kidding. Anyway, he was in the way, especially since I have so little space to work with." She sent Kara a disgusted look that said, without words, just what she thought of the space she'd been allotted. "Keep me company for a few minutes. How'd you like watching a real match?"

"It was terrifying. Watching the others go was bad enough. But Graham?" Kara shook her head. "Horrifying. I think this is just something we will have to agree to disagree on in the future. He can keep his hobby, and I'll stay home where I can be blissfully unaware of when he gets hit or knocked around. Better that way."

"You're talking in future terms. This is good. This is very good. I'm happy for you." She took a singularly ugly fanny pack from under the table and began to load it.

"Why are you packing a bag? You're, like, a hundred yards away from the action in here. Can't you just come back for a roll of tape? And why do you have to wear a fanny pack?"

"Fanny packs are coming back in style. Didn't you read last month's *Vogue*? No? Oh well." The AT put a tube of some ointment in the bag. "Because I need to have some stuff immediately accessible, not have to run back here for it. You've seen how little time they have between rounds. If I need to tape something, or staunch bleeding, I don't want to run back here. Plus, sometimes these doors stick. I could barely get in here the first time. One of the other trainers had to show me how to wiggle the key just right."

Kara shrugged. Not her domain.

"Now, the next round is going to start in about ten minutes. Are you staying, or heading back to your hotel?"

"Staying. At least until I tell Graham where I'll be." She checked her watch. "It's been fifteen minutes. Where is he?"

"Debriefing with Coach Ace, I imagine." Marianne didn't look up as she continued to pack the fanny efficiently, and with practiced ease. "He does a quick analysis with the guys after every match, while it's fresh. He'll give them more in-depth advice later."

"I see. I'll let you finish packing. Thanks again for picking me up from the airport." She started to walk out the door, then turned around. "Oh, and I accidentally told Reagan that you borrowed her car to pick me up. Sorry. Bye!"

She raced from the room just as Marianne's head snapped up. *"What?"*

But Kara was already gone, swallowing a giggle. Then she caught sight of him. He stood, in a Marine Corps boxing T-shirt and simple navy mesh shorts, just inside the security rope.

She couldn't help the grin that exploded over her face, probably matching the same one that he wore. He ducked under the security rope and pulled her into a big hug. Kara wrapped her arms around him and squeezed until she wasn't sure either of them could breathe. He arched his back, pulling her up until her toes barely touched the ground.

"I've missed you," he said into her hair. "Missed you so damn much."

"I missed you, too. I'm sorry," she added, feeling like she was going to start crying. *Swallow it back, girl. Now is not the time to get emotional.* "So sorry."

"Shh." Hand running down her hair, down her back, he soothed. "Shh. We'll talk later. The whole team has to stay until the last match, but then we're free until our twenty-one hundred curfew tonight. Nine o'clock," he clarified when she pulled back and scrunched up her nose.

"I could have done the math, you know," she said defiantly, then shrugged. "Nice that I didn't have to. I have a hotel room already. Do you think you could come over there?"

"I'll see if Reagan can give me a lift over. Or a cab. Is it close?"

"It is. It's not the best place, but a lot of the nicer ones were sold out. I had no clue this was such a big deal," she said in awe, looking around the gym full of spectators. Family who had probably come in from all over the country to watch their son, their brother, their husband compete.

"It is, yeah. Biggest thing I've ever competed in, for sure." He kissed her temple as the announcer gave a five minute warning before the next match was set to begin. "I have to sit with the team. Text me the hotel and your room number. You don't have to stay if you don't want to. I'll get myself over there somehow."

"I'll probably head over and do some work, maybe check in on Zach." But she cupped his face in her hands, turning it this way and that to inspect him closely. "No real damage." But her finger brushed over a small bruise on his cheek. "Not yet, anyway. You've got more of this to go."

"Several more, if I have any say in it. I'm fine." He captured one hand and pressed a kiss to her fingers. "I love you."

She wanted to say it back, so much. But a crowded gym that smelled like sweat, musty laundry and—oddly—rubber was not the place for her initial declaration. "I'll see you later. Good luck to Brad and anyone else who hasn't gone yet."

"Thanks." He kissed her temple, then ducked back under the rope and headed for his team. They were too far away to hear, but she saw Tressler say something. Graham pushed him out of his seat so that he tumbled to the ground. The rest of the team laughed while Tressler gave him a dirty look. Graham sat beside Greg, looking pleased with himself.

Men, she thought. *No, not men. Just one. Mine. My man. My man.*

It was a beautiful thought.

GRAHAM wiped his damp palms on the back of his shirt. He hadn't been this nervous since he'd asked Jessica Calbert to the prom. And there was so much more riding on today than a corsage and a coordinating cummerbund.

When he knocked on the door to Kara's hotel room, it took her a few moments to open the door. When he did, she was on the phone. She smiled and held the door open. He closed it behind him quietly.

"Uh-huh, then what?" She waved him in, then just took his hand and led him into her hotel room. It was a lower-end hotel chain. A step above a roadside motel, but not a very large step. When she'd said she wasn't coming, he'd cancelled the hotel reservations at the decent hotel just outside the main gate. Now he wished he hadn't.

"Well, I'm glad you stood up for yourself. Oh, really?" Her smile grew as she sat on the corner of the queen-size bed. Other than the lone desk chair, it was the only place to sit. "I'm sure he'd love to hear that. Do you want to tell him? Yeah, he's right here. Okay." Eyes bright, she held out her phone. "It's Zach. He wants to say hello."

Everything inside him lit up. "Hey, Zach, what's up, bud?"

"I almost got in a fight at school!"

That made him blink, then look at Kara. She smiled expectantly. "Almost?"

"Yeah, a kid was making fun of my EpiPen case, calling it a purse and sh—stuff. And I wanted to hit him."

Oh boy. He pinched the bridge of his nose. "Zach, that—"

"But I didn't, 'cause I remembered how you were talking about not beating up on people who aren't at your same level. Like when you took it easy on that guy during your scrimmage. And Danny's not at my level at all. He's an idiot."

Graham's lips twitched. "Really."

"Uh-huh. But then someone else heard him and told the teacher and he got in trouble anyway for being a bully and I didn't even have to rat him out or throw a punch. And I thought about you."

His heart simply swelled in his chest until he thought he might pass out. Sitting beside Kara on the bed, he wrapped an arm around her and pulled her in tight. He had to force the words around the lump in his throat. "I'm proud of you, kid."

"Thanks. I'm proud of you, too." He paused. "Is that stupid of me to say? Because I'm a kid and you're a grown-up?"

"No," Graham said hoarsely. "Not stupid at all."

"Mom said you won today. So, like, good job. Did you remember to bring the good luck box?"

"I sure did. There's no way I could have done it without the box." He reached in his back pocket and pulled out his wallet, then slid the photo he'd scanned and copied from his wallet. The young Kara, and infant Zach, stared back up at him. Kara sucked in a breath beside him. When he looked at her from the corner of his eye, she had one hand over her mouth, another on her heart.

"I wish I could have gone. School sucks sometimes."

Clearing his throat, he bit back a moan when Kara pressed a kiss to his neck. "Yeah, sometimes. Hey, I'm going to give you back to your mom now, okay? Keep up the good work. You're an awesome kid, Zach."

He handed the phone back to Kara before he unmanned himself and cried. With a deep breath, he listened to Kara finish the call while he put the photo back in his wallet. She instructed him to listen to Mr. and Mrs. Cook—which explained how she'd managed to get away—and be careful. Then she hung up.

"He was so excited," she said softly. "So excited to say he'd been like you. Like his hero." She smiled a little, though it wobbled, and she looked at the wall across from the bed, as if she couldn't quite look him in the eye. "His hero worship knows no bounds."

Her voice was a little off, and he couldn't tell if she was pleased with Zach's hero worship, or disappointed. "I'm proud of him. He made a great choice."

"I would love you for that alone." Her voice trembled, and she covered her lips for a moment, still not looking at him. "For giving my boy a great man to look up to. I could love you for just that. I love Brad and Greg for that. And Mr.

Cook. Good men that my son can emulate, learn from, grow into."

Had she put him in the same category as his buddies, as an old man?

"But I don't just love you for that." She shifted now to look at him, one leg on the bed, one off. "I love you because you make me feel alive. Because you woke me up, and made me want to be more than just Zach's mother again. Made me realize I could be more. And because you don't look at me and see a broken woman who needs to be taken care of. You see something precious you want to care for. There's a difference."

"Kara." He couldn't say more. Just couldn't.

"Let me finish, please. I won't get it out, otherwise. I was wrong, the day before you left, to be upset with you. I wasn't wrong to be surprised, because clearly you'd done something without telling me first. That's not unreasonable."

"No, it's not."

"Shh. But my anger was misplaced. I had to work through it first. That whole 'being precious' thing? It's new to me. Having someone swoop in and try to take over, or control me . . . that's not new. And so I reacted poorly."

He waited, because he didn't want to be shushed again.

"And so," she said after a deep sigh, "it was with great reflection and a good chat with my lawyer—who likes you, by the way—that I came to realize we were shooting for the same thing, and to get mad about what you'd done was to cut off my nose to spite my face. You got a reaction out of Henry. A good one. He's officially amenable to the termination."

For a second time, his heart swelled. "Thank God."

"Yes, exactly. But I want to make something clear. I was doing it myself. I'd met with Tasha that same day to get the paperwork started. Before—or maybe right at the same time—you went to Henry's home to confront him. I'd made the choice to do so. Do you know why?"

He shook his head, though he hoped he did.

"Because I wanted to be free. Free to make the choice. Maybe we wouldn't work out, for whatever reason. Maybe I wanted to get married to someone who lived in Boston, or Copenhagen."

That made him roll his lips in to keep from smiling.

"Or maybe I just wanted to take my son to see the Grand Canyon. I wanted the choice, without an axe being held over my head. So I decided to take the controlling step. The step that gave me my power back. The one where I got my choice back."

"And?"

"And I choose you. I love you. Zach loves you, too, which is nearly as important as me loving you."

"Nearly," he agreed, itching to reach for her.

"But even if I didn't love you—which I do—you would forever be special to me as the man who influenced me, who encouraged me, who made me want to take that step toward independence. Now I get them both. My independence, and you."

"Hell yeah, you do." He reached for her then, because he couldn't do anything but that. She wanted the choice, but his choice was long gone. She was it for him, come hell or high water.

Her tank top came off almost by magic, with her bra quickly following. They rolled and slid around the slick bedspread, tearing off each other's clothing until they were naked as the day they were born. He entered her in a slow thrust, hooking one of her knees with his elbow to change the angle and deepen his penetration.

Her head tossed around on the pillow, thrashing and causing her hair to spread in a wild tangle. "More, more. Here." She took her leg and bent until her thigh was all but parallel with her torso, her knee next to her ear.

Hot damn. Thank you, yoga.

He slid out, until just the head of his cock remained in her entrance and her eyes widened, then sank again slowly. They had hours alone, and no worries about a young son to run in and interrupt them. He intended to eke out every ounce of pleasure he could before he had to be back.

"Harder," she begged. "Graham . . . Graham, please."

"Trust me," he whispered, pulling out again at an achingly slow pace, and back in again. He was so deep inside her, so tight against her. Nothing could separate them. Nothing would. He would love her forever, make her his forever. Use this lovemaking to cement in their minds the commitment their hearts had made to each other.

He could have stayed like that for hours, simply slipping and sliding in and around her body. Toying and teasing until they were sweaty and panting and near-crazy with need. Another day, another time, he probably would. For now, he contented himself to watch her face every time he pushed into her. Her eyelids twitched, her lips curved and she made a little humming sound of pleasure. As if she were napping in a hammock, and a gentle breeze rocked her.

But even his heart couldn't fully control his body, and soon he felt the buildup of an orgasm he was helpless to tamp down. Reaching under her raised thigh, he massaged at her clit with his thumb, taking his cues from her changing expressions, until her eyes flew open and met his.

"Graham," she whispered, just before the wave crashed over her and she climaxed. He flexed and held on as long as possible, wanting to give fully to her, before he could hold out no longer, and followed.

CHAPTER

22

"I don't know what kind of prize you get if you win this boxing tournament," Kara said, idly scratching Graham's back, "but you get my vote for the gold medal in making love."

"Aw, thanks baby." He kissed her shoulder, as if that were the only part of her he could reach without moving. He was exhausted, that much she could see. But still, he'd managed to rock her softly into an amazing orgasm. The man's talents knew no bounds.

Snuggling against him, she sighed. "I'm sorry I can't stay for the finals. I changed the ticket you bought me to take me home day after tomorrow. I could only get three days off from work . . . and I had to beg pitifully for that." Not to mention, she couldn't justify missing more than that, budget-wise.

"You came. That in itself is a miracle to me." He nuzzled at her temple. "I love you."

"I love you, too. Maybe I shouldn't say that right after you rocked my world downstairs, but it's true."

"'Rocked your world downstairs,'" he repeated on a laugh. "That's a new one. But I believe you."

"Good." She waited to see if he would add anything, but he seemed content to just lay with her in his arms. "You've got another hour or so, right?"

"So sayeth the clock."

"Maybe we could talk a little about the practicalities."

"Practicalities. Not sure if I can manage it, since I think my brain is still liquid. Can I just say how much I appreciate your job? This whole flexy-bendy thing is really growing on me."

"I bet," she said. "But I mean, what happens when we get home. The termination is going to happen, but it takes a while."

His body went from lax to stiff. She hated the change.

"Uh-huh. Usually it's at least six months, maybe more. The courts don't take it lightly, as well they shouldn't. But if he's agreeable, and you've got a good lawyer, it shouldn't be a huge problem."

"Good. But I'm saying that things will have to change for me and Zach. I'm looking for cheaper places to rent, and I might have to pick up another couple of private clients for personal yoga in their homes. Zach's almost to an age he can stay by himself for a few hours if I have an evening client, so that will help, but—whoa!" She barely managed to clamp down on a shriek as Graham rolled her on top of him straddling his chest.

"There's a cheap place out in Hubert. My place. And if you want to take on extra clients, that's fine, but it's not necessary. Zach could stay by himself, but why, when he can stay with me at home?"

This is what she'd wanted him to bring up again. Finally. "Well, you hadn't mentioned that part. Besides, I'm not sure if it's smart for me to go directly from receiving child support to having a live-in boyfriend. Or would I be the live-in girlfriend? Never mind. The point is, maybe I should try to do it myself for just a little bit first."

"You could," he agreed, and her heart dropped like the Tower of Terror ride. A little fall, then a catch. Then another little fall, and another catch. "Or you could accept that we're going to be together forever, and just suck it up and move in with me. You have nothing to prove. And even if you did—which you don't—you've proven it for ten years. Jesus, Kara, you were eighteen, pregnant and alone. You figured it out. You've done it. You would have done it even without child support . . . or what measly child support he's let trickle in over the years. Give yourself some damn credit for past achievements, would you?"

Just like that, her heart rose again. "I see your point."

"Then hear this next point. I want to marry you. I was going to ask you again when we got back home. You weren't escaping me that easily. I figured on planning out something soft and romantic and flowery. The kind of proposal you deserve."

"I don't think anyone *deserves* a certain kind of proposal."

"You deserve the best. The absolute best. And I was going to talk to Zach again, man to man. Give him the heads-up. Maybe take him with me ring shopping if I could sneak it past you."

"Oh." Her heart made the trek up now, into her throat. "Oh."

"I'm not asking a ten-year-old permission, that's weird to me. But Zach and I are cool, and I figured having a good talk about it, one-on-one, would be the respectful way to handle it. The kid deserves respect."

"Why are you so perfect?" she whispered, watching his dark brown eyes soften. He rose up, shifting her back to sit on his thighs, and kissed her. He was so gentle, so tender with it.

"Perfect for you, like you are for me. Not a perfect man, just a perfect match. I was going to wait. I still will, if you want me to, though at this point it feels almost like a technicality than a necessity. Do you want me to?"

She shook her head no. "Now, please."

"Buck naked, in a cheap hotel room right after having wild sex. Yup, this is one for the grandkids."

She pinched at the small space of skin between his pectoral muscle and his armpit. That caused him to yelp and palm her ass cheeks with both hands, squeezing in warning.

"If you want to do it again, I won't stop you. But I don't want to go back to North Carolina without the promise, Graham."

"In that case . . . Kara LeAnn Smith, will you marry me?" He pressed his finger to her lips before she could answer. "Will you let me be a father to Zach? Will you make a few siblings for him with me? Will you trust me with your and Zach's lives?"

"Well," she said after a minute, blinking because he'd become blurry in her vision. "After that, I'm not sure what woman in her right mind would say no."

"That's a yes?"

"You idiot." She kissed him, pulling him tight against her. "Yes. Yes, yes, yes."

"I love you. I love you both."

"We love you right back."

THE knock on Graham's door at exactly twenty-one hundred hours made him smile. He got up and expected to see one of the coaches standing there, doing a head count. Instead, he found Reagan. "Hey there, pretty lady. Does your guy know you're knocking on my door instead of his?"

She smirked. "Bed check was relegated to me tonight. Coaches' meeting. You all set? What?"

He tilted his head to the side. "What do you mean, what?"

"You're smiling. Like, loony smiling. What . . . did something happen?"

He could tell her, but he had a feeling Kara would want

to share the news with her girlfriends. So he simply shrugged and said, "I got a win, I got to see my girl . . . no reason not to be smiling."

"Hmm." Her tone said *I'm not buying it* but she simply waved and walked down to the next room to knock. "Bed check!"

He pulled back in his room, prepared to close the door, but the door across from him opened and Greg poked his head out. "Bed check Nazi gone?"

"I can still hear you," she said from down the hall.

"Love you!"

"Get back to bed!"

There was laughter from the other rooms in the hallway.

"Okay, quick, before the drill sergeant comes back. What happy pills did you take?"

The door next to Greg's opened and Brad's exasperated face stuck out. "Both of you shut the gossip train down, would you?"

"Sweeney's got news. I can smell it." Greg turned his eagle eyes back at him. "'Fess up."

"Wow, third degree much?"

"I still hear you," Reagan sang from around the corner.

"God, she's a pain in the ass." Greg grinned from ear to ear. "Mine. Now spill. Fast."

"I . . . might have asked Kara a very important question."

Both men stared at him, dumbfounded.

"She might have had a very positive reaction to that question."

"Jesus H.," Brad breathed out. "You really went for it."

"And it paid off, apparently." Risking it, Greg stepped out into the hall and held out an arm for a guy hug. "Congratulations, man. You're a lucky guy."

"Yeah, lucky. Congrats and stuff. Night," Brad said, zipping back in and closing his door silently.

Greg and Graham both smiled and shook their heads. The man was crazy about rules and not breaking them.

"Let's follow Grandpa's lead and hit the rack. We've got a huge day tomorrow."

"Yup. And you wouldn't want your fiancée to see you lose like an asshole, would you?" Greg nudged his side with an elbow. "Night."

Graham shut his door and headed for bed. Ten seconds later, there was a soft knock.

"Uh, Graham? I'm locked out."

"Gregory Higgs!" Reagan yelled from down the hall. "Your ass is grass, Marine!"

"Fuck," his friend croaked.

Graham laughed quietly and tucked himself back down.

CHAPTER

23

His first match had been easier than yesterday's. After a third round KO, Graham advanced to the next round, as did most of his team members. They had a three hour break for lunch, which Graham intended to use to spend as much time as possible with Kara. He had one more day with her before she headed home. She'd miss the finals, but just having her there at all was a dream come true.

He took her out to lunch, picking somewhere close where he knew he could order the right combination of protein and carbs to keep his energy up for the next round. Kara stared at him when he ordered his chicken dry, no seasoning.

"Hidden salt," he explained. "Normally I wouldn't care. It's just this week. Brad, now he's a stickler for that junk." Handing the menu to the server after Kara ordered—the much more appetizing sounding classic burger and fries—he reached over and held her hand. His thumb rubbed over her left ring finger. "Any requests?"

"What, like karaoke?"

"No, for your ring."

She scrunched her nose. "I don't know. I'm not big into jewelry so . . . something small? Like, not set too high. And nothing flashy, or with stones all the way around. Just the single stone on top is good. But not an oval or a pear. Emerald or princess is fine."

He snorted. "But you don't know."

She blushed. "Okay, so once you think about it a little, stuff comes to you. I haven't been designing my ring for years or anything. I don't have any hidden sketches of wedding dresses anywhere. It just wasn't on my mind. Even when I got pregnant, my first thought wasn't to rush down any altar."

He played with her fingers a moment while their server dropped off a bread basket. He pushed it towards her, but she just set it aside. "No regrets? You weren't anti-marriage before this?"

"No. I just didn't think I'd get to experience it. I didn't think I'd be this lucky." She squeezed his hand. "You are so unexpected in my world. So out of left field."

He picked up her hand and kissed that same ring finger. "You blew me away from the start. I only wish I'd started seriously pursuing you sooner. I feel like we wasted weeks of time."

"Not wasted. I have to be more cautious, naturally. I got to see you as a man first, before seeing you as a potential . . . something."

"Is that what I am now?" he teased. "A something?"

"You're an everything."

She humbled him. And he could not wait to get through the tournament and get home to continue his life with her and Zach.

KARA stood beside Marianne as Coach Ace called the Marines over for a chat. Even those who had been knocked out from the tournament were sticking to the team like glue. They were a unit. It was awesome to watch.

"I love my job," Marianne said with a smile, arms crossed over her chest. "I'm going to miss working for the Marines, but I've already started sending out my résumé."

"Really? Where?"

"California." She leaned her head over to rest on Kara's shoulder for a moment. It was a gesture Kara remembered from their teen years, when they'd talked about boys, or needed to bitch about life. It was a call for support. "He asked me to move in with him last night."

"I love how you say that. Move in, like you just have some friends come over one day with a few pickups and haul your stuff a few blocks over." Like she would be doing.

"He's got an apartment full of stuff. I've got a furnished rental here. It won't be hard. Leaving here will be," she added, wrapping an arm around Kara as the guys huddled in tighter. "Leaving Mom and Dad, and you. I've always been less than two hours away from home. But just look at him," she added with a sigh.

It shouldn't have surprised her, but somehow, the thought of Marianne not being on the east coast, within an hour or so drive, was sad.

"I can't believe you won't be nearby. It's like the end of an era."

"I know it. But how could I say no to that man?"

"No clue," Kara said, deciding now was as good a time as any. "Since I couldn't say no to mine. He asked me to marry him."

Marianne jerked against her, her hand tightening at Kara's waist. "Say what? He . . . what? You . . . what?"

"New rule: You can't say 'what' for the rest of the day. He asked me to marry him, and I said yes. Don't tell your parents though. I don't want them to accidentally spill the beans to Zach. We want to tell him together, in person, when Graham comes home from here."

"No, of course not. Wow . . . my best friend is getting married." She paused. "You're not going to make me wear an ugly bridesmaid's dress, are you?"

"What, as opposed to your usual haute couture polo and khakis?" Kara laughed. "No, no bridesmaids. Small. Simple." She thought for a moment. "Actually, I should probably check with Graham first, shouldn't I? He might have some ideas of his own for the wedding."

They both looked at each other for a moment, then together said, "Nah." And laughed.

"God, I'm going to miss you." She hugged Marianne once more. "Now, they look like they're about to get started. Should I grab my seat?"

"First, would you mind doing me a favor? Levi is a no-show today. He's probably in a corner somewhere listening to depressing music and mourning the loss of Nikki. Again." She rolled her eyes and dug out a key with a temporary plastic tag. "They gave us a storage closet each for supplies. Could you go in there—third door on the left behind the bleachers—and grab the cardboard box labeled 'gauze'? It's pretty small, but they're breaking the huddle so I need to get started and I'm going to run out of gauze soon. Wiggle and jiggle if it doesn't automatically open."

"Sure." She took the key and put it in her pocket. They both watched as the Marines gathered together, hands all gathered up high in the center. Someone in the middle counted down, and together they let out a booming "Oo-rah!"

Kara rubbed up and down her arms as the hairs stood on end. Graham and Brad wandered by, giving her and Marianne a wave before walking toward the locker room to get changed from their street clothes into their boxing uniforms.

"Okay, that gets me, every time."

Marianne nodded. "Ditto. Thanks, I'll see you in a sec.

Gotta prep the room!" And her friend was off, jogging away in her bright white athletic shoes, blonde hair bouncing from her tiny ponytail. With a smile, Kara walked over to the storage to get the box of gauze. She counted the third from the left, struggled with the key in the lock a little, then struggled to push the door open—well, Marianne *had* warned her the doors sucked—then walked in. As she felt for a light switch on the side by the door, she sniffed.

"What . . . is . . ." She spotted the small flame in the corner just as the door slammed shut behind her. She turned, fighting to find the doorknob, but in the dark it was nearly impossible. She took a deep breath to yell, but something covered her mouth. A hand, she thought dimly, as she was pulled away from the door.

"Shut up," a male voice hissed by her ear. "Just shut the fuck up. I'll let you go soon, you just have to shut up and stay here awhile."

Levi. She was 90 percent sure. Between the slender body being pressed up against her and the voice, she would have bet Zach's tiny college fund on it. She shook her head, trying to tell him who she was, trying to tell him about the fire, trying to get any words out, but he only squeezed her jaw until it hurt.

"Fucking shut up. God, you're as bad as them. We're just going to wait until this pile has burned, then we can go out and you can go on your way."

He'd started the fire? Deliberately? *Inside?* What the hell was the matter with him? He had to be crazy. She couldn't tell what exactly the fire was feeding on, but it grew quickly, growing fast, burning in a blackening cardboard box that was surrounded by nothing else on the concrete ground. She was no Smokey the Bear, but even she knew this wasn't a fail-safe way to contain the flames. Crazy Pants apparently didn't know that. Or maybe didn't care . . .

And it was getting hotter. Perspiration beaded her

forehead. Behind his smothering hand, it was harder to catch a breath. "Please," she moaned, though the word was garbled, nearly inaudible.

"Please? Please what? Let you go? Did the Marines let my brother go when he wanted to get out? No, they recalled him. They killed him. They murdered my brother. Why would I let you go?" His voice was low, and as she twisted just a little, she could see him staring intently at the fire, as if needing to see every last bit turn to ash.

"They're all assholes. All of them. They've made Nikki and I feel like nobodies, looking down on us. Hell, your own boyfriend screamed at her, and then turned her in for that stupid prank. Just a prank!"

His hand tightened reflexively, and she squeaked.

"I'm not like them. I don't kill. I show mercy. But mercy and forgiveness aren't the same thing, are they? Sometimes, you have to pay for your mistakes before you can be forgiven. Little ways, you know?"

She wriggled a little, testing his hold. He cinched his arm tighter, but she instinctively fought harder, clawing at his arm now in an attempt to find one millisecond of weakness she could break out of. Then he moved up to grip under her chin. His forearm cut into her windpipe, making the effort to breathe around his hand almost impossible. She quit struggling in order to save her breath.

"Yeah, you'll calm down. If they don't have uniforms, they can't compete, right? That'll hurt. They should have disbanded already. I don't know why they kept going. The MPs are idiots. Taking Nikki away. She's innocent!" he said in a guttural voice, and he squeezed with the final word. "One more mistake."

Seeing stars, Kara knew even if he didn't intend to, he'd suffocate her. The air was too close. Too thick now. She wouldn't make it. Weak with lack of oxygen, she went completely lax against him, which forced his hold to shift just enough that she swung her arms back and dug her thumbs into his eyes. Or as close to his eyes as she could reach. Simultaneously, she arched her back away and swung her heel up between them, aiming for his crotch.

Thank you, yoga, for giving me this range of motion.

She missed the crotch, but landed a solid blow somewhere on his inner thigh. And he let go enough that she could fall to her knees and crawl for the door. He lunged for her, landing on top of her and flattening her to the cool concrete of the storage room.

Opening her mouth, Kara fought to scream, but choked on a cough instead.

Gotta get out. Gotta get to the fresh air.

Hysterically, she thought she'd never before considered the stale, humid air of a gym to be fresh before. But she'd have given everything she had for one gulp of it now.

She bucked and fought, rolling with Levi for every inch. Boxes rained down around them, some on top of them. Her temple hit the metal edge of something and she retched, stomach heaving from the pain. But she kept fighting, even as her lungs burned and her limbs weakened.

And from the corner of her eye, she saw the flames rising higher.

"WHERE the hell are the uniforms?" Tressler walked back out of the locker room, nearly bashing Greg in the head with the door as he shoved out. "Do you guys know where they are?"

Greg looked at Brad and Graham, then shrugged. "I don't know. I put mine in the hamper last night to be laundered, just like they said."

Graham looked around, wondering who actually did the laundering. "I'll ask Coach."

"We better find them soon. I'm third up, and I can't go

out there in my damn underwear." Tressler stormed back in with a scowl. Brad rolled his eyes, shook his head and went to Marianne's training room. He wouldn't fight until last and had plenty of time to kill.

Graham was toward the middle of the day, with another potential match later in the evening if his first was a win. He jogged over to where Coach Cartwright and Coach Ace stood, heads together, discussing something.

"Coach, sorry to interrupt. Do you know where the uniforms are?"

Coach Ace raised dark brows, while Coach Cartwright turned in a circle, as if they were going to magically appear within arm's reach.

"Cook was in charge of those. Or maybe Ms. Robilard. Check with one of them." Dismissing him, the coaches went back to their discussion.

Okay then. He looked around the gym, spotted Reagan standing beside the site manager—the event staff had been introduced to the teams on day one. He walked over. "Reagan, hey, sorry to bother you."

"No problem. Al, we'll talk later?" She took Graham's arm and walked a few feet away. "What's up?"

"Looking for our uniforms. They're not in the locker room like they were yesterday. We were told to leave them in the hampers and they'd be laundered and ready for today."

"Yes, I gave them to Marianne's intern. He might have left them in the training room. Let's go check." She hooked an elbow with his, partly for stability, he knew, because of the sky high heels she insisted on wearing, and partly because she was just a friendly person. "You're doing well so far. How are things?"

"Things are good." He waited for her to ask about the engagement, but she didn't. So Kara hadn't shared the news yet. He'd let her do so when she was ready. They entered the

training room together, finding a harried Marianne taping
Simpson's ankle and looking around with wild eyes.

"You," she said, pointing a finger at Reagan. "You have to
help me. I'm alone, and I ran out of gauze. I'm using what they
have," she added, waving a hand at the Army and Air Force
trainers, "but I like my stuff better. I sent Kara for the extra
box in the storage room, and she hasn't come back. Either she
forgot, or she couldn't find it, or someone abducted her and
took her to the Bahamas where she will live forever and ever."

"Since I'm the guy who would be abducting her and taking her to the Bahamas, that's off the table," he joked.

Reagan smiled soothingly. "I'll check."

"No, I'll check," Graham said. "If the uniforms are there,
I'll take them back to the locker room with me."

"They're not in here," Marianne said, finishing up the
tape and slapping a hand on Simpson's back. "Off you go,
big boy. Good luck."

"Thanks, Cook." He slid his feet back into his untied
running shoes and headed out.

"I'll check here for the uniforms," Reagan said, "and you
look in the storage room with Kara."

"She's got my key, so if she's not in there and the door is
locked, search the stands or call her cell," Marianne added.
"But I don't have the uniforms."

"I'll check," Reagan said again, pushing Graham out of
the door. "She's stressed," she whispered. "Her intern turned
into a huge flop down here. Let's not put more on her plate
than necessary."

"Got it." He turned and jogged across the gym to where
the storage rooms were. He'd helped Brad carry in Marianne's supplies the first day when she'd been setting up shop
and knew which one it was.

But as he neared the storage room—door closed—he
noticed a thin tendril of smoke coming from the door. Not

wanting to panic anyone if it was as simple as someone smoking in there—though the odds were low—he tried the door handle. Locked. He looked around for someone and grabbed the nearest person who looked like they worked there. "Do you have a master key?"

They stared at him, bewildered. "No, that would be Al."

"Get Al over here. Now!" he barked when the employee just stared at him. He pointed at the door, and the man hurried to call on the walkie talkie for Al to come over ASAP.

He felt the door handle more closely now—warm, but not hot—and listened. Then he heard it. Something rustled inside. Someone was in there. "Hey." He banged on the door. "Hey! Open up!"

He heard more scrambling, scurrying, and another noise that could have been the shriek of metal across a floor. Or a woman crying. It was impossible to tell. He tried the handle again, but it hadn't magically unlocked. "Where the fuck is Al?" he yelled, then tried to shoulder the door open. But there was no busting it down. The door was thick, and designed to open out, which meant it would be impossible to break in without a battering ram.

Al, the paunchy middle-aged site supervisor, hustled over, breathing like he'd run a marathon instead of just across the gym floor. "Let's not panic," he started to suggest, but Graham shoved him at the door.

"Open it. Open it now, God damn it. Someone's in there." And he had the worst feeling possible it might be Kara.

CHAPTER

24

Graham's entire body quivered with unreleased anxiety and the need to *do* something, without being able to. "You," he said, pointing at the employee who had radioed to Al. "Go get a fire extinguisher. Get two. Bring help. Don't start screaming about a fire, just get help. Go!" he yelled, shoving the employee in the back when they simply stood, frozen. He scurried off, looking terrified enough to piss his pants.

God knew if he'd actually do it. Graham focused on waiting for Al to find the right key, then heard something slap up against the door. It sounded like knocking from the inside. "Jesus, get the door open. Get it open."

"I'm trying as fast . . ." Understanding the severity now, as more smoke made its way through the opening around the door, Al's hands shook as he tried to push the key in. Finally, Graham shoved him aside and unlocked it, throwing the door open simultaneously. He felt as if he could rip the whole thing from the door hinges.

Smoke poured out in a wave, gray and thin but choking nonetheless. He bent over, sucked in a breath, then ran in.

And found Levi on top of Kara, pulling at her arms and tangling his legs with hers. A cardboard box lay over them, more scattered on the floor. And in the corner, a fire burned. His main focus became Kara. He rushed Levi, bulldozing him like a linebacker so the kid flew off his woman and several feet back, smacking into the back wall of the closet.

Graham crouched between Levi and Kara, shielding her with his back. "Baby, can you stand? Can you walk?"

She looked up at him, glassy-eyed, and coughed.

That was enough for him. He bent down and scooped her up. He made it two steps toward Al, toward the open air of the gym when he felt something hit the center of his back. He stumbled forward, balance thrown off with Kara in his arms, and went to his knees. One cracked hard against the floor as he twisted to keep from landing directly on Kara.

Levi beat against his back, kicking and punching and scratching while screaming something incoherent in a raspy, hoarse voice. Kara curled into a ball, sheltered by his arms and back, and tried to crawl toward the gym.

He heard shouting, yells, saw light and felt relief as he waited for Kara to make her way to safety. And then, he saw red. Turning, he pushed Levi off, then swung out with a fist hard enough to send him flying back. He stumbled, tripped over one of the boxes, and landed ass-first into the fire.

Graham hesitated—and for the rest of his life he would hate himself for it—then reached back in and pulled the man out, rolling him to extinguish the flames that ate at his shirt and pants. His own hands burned with the effort, and something scorched his calf. When that wasn't enough, Graham ripped his shirt off and used it to beat down on the remaining sparks until the man only smoked.

Dimly, from somewhere else in his brain, he saw others burst in with the fire extinguisher. Heard the fire alarm sound. People yelling, thundering down the bleachers in an effort to get outside. Heard someone yell his name. Saw someone shoot white foam from an extinguisher at the fire.

And then felt hands drag him from the closet. He squinted as though he'd been living in a cave for a year as Brad and Tressler hooked him under each arm and dragged him back into the gym, then toward the nearest exit. He could walk. He *was* walking. Wasn't he? Or was he floating? And why didn't his left leg want to hold him up?

"Sweeney." Coach Ace was on them as soon as they left the building. "Look at me, son. Look at me. Let me see your eyes."

"No, look at *me*." Marianne pushed the huge coach aside. For a tiny thing, Graham thought with a loopy smile, she was a bulldog.

Ha. Bulldog. Marine. So fitting.

"Hey. Hey, buddy. Woo hoo." She snapped and brought his attention back down to her. And he sat with a thud on a curb. "Hey now. There we go. Eyes on me. Follow the finger."

He did, though it felt like his eyes wanted to cross instead. "Where's Kara?"

"What's today's date?"

"Kara," he said again, coughing with it.

"She's with another trainer. Look at me. Focus. Date, please."

He just looked at her, into those blue eyes, full of concern and near tears. "Kara," he whispered.

Marianne looked up, then said, "Bring him over to her. If he's sitting next to her, maybe I'll actually get something done."

He felt himself be hefted back up—floating again—and let himself glide to another clump of people. Kara lay in the grass, half-propped in Greg's arms, being attended to by a man dressed much like Marianne, only wearing black and gold. Army colors. He seemed competent and caring, and Graham could kiss him.

Brad and Tressler settled him down next to her, and he immediately grabbed for her hand. It hurt, thanks to the raw burns from the fire, but he couldn't have cared less. She squeezed weakly, looking at him with those glassy, unfocused eyes again. The man held an ice pack to her temple, another at her shoulder.

She tried to say something, but he heard nothing. He leaned in, fighting when Tressler tried to keep him upright. "What, baby? What is it?"

She whispered, nearly toneless, "Did you win?"

He blinked, then looked at the trainer attending her. "What?"

Marianne sat beside him, settling an ice pack on his left knee. He hissed in at the cold.

"She's got a concussion, probably. The ambulance should be . . . there. There we go. I hear them. They're going to take her to the base hospital. You, too, sweetie."

He watched her a moment, saw a silent tear track down her cheek. Marianne was normally so strong. So formidable. She had to be, to keep up with a group of hardened Marines. But just now, he saw the soft side. And it worried him that she was struggling to hold on to her professional, tough exterior. It meant there was something to worry about. "I'm going with her."

Brad started to speak, but Marianne shook her head. "That's fine. I only see two ambulances anyway, and Levi's going to need the other. Go with her. Your knee will be fine. Keep this on it, and then twenty off. Ask for another one at the hospital when you get there. And have them wrap your hands with some ointment. Don't you dare argue."

Marianne stood as paramedics raced over, one carrying a straight board.

He leaned down, near her ear as Kara watched the proceedings with wide eyes and an uncomprehending look on her face. "It's going to be fine, sweetheart. I promise. I'm not letting you out of my sight." He kissed her gently, careful not to move her head at all. "I love you."

"I love you," she mouthed back, before he had to scoot away to give the paramedics room to work.

KARA awoke, for the nineteenth time it seemed like, to dark. Finally. Too many people poking, prodding, invading her personal space, shining bright lights and not letting her close her eyes had left her angry. And she was hungry. So hungry she'd morphed to "hangry."

The thought made her smile a little, and miss Zach so much it hurt. She tried to roll to her side, but that hurt, so she turned her head very slowly. She'd made the unfortunate decision when they'd first brought her in to try and sit up too fast. That had resulted in dry heaving and more pain. Lesson learned.

The sounds of life hummed outside the curtain, but at least the lights in her own little cubicle were lowered, and the curtains seemed to help block most of the rest. There was no clock though. It could be four in the afternoon, or three in the morning. They'd removed all her jewelry when she'd come in for the MRI and CAT scans. She'd fallen asleep before they'd given her the results. Given she wasn't in surgery, or on some special head trauma floor, she could safely assume she was going to make it.

Graham sat beside her, as he had since they'd brought her in. Slumped over in an uncomfortable position for sleep. She'd tried in vain to shoo him out the door to make it to his match, which he'd laughed at. While she'd been getting an MRI, he'd been in the ER himself getting his knee X-rayed and his hands bandaged. He'd fractured his patella, alongside minor burns on his hands. No boxing for him, and likely no exercise for several weeks. The fact that he got hurt assisting her made her stomach cramp. But God . . . thank God he'd been there.

She studied him, while she had the chance. His face was slack, mouth open just a little. The man was gorgeous, and looked like a little boy while he slept. His left leg was extended straight out, and a pair of crutches propped up in one corner. His hand held hers, fingers entwined as much as they could through the gauze wrapping around them. More than once, a nurse had come by and had had to ask multiple times for him to let go before they could check vitals. He was so worried, even if he didn't say it. She saw it in his eyes. He didn't want to let her go.

"Knock, knock." Reagan's voice came through the thick curtain, and she stuck in one hand to wave. "Can I come in?"

"Yeah, but shh." There was no way for her to make herself more presentable, so she just looked down to make sure the hospital gown covered everything it could, and smoothed her hair from her face. "Graham's sleeping, finally."

"You're worried about him? Oh, honey." With a tsking sound, Reagan came in and pressed a tender kiss to the top of her head. "You're such a mom."

"Guilty." After a moment, she asked, "Has anyone called the Cooks? Or Zach?"

"Marianne called her parents to explain, and asked them not to mention it to Zach. We figured you would want to explain what happened after you get home, when he can see clearly you're okay."

"Thank you." Starting to tire, Kara let her eyes close for a moment. It felt soothing to her brain. Like spreading cool aloe over a sunburn. "What time is it?"

"Seven."

"AM or PM?"

"Wow, you really were out of it. Only PM." Reagan's hand rubbed her forearm a bit. "How are you feeling?"

"Exhausted, which is ridiculous since all I've been doing for the past, I guess, eight or nine hours is lying here and sleeping on and off."

"Hospitals aren't restful places. Even if you were asleep, it probably wasn't a good deep REM," Reagan pointed out. "But let's ignore that. Have the MPs come to speak with you?"

"Yes, and the Feds, which shocked the hell out of me. But I guess it's looking like it might be considered a terrorist threat, in the legal sense. I don't think that's what it is, though."

"It's crazy, is what it is."

"No doubt about that." Kara opened her eyes briefly, took in her friend's less-than-pulled-together look. Her skirt was rumpled, her shirt half-untucked, her hair was falling from its formerly tidy chignon, and her eyes were rimmed in dark circles. "You look like hell."

"Hey, at least I'm wearing real clothes."

"Touché. What's going to happen with the event?"

"It's still going on, just at a new location. The first one, most of the damage was contained in the storage room, but the fire folks don't want anyone going in there for a few days while they do a thorough check."

"Sensible."

"Sensible, but inconvenient. Luckily, Hood is big enough that we can change to a different gym. It's tighter, not as nice, but it'll suffice. These guys spend months in tents and little metal boxes in the desert. Competing in a boxing tournament in a second-rate gym is hardly going to stop them."

"But he burned . . . something." She tried to remember. They'd told her. What had they told her? "Something."

Reagan's voice softened as she said, "He burned their uniforms. No problems there, though. The Army and Air Force teams stepped up and are loaning our guys their practice gear so they can continue." She paused a moment, and Kara closed her eyes again to let her friend's voice drift over her. "It's interesting. There's this insane rivalry, almost like high school all over again. You know, two football teams from across town meeting up on homecoming night. Everyone's got blood lust. But, you know, the adult version of that."

Kara smiled, but kept her eyes closed.

"And yet, the second there's trouble, when they could have said, 'Aw, too bad, so sad, Marines. Better luck next year,' everyone scrambles to help instead. Because everyone knows how hard everyone else worked to get here, and nobody wants to win by default."

"Brothers in arms," Graham said in a gravelly voice, waking up in inches. He wiped at his mouth with the back of his hand, as if worried he might have drooled. He sat up and rubbed a thumb over Kara's cheek, and she smiled at the caress. His touch erased so much pain.

"How you feeling, baby?"

"Tired."

"We'll get you out of here as soon as we can."

"Graham, Greg and Brad are out in the waiting room. They didn't want to come back in case she was sleeping, or not up for it. Why don't you go keep them company while Kara and I chat a bit?"

He looked at her, uncertain. But Kara knew he wanted to hear how the matches had gone on in his absence. He simply wouldn't admit it in front of her.

"Go." She pushed weakly at his arm. "Go away so we can have girl time."

"If you're sure . . ."

"Very. Shoo. And call Zach for me, would you? I can't handle it right now; it would give me a headache. He'd love to hear from you, though."

"You got it." He brushed a kiss gently over her forehead, then stood, grabbed his crutches and hobbled out.

"He is so in love with you, girl."

Kara grinned, then dialed it back when it pulled on her bruised face. "I'm going to marry him."

"Marianne told me," she said. "What? She wanted to make sure I knew in case it came up while you were unconscious or something. She was just covering her bases. But thank you for telling me."

"I need to close my eyes now," Kara said, feeling the beginnings of another headache. Not being the type to suffer silently, she reached for the little clicker the nurse had shown her and pressed for more pain medication. "Talk to me for a few while I keep them closed?"

"No problem. Let's start with how the site director, Al, hit on me this morning."

Kara let the darkness act as a balm, and her friend's voice ground her.

GRAHAM hated crutches. They were a menace to society. He hobbled as best he could, keeping an eye out for his friends. As he rounded the corner, he saw not only Greg and Brad, but the entire damn team filling the waiting room. They stood as one when he came into view, and several let out an "Oo-rah!"

"Shh!" hissed the nurse at the nearby desk.

"Sorry," one of them called out from the back, earning another evil glare from the desk nurse.

Greg pulled out a chair like a waiter in a fancy restaurant. "Your seat, good sir."

"Buzz off." But he sat, because his armpits hurt. That was the worst part about crutches. He remembered now.

"How's Kara?" Brad asked as the team members settled themselves again.

"Concussion, lots of bruises, raw throat. She'll be sore for a while, but okay. She can't fly home, for sure. Not yet. I'll be renting a car and driving her home."

"With a bum leg?" Simpson asked, looking confused.

"It's my left leg, numbnuts." He tapped the side of the thick knee brace that ran from the middle of his thigh down to the bottom of his calf. "I can drive with the right. I'll be fine. No other choice, really. Tell me what's going on with the games? I'm sorry I hurt our chances." His dropping out of the competition left a gaping hole in their roster, and a lot of ground to make up.

"First, let's just clear this up." Coach Ace stood. "I trained you all to be warriors and fighters. Boxing is one way to showcase that, but it's not the only way. I'm damn proud of you, Sweeney. You did what you were trained to do. Fight for the right side. You probably saved that woman's life. So I don't want to hear about letting anyone down, or being sorry. That's damn stupid, and you're not a stupid guy."

Graham watched as Coach Ace sat back down with a decisive nod. "Uh . . . thank you, Coach. So . . . results?"

Brad had been knocked out of the running that afternoon. He was serious enough about the sport and the team, Graham expected to see more disappointment. Brad shrugged. "When you've seen a life-or-death situation not long before, it suddenly puts things into perspective."

Greg was in the finals for his weight class, as was Tressler and several others. It looked as though their chances of bringing home a team win were almost nil. But their spirits were high regardless.

Maybe Brad was right. Having watched one of their own— as Kara was certainly their own now—nearly die had given everyone a little perspective about the games themselves.

Team members slowly trickled out after shaking his hand. Many asked him to tell Kara they were thinking about her. They had come to consider her a member of the team, as she'd supported them, taught them, and come to be involved with one of them. She was family. That conclusion was cemented when Coach Willis walked past and dropped a small T-shirt in his lap. "For Kara," he said in his gruff voice, beard shaking. "I really like that girl."

Graham nodded, then looked at the shirt. Marine Corps Boxing Team, size medium. For her. He couldn't talk around the lump in his throat, so he resorted to handshakes and head nods as the last of the team filed out. All but Greg and Brad.

He sat back, wishing he had one of those pain med IV drips like Kara did. "You'll miss the bus."

"They're leaving us here. Reagan's gonna take us home." Sitting forward, Brad laced his fingers together beside his knee. "Marianne's gotten some of the story from the MPs when they interviewed her, but not all of it. Apparently his older brother was in the Corps about four or five years ago. Ready to separate and move on, and he got recalled for one last deployment. Was killed in action in Afghanistan."

Graham dug his thumbs in his eyes. It jived with what they'd told him thus far when they had come to take Kara's statement.

"Levi and his brother were close, and he took it hard," Greg went on. "Blamed the military, the government, and anyone else he could for his brother's death. His parents thought, when he accepted the internship with Marianne, that he'd gotten over it."

"Apparently not," Graham said dryly.

"Apparently not," Brad echoed. "So he's been looking for ways to 'punish' Marines. Little ways here and there. I think they believe him when he says he never wanted to hurt anyone. Not really. Just embarrass us, inconvenience us, and eventually make it so we couldn't compete."

"Hurting us, just in a different way. Because from his fucked-up viewpoint, if he didn't physically hurt us, he was better than the Marines, who killed his brother." Graham had seen enough trials with nut jobs to know how they rationalized anything and everything.

"Exactly. The current theory is the fire was meant to stay contained, just to get rid of the uniforms. He has a thing for fire," Brad added with a roll of his eyes. "But nobody thinks he honestly meant for it to get as out of hand as it did. Or to hurt anyone."

Graham's hands tightened around the chair. Whether he'd meant it or not, Kara's life had been well and truly in danger thanks to that fuckhead's actions.

"But he's not getting out of jail for a long time. Well, hospital first, because he got burned worse than Kara. I'm guessing they'll do a psych eval while he's here. Hopefully he gets the help he needs far, far away from Lejeune, but either way, he won't be bothering us."

Greg yawned and stretched out his legs in a way that made Graham long to do the same. Reading his mind, his friend asked, "What's the prognosis on the knee?"

"Fractured patella, but the best kind of fracture, if such a thing exists. Not displaced, so should heal without surgery as long as I stay off it. Six to eight weeks."

"You'll be back up in six."

Graham appreciated Brad's confidence in his healing powers. "I should get back to Kara. I don't want to leave her for too long."

"Understood, man." Brad waited until he was steady on his crutches, then asked with a grin, "I guess we won't see you back on base tonight?"

"Guessed right. Keep me updated," he added when Brad gave him a back slap, then steadied him as he pitched forward a bit.

"Sorry," Brad said sheepishly.

"Good luck tomorrow. Kick some ass," he told Greg who came in for a quick guy hug.

"Goes without saying. Now, go give Reagan the boot so she can drive us home."

"Already booted. She's sleeping," Reagan said, placing a light hand on Graham's shoulder. "And it looks like she's actually resting, so try to be quiet when you go back in. I'll come check on you in the morning and hopefully I'll be able to drive you back to her hotel, but call me if anything changes."

"Thanks. You're the best." He kissed her cheek, which had Greg raising a brow.

Then Reagan linked arms with Greg and walked between him and Brad toward the exit, heels clicking on the worn linoleum flooring the whole way.

CHAPTER

2 5

They left after breakfast, once the morning doctor had cleared her to check out, and managed to make it into Shreveport, Louisiana, before Graham called it a night.

"I could have figured out how to get home." Kara reclined on the hotel bed, feeling foolish and not a little guilty that Graham had left the games early to drive her back. He wasn't 100 percent healed himself, but insisted he'd rather drive her than risk her flying so soon after a concussion. She hadn't had the energy to argue at the time, but having slept most of the first day's drive, her fighting form was back.

"Yeah. Fly home, and watch your brain explode mid-flight. Great option." He rested his crutches next to the bed and slid down beside her. His knee was still in its brace, which was much thicker and longer than the one Brad wore.

"How long do you have to wear that?"

"Only until we get back and I can get into a doctor at home. They knew I'd be traveling home so they gave me a sturdier brace than I'll probably need on a regular basis. How are you feeling?"

He'd checked in with her every step of the way, insisting they pull over often, and that she sleep when she could instead of keeping him company. Being coddled should have annoyed her . . . but she was still in pain enough to admit it felt wonderful.

As he shifted and rolled, she let him settle down on the bed with the TV remote, then snuggled up against him. He'd been so careful to touch her, avoiding contact beside a whisper of a kiss here or a light graze of the fingers there. Now she needed the comfort of his heat, his skin, his touch. Needed it more than her next breath. When his arm opened and gave her more space to cuddle closer, she did without hesitation. Her head jostled slightly as he wrapped his arm around her back to pull her in tighter, but she bit back the moan. If she said anything, he'd insist they sleep separate. She couldn't handle another night without him.

"Zach sounded okay, didn't he?" she said as he turned the TV on to a nightly news program, closed captioning on and sound muted. "He wasn't suspicious of us taking a car back, and being a few days late?"

"Not really. He sounded more depressed that I 'lost' than for you to be late getting back."

"I need to find a way to thank Frank and Mary for taking him in in the first place, and then keeping him longer than planned without warning."

"We can invite them over for dinner. Or a bottle of wine. Check with Marianne."

"He sounded like he was having a blast though," she said, relieved.

"Face it, Mama. He's having fun without you."

She pinched his side and had the satisfaction of his grunt, though he didn't budge. "I'm still his Important Person."

"Of course you are." He kissed the top of her head, then started surfing channels, still on mute.

"You can be an Important Person, too."

He was quiet for a while, still flipping. Then he whispered, "Thank you."

She nearly fell asleep with the warm, reassuring sound of his heartbeat and the pain medication she'd taken home with her coursing through her veins. But then he squeezed her gently and asked, "Will you guys move in with me when we get home?"

"That's . . . wow." She took a moment to think. Because she'd been focusing on his heartbeat to lull her, she noted that it had sped up exponentially. "It's a big step."

"You already agreed to marry me. I'd say moving in together is sort of a half step back from that."

Reasonable. But still . . . "Engaged isn't married. I figured we had several months before we'd hit that point. I figured you'd want to wait for the termination paperwork to come through."

He reached up and played with her hair, careful of the side that had hit the metal rod in the storage room and caused the concussion. "I want you and Zach now, and later. Whether the termination comes through in a month or three days before Zach turns eighteen, he's still going to be yours, and mine. Paperwork changes nothing but logistics."

With a sigh, she nodded. "Slowly. We'll do it in stages. Zach will love it, I'm sure, but just in case, I want to make the change slow. Set up a bedroom in your place for him, try some weekends over there."

"And I want to get a dog."

"What?" She sat up so fast her head spun. Closing her eyes, she moaned and rested her forehead against his shoulder. "Damn it. You can't do that to me right now."

"It's a dog. How was I supposed to know you'd react that

way?" He rubbed up and down her back while the urge to vomit passed. "I've wanted a dog for a while. I'm a dog guy. Zach's a dog guy. Now that I know someone would be home to take care of one if I have to work late, it seems like a good time to get one."

"A dog," she said again on a pained moan . . . but it had nothing to do with her concussion. "Changes everywhere. Wait . . . you're in Hubert. It would mean he'd have to change schools, too. That's not easy, with his restrictions."

"Luckily, you've got a guy who knows the legal requirements for accommodations. What?" he asked when she looked up at him. "I read your blog. I've done a little research of my own. I know what you have a right to ask for."

"Maybe I should have you write a guest column for the website," she teased. "Ask Graham your legal questions."

"I'd do it. I think the blog really has a shot at taking off, if you wanted to devote more time to it."

"I do. I love yoga, and I'll still always want to practice, and teach. But less classes. More time for Zach." It sounded like heaven, especially when she was so tired.

"Perfect. Find the balance and go with it. It's not about the money," he added when she started to bite her lip. "It's about the life. You've worked so hard for so long. I know you want to be there with Zach. With other kids, as they come along."

Another baby. She cupped her belly in hope. A baby wanted, loved, adored, cherished by both parents from the moment it was created. "You're right."

"Music to my ears. Woman!" he yelped as she pinched him again. "If you were back up to full speed, you'd pay for that."

"So I better take advantage now." He flattened his hand over hers against his chest, staving off any additional pokes or prods.

"I really love you, you know," she said, pressing a kiss to his chest. "What's with the shirt, by the way? You always sleep without one."

"As we're not going to be getting into any funny business, the shirt stays on."

"Aw." She slid her hand under the hem, loving the feel of his skin under her palm. "Shame. Looking at your body is one of my favorite pastimes."

"Not tonight, oh, horny one." He gripped her wrist gently and pulled it back out. "You're concussed still. No physical activity for two weeks. Doctor's orders."

"Shame, since tomorrow's our last night alone together for a while."

"Such is life. I've spent the last two months—stop—building up endurance and—Kara—learning how to cope with—okay, you have to quit."

She looked up from where she'd slithered down—gently, of course—to tug at the drawstrings of his athletic shorts. "Spoilsport."

"That's me, running around ruining the fun for everyone. Well, not running," he added with a grimace. "Get back up here. We want to make decent time tomorrow, so we're starting early."

"Yes, Mr. Bossy Pants." She curled back up against him again. As his breathing evened out, she whispered, "I love you."

"Love you too, yoga girl."

THREE MONTHS LATER . . .

Graham walked in to chaos. He'd come to expect the chaos, as it was a near-daily occurrence anymore after Kara and Zach had fully moved in two weeks earlier. Her fears of Zach handling the news about their engagement had been overblown. The boy had taken their news with a whoop and a fist pump, along with an immediate request for a puppy. He'd also handled the shifting of schools like a champ, and with Kara's firm but calm request for accommodations for his allergies in place, he'd begun to thrive in the new environment.

Kids. Resilient, demanding suckers.

When Zach had asked if Graham wanted to be called Dad, Graham had looked to Kara for advice. She'd given him free rein, and in the end he'd left the decision up to Zach. Zach chose to stick with Graham, as he liked feeling more adult by using an adult's first name. Later, in private, Zach had told him even if he called him Graham, could he still think of him as Dad? Graham wondered how one kid could make a grown man want to cry.

Mom, however, would still always be Mom. No debate.

They'd moved in, gotten a puppy—much to Kara's dismay, as she'd lobbied for an older dog past the chew-and-accident stage. She talked a big game, and had feigned disgust when her son had picked the ugliest, hairiest dog at the rescue shelter. But she spent a majority of her free time carrying around and snuggling with the shaggy mutt Zach had picked out. The love was mutual, as the pup had imprinted largely on Kara, following her around the house like a fuzzy shadow whenever he wasn't wrestling with Zach.

"Zachary! Zach, get back in here now!" Kara bellowed from the kitchen window into the backyard. "And wipe that dog's paws off on the towel before you do. You've left your school crap everywhere!"

Graham grinned and let his own bag drop on the sofa beside the front door. His cover received better treatment, placing it on the bookshelf where he always did. "Hey."

Kara whirled on him, her face red and her hands covered in yellow rubber gloves. The front of her T-shirt—the boxing team shirt she'd been given in the hospital—was splotched with wet patches, and her yoga pants were cuffed up, too. "That dog of yours—"

"Zach's dog."

"That dog of yours," she repeated, "has driven me to the

mad house today. And that kid has lost his mind if I am going to think for one second about adding *another* dog so the first one isn't 'lonely.'" She blew out a raspberry. "I kicked them both out of the house, only to realize he'd left yet another mess for me to clean up."

"The dog or Zach?" he asked with a smile. "Okay, okay. Let me change and I'll come help. Just point me in the right direction and I'll help clean up."

"Just pick a spot!" she yelled after him as he went back to the bedroom to change from his uniform to jeans and a T-shirt. As he came back, she pointed with one gloved hand at the table. "What's that?"

He picked up the thick envelope, and the small but heavy box. "The box is our wedding invitations. The printer called before I left work, so I swung by and grabbed them."

"Oh." She ran to the kitchen sink and tossed the gloves under the cabinet, washing up before hurrying back to sit with him at the kitchen table. "Let me see, let me see. Gimme."

"You know," he said conversationally as he pulled out his pocket knife and slid through the tape sealing the box, "for a woman who avoided my advances for weeks, and insisted we couldn't get married, you're very attached to the planning of this wedding."

"Well, I'm only doing it once. You're stuck, buddy. And I want to make sure it's right. Oh," she breathed as he opened it fully and she saw the top invitation. Printed with silver lettering, it was delicate, simple, classic . . . exactly what Kara exemplified in Graham's mind. "They're perfect."

The wording had been difficult, as custom dictated the invitation include both sets of parents' names. Graham felt odd having just his parents included, and had been grateful when his mother and father had agreed to be left off the formal invites to spare Kara the awkwardness. They'd loved her when they'd come to visit two weeks earlier, and had been delighted with Zach.

Not as delighted with the puppy. On that, they sided with Kara.

"Three months from tomorrow," she said, running her fingertips over the raised date. "Fast."

"Not fast enough, far as I'm concerned." He kissed her cheek, then pulled the other envelope out. "And this, I picked up after the printer's."

"You're quite the errand boy," she said absently, still looking through the invitation box, now focused on the envelopes.

"It's not wedding invitations, but it's something. I picked it up from Tasha's office."

That got her attention. She pushed the box of invitations to the side and scooted her chair closer. "What is it?"

"Papers are signed, and a court date has been set. It's not a guarantee, but it's going in the right direction so far. She's confident it will all turn out."

Her eyes filled as she looked through the copies of original paperwork that would forever sever the ties she and Zach had with his biological father. The man was a first-class asshole, and he'd never have a place in their lives. But Graham understood that even with a situation like that, there were emotions involved. "You okay?"

"Hmm? Oh, yes. I'm good. This is a good thing. Sorry." She knuckled away a stray tear. "Just really, you know . . . it's a lot."

"It is." He held her a moment, let her gain her composure. "I talked to Greg today, gave him a heads-up on the wedding date so they can plan ahead. He said to count him and Reagan in."

"That's funny, because I talked to Marianne. It sounds like California agrees with her . . . though I have a feeling much of that is being with Brad and less about the geography. She's settling in nicely at the university. Division II athletes seem like a breeze after handling you guys."

"Yeah, no kidding. We were a pretty high maintenance bunch."

"And no interns," she added with a grin.

Zach stormed in then, the puppy scrambling to make the same turn and follow.

"Zach, did you wipe that dog's feet off?" Kara demanded.

"Yeah, I did. What's for dinner? Hey, Graham."

"Hey, kid." Graham held out a hand for a high five as Zach passed by. "Homework done?"

"Ye . . . no. Dang it." Looking sullen, he headed for his room. "Forgot math."

"Finish it before dinner," Kara suggested, "and you can FaceTime with Matt." His best friend from his old school.

"Got it. C'mon, Boscoe, let's go play with numbers."

The pup, hearing the key word "play," yipped and raced off behind him, running into a wall before making the final turn for Zach's room.

"That dog is going to leave dent marks in every piece of drywall we have." Shaking her head, Kara stood and went to the fridge to start pulling out the fixings for dinner.

Graham walked up behind her—his knee had fully healed, thank God—and pulled her back against him. Nibbling on her neck, he asked, "How long do you think he'll be preoccupied with math?"

"Since he's more of a word nerd than he is a math geek, a while."

"Hmm." His hand worked lower, grazing the waistband of her yoga pants. "Maybe we should go discuss tonight's meal plan first. Alone."

"I could be up for a discussion of such." She twisted around to lock her lips firmly on his, holding him down so she could fully take advantage. "Yup, let's go 'meal plan' for a bit. I'm thinking about something spicy."

He followed her to the bedroom. "Whatever you say, yoga girl."

TURN THE PAGE FOR A
PREVIEW OF JEANETTE MURRAY'S NEXT
SANTA FE BOBCATS NOVEL

COMPLETING THE PASS

COMING SOON FROM INTERMIX!

Josh Leeman walked into the Bobcats headquarters and gave Kristen a wary smile. "Hey, I think someone is expecting me for . . . You okay?"

Kristen, the front office's high-octane, almost unbelievably efficient administrative assistant, gave him a weak smile in return. "Sure, I'm fine. Thanks for asking."

Josh couldn't help noticing she was wringing her hands as she said it. And for the first time since he'd met her several seasons ago, she was missing that certain polish that she carried around with her. Her hair was down, rather than back in its typical smooth bun, and looked a little tangled, as if she'd forgotten to brush it before heading to work. Her sweater was baggy, and if she wore any makeup, he couldn't tell.

"Right. That's good." He rocked back on his heels, taking in the front lobby. It was a rare day he ended up in the front offices. Not much call for him here. He was the guy who stuck to the shadows of the team. Forgotten, until called upon. And he'd never wanted to be called upon.

Somehow, it had happened anyway.

"So, I think Coach Jordan is expecting me."

She nodded, nibbling on her lip and making a quick call to announce him. When she waved him on toward the double doors, she looked . . . worried.

Kristen was a known mother hen for the team. If she was worried, there was something to worry about. With this career, the options were pretty limited. He was being traded, or just straight cut. Try as he might, he struggled to think of a worse situation than being cut from the team he'd spent four years with.

He walked through the hallways, feeling insignificant beside the team photos of Bobcats past. Not to mention the few gigantic portraits of the NFL MVPs the Bobcats had held on their rosters over the decades.

As he entered the main bay of offices for the coaches and the owners, he approached the desk that sat in the middle of the open space with trepidation. There was something about Frank, the man who manned the desk, that terrified him. Maybe that was a pussy thing to say, that he was terrified of an old guy who might have been sixty-five, or maybe ninety-five . . . but it was also the damn truth.

"Hey, Frank." The man didn't look up from his typing. With hands that looked gnarled as tree roots, he was typing what had to be at least eighty words a minute, and he wasn't stopping anytime soon. "Uh, Kristen sent me back."

"Coach Jordan's office," the older man barked, nodding his head toward the left back corner office. His fingers never stopped. "Go on in."

"Right." Josh paused a moment, then said, "Thanks."

Might as well have said nothing at all, for all the attention Frank paid him. Heading back, he wiped his damp palms on his jeans before knocking on the door.

The worst they can do is cut you. You try out for another team, or you go on to something else. Calm down.

"Come on in," he heard Coach Jordan say. When he entered, he saw the quarterback coach sitting across from the head coach in a comfortable leather high-back chair.

The head coach and the quarterback coach. This . . . was unexpected.

"Kristen called and said you needed to see me?" Josh took a few steps in, pausing by the door.

Coach Jordan nodded at it. "Go ahead and close it. Have a seat."

He closed the door and took a seat beside Clayton Barnes, the quarterback coach who'd joined the team last year. Clayton reached over to shake his hand, but said nothing. No smiles, no friendly winks, nothing.

The worst they can do is cut you.

Coach Jordan glanced at his wall a moment, as if still gathering his thoughts. His naturally tanned skin—thanks to his Hawaiian ancestry—seemed even darker. Likely he'd been on vacation with his two teenage daughters, one of whom Josh was pretty sure should be heading to college this summer. He followed his coach's gaze to the wall of photos. There were ones of his two teenagers, when they were younger. A few of him and the girls with his now-ex-wife. Awkward. And a few newer additions with Cassie Wainwright—now Cassie Owens—his daughter from a past relationship with whom he'd only recently connected.

In the center of the grouping was a large photo of Cassie, her father, and two sisters on Cassie and Trey's wedding day. The bride wore white, and a smile that could light up the Bobcats stadium for *Monday Night Football.*

"Nice picture," he said, because the silence was killing him. When Coach glanced at him, he pointed to the wedding photo. "She looks happy."

That brought out a small smile on his stern face. "She was gorgeous. Prettiest bride you could ask for. Perfect day."

Josh nodded, because it was polite. He hadn't been

there—hadn't been invited, not that he minded. No way could the couple invite the whole team, and while he and Trey—the Bobcats' star quarterback—were friendly given their positions, they weren't really friends.

"That brings me to what we need to discuss." Settling back in his chair, Coach Jordan steepled his hands together and tapped his chin a few times.

The worst they can do is cut you.

"Cassie and Trey are currently on their honeymoon," he went on. "They delayed the trip because Cassie had some conferences and such. Nerd Herd stuff." Josh nodded again. "There was an . . . incident."

Josh blinked, then looked over at Coach Barnes. But the quarterback coach simply sat, stone-faced.

"Incident?" He wiped his hands on his jeans again. "Is everyone okay?"

"Nothing life threatening. Cassie is fine. I'd have had to kill him if he brought my daughter back hurt," the coach muttered. "But no, the injury was Trey's."

Those hands that had continued to sweat started to feel clammy. "Nothing major, I hope."

"A sprain," Coach Barnes said, sounding annoyed more than upset. "Left ankle. Who tells a multimillion-dollar quarterback hang gliding is a good idea?"

"Easy," Coach Jordan said. Coach Barnes glared, but settled back in his chair. "It's a pretty bad sprain. We can hope he'll be back for Game One."

Josh nodded again.

"You get where he's going with this?" Coach Barnes asked.

"Uh . . . Trey's hurt." Barnes gave him a disbelieving look. "But he's going to be okay. Right?"

"It's a sprain. His foot didn't fall off." Coach Barnes looked at Coach Jordan with a *What's with this guy?* look.

"We can't guarantee he will be back by the first game.

He definitely won't be playing in the preseason matchups. So that means we're looking at you to carry us forward."

Josh froze, looking between the two coaches. "I'm sorry, what?"

Coach Barnes just rolled his eyes.

Coach Jordan seemed to have found some Zen in the whole thing. "Leeman, we're saying you're our go-to guy right now."

"But you're looking for a replacement. Right?" His hands started to shake, so he shoved them in the pockets of his jeans. "To step in."

"*You* are the replacement. It's what you're paid for," Barnes snapped.

"With Trey only missing preseason, and maybe a game or two, we don't feel it's prudent to grab another quarterback at this time," Coach Jordan said more diplomatically. Then he paused. "That's code for 'It's not in the budget.'"

He could respect a budget. He was raised with the words "it's not in the budget" being a weekly mantra from his single mother.

"So you're it." Coach Barnes stood and slapped him on the shoulder. "I hope you're ready for the spotlight. Because when it becomes news Owens isn't starting Game One, you're going to be the person everyone starts watching. Closely." He stood and left without another word.

Coach Jordan just gave him a wan smile. "We told you this now, in May, so you're ready to put your nose to the grindstone in July for training camp. Don't put on twenty pounds of fat we have to work off of you before you're any good to us."

"Yeah. Sure. Right." He was nodding again like a damned bobblehead. "Don't get fat. Got it."

"Stay healthy. Stay in shape. And for the love of God, don't go hang gliding." His coach motioned to the door with his head, and Josh was dismissed.

As he walked back down the hallway, he paused in front of the 1989 Super Bowl championship Bobcats team photo. He took in the mullets, the pornstaches, the out-of-control curls . . . and wanted to vomit.

Apparently, cutting him *wasn't* the worst thing they could do.

CARRINGTON Gray walked into her father's hospital room with a quick *knock-knock*.

"Hey, Daddy." She set flowers on the table and walked over to the chair she knew her mother would have vacated only for an emergency bathroom break or sustenance run. Maeve Gray was a loyal, loving wife. Stooping down, she kissed her father's cheek with care. He'd lost weight.

He turned eyes that seemed a little too cloudy for comfort toward her. The top of his head was still wrapped in bandages from the severe sunburn he'd received. Monitors beeped, and the IV that provided hydration ran into his reddened, bandaged arm. "Hello."

"Daddy?" What kind of medication was he on? "Dad. How're you feeling?" She hesitated—not wanting to hurt him—then gingerly took hold of his hand, which was pink, but not burned at least.

He shook his head, then nodded, then shook it again. "Hello."

Carri blinked. "Daddy. You know who I am, right?"

He blinked back, as if in a copycat gesture of her own. "Of course. Maeve, sweetheart. You shouldn't be in my room. If my father catches us—"

"Herb." Maeve walked in quickly, coming to stand by the other side of the bed. "It's Carri. Carrington. Your daughter. I'm Maeve." In a gesture that made Carri's throat clog, her mother carefully brought her father's hand up to cup her cheek.

"Maeve," he whispered, eyes watering.

Carri felt awkward, as if intruding on a private, personal moment. With shaking hands, she stood and walked out to the hallway, sinking onto a chair. The cracked vinyl and plastic scratched at the backs of her thighs. A woman in blue scrubs and a white coat walked into her father's room, and a moment later, her mother walked out to sit beside her.

Maeve sighed as she settled down into the chair beside Carri's, then reached over to place a hand over Carri's shaking ones. "I'm glad you could come, Carrington. How was the drive from Utah? Or did you fly?"

"Mom." It suddenly made sense, why her mother had been so vague about the "accident" that had put her father into the hospital. Who rushed to the ER because of a simple sunburn? "I'm here now. Can you please tell me what's going on? The whole truth this time."

Maeve's lip trembled, but she firmed it up and nodded once. "I was at work when your father . . . wandered away."

Wandered away, like a puppy that slipped out an open gate? Like a toddler who jimmied the safety lock? "Mom . . ."

"He was gone for nearly twenty-four hours. In this heat, he was pretty dehydrated, and very sunburned." She laughed, but the sound was watery. "You know how he always forgot to bring a hat with him when he'd go to your soccer games. With that bald egg he calls a head—"

"Mom." She said it firmly now, because she was afraid if her mother kept going, she'd break. "Tell me the truth. What's going on?"

"Dementia," Maeve whispered, looking back toward her husband's open room door. "They'll run a few more tests, but it's nearly impossible to deny at this point. He's been . . . forgetful lately. Calling things the wrong word, calling me his mother's name a few times. I just thought, 'Hey, old age, right?'" Her mother reached up one hand to wipe at the corner of her eye. "I thought maybe retirement was getting to him; he was watching too much television. I started bringing home those crossword puzzles and the . . . oh, the numbers in the boxes."

"Sudoku."

"Yes." She laughed again, but it was less watery this time. "See? Happens to everyone, the whole forgetting words thing. It wasn't often, but it had started happening with enough frequency I'd convinced him to head to his doctor. They confirmed it. We were going to tell you when you came to visit next. It's not the sort of thing you talk about on the phone. Then this . . ." Maeve covered her mouth on a sob.

Carri clenched her hands in her lap. They'd deliberately kept her out of the loop.

Her mother continued. "He was . . . was gone. Alone. For hours, Carrington. Hours. Wandering around, no clue where he was going. In just his house shoes, a T-shirt and shorts. They found him at a park, watching children play a junior league soccer game. A parent saw him, spoke to him, saw the burns and called 911." Her mother swallowed and smiled, though her lips quivered. "He told the police he was watching his daughter. It wasn't even a field you'd ever played at before."

Carri reached up to knuckle away a tear of her own. "Oh, Mom. Oh my God."

With a puff of breath, Maeve pulled herself together quickly. "We'll figure this out. We have some long-term care insurance. I can't come home permanently. We can't afford for me to retire right now. But we've been paying those insurance people money for years. They can send a professional to sit with him while I'm gone, make sure he's safe."

"Of course they can." Not sure at all what long-term care insurance did or didn't do, Carri quickly made a mental note to look it up, and see if she could help. "I'm guessing you need an official diagnosis first, right?"

"We were still in the testing stage with his neurologist, but I think this should seal the deal on that front. He should be released from the ICU tomorrow afternoon." Suddenly,

Maeve threw her arms around Carri's shoulders. "I'm just so glad you came."

Carri patted her mother's back and decided to not think what it meant that her mother had doubted their only child would come home when her father was in critical condition in the hospital.

It wasn't flattering, that was for sure.

ALSO FROM
JEANETTE MURRAY

AGAINST

THE

ROPES

As a troubled teen, Gregory Higgs channeled his energy
into boxing instead of breaking the law. The ring gave him
purpose and something to strive for. So did the Marines.
Combining the two seemed like a natural fit.

Another natural fit? Reagan Robilard, the sweet athlete
liaison who keeps all the fighters out of trouble and man-
ages their PR—a job that gets more challenging when
someone digs up the truth about Greg's not-so-shiny past
after equipment is vandalized at the gym.

Even if it weren't her job, Reagan couldn't let Greg take
the fall. Because passion doesn't pull any punches when it
comes to matters of the heart…

ALSO IN THE SERIES
BELOW THE BELT
FIGHT TO THE FINISH

**"This is one series that readers should
check out as quickly as possible."**
—*RT Book Reviews*

Available wherever books are sold and at penguin.com